LORA LEIGH

USA Today Bestselling Author

BROKEN WINGS

Cerridwen Press

$\mathcal{W}$hat the critics are saying...

ଵ

5 *Cups* "Ms. Leigh is a talented author with an extremely creative imagination. This book is a departure from her usual erotic style, however, as always, the writing is superb. The story is absolutely wonderful and touched me deeply. I highly recommend this book to anyone who enjoys tales of fantasy and mythical creatures. Broken Wings is an extraordinary read that I am sure many others will adore just as much as I did." ~ *Coffee Time Romance*

Recommended Read, 5 *Angels* "Oh my lord this story was amazing. The characters are so vibrant you can feel every tear; every bit of heartbreak is amplified tenfold...Lora Leigh's Broken Wings is a nail biting, breath holding, tear jerking, absolute must read story. You know the saying that each page is an adventure, well in this story it is the absolute truth. Get this book! If you don't you are going to hit yourself over the head for your lack of foresight!" ~ *Fallen Angel Reviews.*

"Broken Wings touched my every emotion. Through Ms. Leigh's beautiful writing voice, I was transported into this fantasy world she has masterfully created. I flew alongside these magnificent winged creatures, felt the pain of loss and the joy of new found beginnings. This is a beautiful love story that is entangled with tragedy from the past, but Matte and Dearn work together to bring peace and hope for a united Winged Clan." ~ *Cupid's Library Reviews*

A Cerridwen Press Publication

www.cerridwenpress.com

Broken Wings

ISBN 9781419954801
ALL RIGHTS RESERVED.
Broken Wings Copyright © 2005 Lora Leigh
Edited by Sue-Ellen Gower
Cover art by Syneca

This book printed in the U.S.A. by Jasmine-Jade Enterprises,
LLC

Electronic book Publication May 2005
Trade paperback Publication December 2005

Cerridwen Press is an imprint of Ellora's Cave Publishing,
Inc.®

If you are interested in a spicier read (and are over 18), check out the author's erotic romances at Ellora's Cave Publishing (www.ellorascave.com).

A Wish, A Kiss, A Dream *(anthology)*

B.O.B.'s Fall (with Veronica Chadwick)

Bound Hearts 1: Surrender

Bound Hearts 2: Submission

Bound Hearts 3: Seduction

Bound Hearts 4: Sacrifice

Bound Hearts 6: Embraced

Bound Hearts 7: Shameless

Cowboy & the Captive

Elemental Desires *(anthology)*

Feline Breeds 1: Tempting The Beast

Feline Breeds 2: The Man Within

Feline Breeds 3: Kiss of Heat

Legacies 1: Shattered Legacy

Legacies 2: Shadowed Legacy

Manaconda *(anthology)*

Men Of August 1: Marly's Choice

Men Of August 2: Sarah's Seduction

Men Of August 3: Heather's Gift

Men Of August 4: August Heat

Moving Violations *with Veronica Chadwick*

Soul Deep

Wizard Twins 1: Ménage a Magick

Wizard Twins 2: When Wizards Rule

Wolf Breeds 1: Wolfe's Hope

Wolf Breeds 2: Jacob's Faith

Wolf Breeds 3: Aiden's Charity

Wolf Breeds 4: Elizabeth's Wolf

About the Author

❦

Lora Leigh is a wife and mother living in Kentucky. She dreams in bright, vivid images of the characters intent on taking over her writing life, and fights a constant battle to put them on the hard drive of her computer before they can disappear as fast as they appeared.

Lora's family, and her writing life co-exist, if not in harmony, in relative peace with each other. An understanding husband is the key to late nights with difficult scenes and stubborn characters. His insights into human nature and the workings of the male psyche provide her hours of laughter, and innumerable romantic ideas that she works tirelessly to put into effect.

Lora welcomes comments from readers. You can find her website and email address on her author bio page at www.cerridwenpress.com.

Tell Us What You Think

We appreciate hearing reader opinions about our books. You can email us at Comments@EllorasCave.com.

BROKEN WINGS

ஐ

Dedication

છ

In memory of my father, Russell Kanawha, who endured endless nights of a pecking typewriting, and a little girl's dreams.

Chapter One

ঔ

It was Dania's screams that brought Mera awake. Shrill and resonant with pain and terror, the child's cries had her out of the bed and rushing ahead of her husband into the family room of the aerie. She came to an abrupt, disbelieving halt just inside the doorway. Her blood thickened, congealing in terror as she saw the creatures awaiting her.

In the middle of the room, grinning evilly in the flickering light of the thick candle on the small altar where the statues of the gods were displayed, stood the nightmares of the past, the vilest creatures ever known to the Winged Clans.

Ralnd, who had rushed in behind her with sword raised, lowered it as the daggers pressed dangerously into the throats of their three babes. Their daughter cried out in desperation, her tiny wings fluttering in terror against the black-garbed chest of the human who held her. The twins, Aaroen and Gable, were silent, desperate to appear brave. She saw their fear, but also their belief that Papa would save them.

With the humans were the Vultures. They were the vilest of the Clans, nightmares thought extinct. Their black wings were dull, as though dirt and oil coated their feathers, large stocky bodies with their thick muscular arms pinning her sons against their chests. They watched her with narrowed, leering eyes, their evil grins tight and promising long-nourished retribution.

"Gods, this is not possible," Ralnd whispered as his sword was jerked roughly from his hand.

One of the Vultures crossed the room. His black eyes were malevolent, his expression cold and cruel.

11

"All things are possible. Is this not what your White Lance priests teach you?" he sneered.

The Vulture Clan had been destroyed centuries ago and sent into the bowels of the Seven Hells. How had such an evil breed been brought back from extinction? And why had they once again aligned themselves with the human, demon-worshipping Elitists?

Ralnd pulled Mera close to his chest, but the warmth of his body, the strength she knew it contained, could do little to comfort her. The Vulture and human force numbered too many, and the tales of old rushed back to her with sickening clarity. Their brutality was remembered well, despite the centuries since their defeat.

"What do you want? We have nothing of value within the aerie. You know that such things are stored in the Fortress." Mera heard the vein of fear in her husband's voice and it caused her knees to weaken. That tone, added to the tearful pleas of her daughter, was more than she could bear.

"Too bad." The leader of the Vultures scanned Ralnd with contempt and loathing. "And here we so hoped such practices had changed in the centuries we've been gone."

"Please." Mera could not keep the terror from her voice. "Please let the children return to their rooms. They are of no threat to you."

The black gaze, flat and devoid of compassion or warmth, turned to her now. Mera watched, trembling as those eyes went over her body, scantily clad as it was in the thin nightgown. She flinched at the cold smile that edged those narrow lips as he paused to survey her breasts. She wanted to scream, to rail at the fates and the gods above that these creatures had chosen her aerie to invade.

It was too late for railing, too late to scream or to plead, but she knew she would do both before the night was finished.

"She's right, the children pose no threat to you," Ralnd said, his voice soft and reasonable. "Let them return to their room. They are just babes."

Mera whimpered as the dagger dragged lightly over her daughter's throat and the child's eyes widened in growing terror. Dania was so frightened she could not even cry now. Shock glazed her eyes and she trembled with her terror.

"We could do that." The leader cast a look to one of his brothers. "Stand silently and still while you are restrained, then we'll send the babes on their way."

Mera felt Ralnd tense. The thought of being restrained, unable to fight or fly in the event of deception, was more than he could bear, she knew. But the jagged whimpers of the babes did what nothing else could have. Ralnd nodded shortly.

The humans tied them with practiced skill, twisting their hands behind their backs, beneath their wings and binding them with rope. Mera's eyes stayed on Dania's, fighting to offer hope, though she sensed there was no hope left.

The Vultures moved behind the humans, watching, their eyes flat and emotionless.

"Let the children go now," Ralnd reminded them.

The smirk that curved the leader's face sent a tear falling from Mera's eyes. Evil, dark and cruel defined that harsh slash of a smile.

"Not yet, but soon." He moved closer, his eyes glittering, and she could not contain her harsh cry as he touched her cheek. She jerked back—the vile smell of his body was more than she could bear, and she nearly gagged at the stench. His eyes narrowed and a gleam of fierce anticipation colored his expression.

"Release the children, my friends," he said softly.

For a moment Mera thought they meant to keep their word as each child fell to the floor. Then she screamed, agony washing over her in waves.

"No!"

The children cried out at first. With each brutal blow, each bone-breaking impact of large fists and each demented kick, they screamed. They fought, their little wings flaring out to beat at their captors, even as Mera struggled for release from the Vultures holding her back, battled to reach her babies and shield them with her own body.

But the hands that restrained her were too strong as a brutal fist to the side of her head rendered her nearly senseless with pain. Ralnd fought fiercely beside her, his own wings extended, beating at the Vultures until a blow from a sword sent him to his knees. The harsh cry torn from his throat joined the last broken screams of her children.

The Vultures and the Elitists now circled the room, laughing at their handiwork. They extended the children's limp wings and brutally hacked them off with their swords as blood sprayed the room. They groped into the mangled and torn flesh of the wings until they pulled from them one of the small circular discs that attached cartilage and bone to flesh.

Mera collapsed as Dania's wings fell to the bloodied floor beside the child's broken body. The sightless blue eyes stared toward her, horror and pain frozen forever in her daughter's shattered face.

Those who held Ralnd continued to rain blows on his weakened body, pushing him closer to the edge of unconsciousness. Mera prayed now for the darkness herself, but the Vultures had yet to strike her with the strength needed to take her from this unbearable moment.

"Damn, they didn't put up much of a fight, Graden." The Vulture leader stood over the broken bodies of the children, his voice filled with disappointment. "I expected more from Eagle whelps."

Mera forced herself to watch them moving about her home, their feet carelessly tracking the blood of her babes across the stone floor.

"Kill while you can, diseased leavings of Cinder. When King Dearn learns of this he will hunt you down and leave your bodies for the winds of Sorin to strip bare of skin and life as you are borne to the darkest reaches of the Seven Hells," Mera cursed him.

Hatred filled her heart. She knew now that nothing or no one could save her and Ralnd. Their fate had been written the moment the Vultures and the humans stepped into her home.

"Ah, such fire and hatred." The Vulture leader walked to her, kicking Ralnd a fierce blow as he passed. "Would you give me a fight, little angel?"

The agonized expulsion of breath that came from her husband's body ripped through Mera's soul. Gods help them, their own horror was just beginning. She watched the Vulture leader's hand move to his crotch and tighten about the flesh there.

"I'll spare your lives for a price, angel." He grinned down at her now. "Spread your thighs and welcome me, and I will spare your husband."

"No!" Ralnd's desperate denial was cut off as a foot landed painfully in the flesh of his stomach.

Mera turned her head, meeting the pain-ridden eyes of her mate, and in them she saw the same knowledge she could feel beating with wings of despair in her belly.

"Like you spared my babes?" She turned back to the monster looming above her. "I would never bow to your diseased and filthy body. I would prefer death to your touch."

She watched his eyes narrow, the black glitter in them more terrifying than anything she had known in her life. It was like watching Cinder himself stare down at her, his eyes filled with lust and contempt.

"Tie her to her bed and let her mate watch."

Hands gripped her arms as laughter roared around her, and Ralnd's desperate struggles finally penetrated the haze that paralyzed her. She fought the blows intended to weaken her as they tied her spread-eagle on her marriage bed. She screamed, she cursed and sought to tear with her teeth what she could no longer reach with her nails. It did nothing to halt their play or their enjoyment of it.

When she felt the first demon tear into her body, she screamed until she felt her throat shatter. After that, no other cries would come from it, only the desperate, mindless whimpers as agony spread through her. She strained against her bonds, her hands forming claws, her legs fighting against the ropes binding her.

Mera could hear Ralnd as well, fighting to aid her, his broken protests of such degradation filling their bedroom. Time after time, they raped her, hit her, cut her with the sharp blades of their daggers. As the last began to loosen his pants, the Vulture leader walked to Ralnd and slowly, painfully, pushed his dagger into her mate's chest.

Mera stilled. She was unaware of the last Vulture as he raped her. Her gaze was locked with the sightless, agonized gaze of her mate. She felt her body tremble; then, slowly, the only life left in her was that of her heart pumping, her lungs filling by instinct. She no longer felt the fists that bruised her body or the knives that nicked at the slow pulse of her veins. All she knew was her mate and the blood that oozed from the edges of the dagger, spilling slowly down his chest as his skin turned ashen.

Distantly, she heard the leader's jeers, but on some instinctual level she also felt his disappointment. He had not gained from this night's work the pleasure he had meant to.

"Worthless white whore." Mera heard his insult as she felt the thick expulsion of his seed into her body once more.

She turned her eyes to him. She wanted to speak, but no words would form. As he gave a final grunt and she felt him pull his weakening member from her body, she sneered and mouthed the words she could not voice.

"Soulless, gutless slither."

She watched him flush. His fist collided with her face, spraying her blood on the wall beside her bed. Yet, she felt no pain now; it was mercifully numbed—only the vibrations of the blow were felt.

"Let her bleed out. Let the whore suffer." He tightened his pants with a jerk of his hands and Mera sneered.

Her death might be slow, but she knew it would not compare to the death this viperous monster would know. Soon, there would be those who would miss her family, and the Vultures' return would be known. Then, Dearn would find them all, and they would suffer as they had never suffered before.

Daggers pricked her flesh, tearing into her with the smallest of slices. Let her bleed out, he had ordered, and she knew then what he meant—a slow, painful death. One that would give her time to remember, over and over again, what he had done.

Mera stared at the ceiling, refusing to watch, refusing to remember, refusing to stare at her broken mate. She would not cry, not while they could see and revel in her pain.

Suddenly, she thought of their newborn, left sleeping in her cradle in the corner. She had a brief memory of an intruder with oddly colored wings lifting the child from its bed. The child had not cried. Its blood had not joined that of its brothers and sister. Gods save her, where was her baby?

Chapter Two

ຄ

Dearn, King of the Winged Clans, stood on the balcony of his rooms and watched the display above him. Against the backdrop of a clear blue sky, the Winged Clans arrived in a blaze of color and prepared to land within the heavily fortified stone walls of the Fortress.

They flew from all directions, their huge wings catching the currents of air as they glided within the enclosed walls that housed the ruling family, a stone fortress set atop the highest mountain of the continent overlooking sheer cliffs and a boulder-strewn valley miles below. The Valley of the Gods, it was called, for it was here that Ashrad, their greatest god, and three of his children—Sorin, Dorin and Aleda—had defeated Ashrad's black-hearted son Cinder and sent him to rule the fiery depths of the Seven Hells.

The Fortress was more than just the home of the ruling Clan, though. Rising above the top of the mountain and spearing the clouds with its upper levels as it rose majestically, its many levels housed hundreds of small aeries and individual rooms accessible only by wing or from the stairways hewn into the inside of the mountain. Below it, caverns cut from solid rock provided more personal aeries and passageways led to storehouses and caves full of goods and gold, dallion stones, weapons and clothing. In times of famine or drought, all the Clans benefited from the stores. Canned goods, dried meats, flour, meal, sugar and all manner of dried foodstuffs were stored away, used during winter storms and replenished each year.

It was a place of safety. The Fortress could house the entire population of the Clans—feed and clothe them and sustain them through crisis, famine or war. It was a symbol of all they were, and all they hoped to be. The Fortress was the heart of the Clans, and it was here they gathered when in need.

Deep in his soul Dearn knew the foresight that had established this refuge eons ago would be greatly needed in the times ahead. In his bones he felt the haunting fear that the past was returning, and the bloodshed of hundreds of years before in a conflict so savage it nearly tore the Clans apart would come once again. They were at war, and they would be fighting against haunting specters that should have been destroyed during those first bloody centuries of battle.

As the first of the new arrivals began to land, Dearn narrowed his eyes, making a mental count of those arriving and adding them to those who had come before. The numbers were coming up woefully short.

From the South came the White Lance Clan. The White Lance was the spirit Clan, a graceful, soft-spoken group with pure white wings that had produced many of the spirit men and healers that inhabited the Fortress. They were called the angels of the Clans, for it was said the spirits of their dead protected and graced the gardens of Ashrad, providing a place of peace and comfort in the eternity of the afterlife.

From the West came the Eagle Clans. Soft shades of golden brown and amber mingled with delicate auburn glowed in fiery splendor on their wings as they banked and turned in the rays of the sun. The Eagles were temperamental, territorial and the strongest warriors of all the Clans. From them the ruling families had always been drawn. Their decisiveness, arrogance and warrior training had sustained them when other Clans had fallen behind. It was this Clan that was lacking the most in numbers.

From the North came the Ravens, their black wings reflecting brilliant blue highlights as they hovered. They were smaller, quicker and fought better during the darkness of night than the Eagle warriors, though they seemed less inclined to competitiveness than their bronze-winged brothers. They excelled as trackers and scouts. They could hide easily in the darkness, and their eyes could pierce the shadows to track their prey much better than the other Clan warriors.

From the East came the Red Hawk Clans, their wings gleaming in shades of mahogany, burgundy and burnished gold. They were a fierce yet often laughing breed, quick to anger and just as quick to forgive. They fought with single-minded determination to quickly finish a battle so they could return to play. Today, however, they were sober and concerned as they landed within the courtyard, searching among the crowds for lost family members.

The Owl, Crow and Falcon Clans had yet to appear in force. This concerned Dearn. Those Clans were smaller, more spread out and less able to defend themselves on their own. Their absence worried him greatly.

The women and children landed first, watched over by the hardened warriors above them. There was an atmosphere of grief and fear. The skies were filled with patrols, extending out for miles. Families drew together; anxious voices called out one to the other, questioning and fearful for missing loved ones. Dearn knew many were confused, their gazes lifting to the sky as the lonely wail of the Call still echoed throughout the mountains. The Call was sounded only during times of great danger to the Clans. Many were unaware of the peril now stalking them.

But he knew. He had seen it firsthand. Had smelled the stench of it in his nostrils, seen the brutality of it with his own eyes. Rage ate at him, spreading like a dark, diseased shadow upon his soul as the memory replayed once again through his mind. Vengeance. His fingers clenched on the railing before him, his body braced against the wash of white-hot agony. His sword would taste the blood of his enemies, and his vengeance would rain quick and true upon their heads. It was all that sustained him now. All that would sustain him until the time of reckoning arrived.

* * * * *

Tamora watched King Dearn where he stood silently on the balcony of the upper floor of the castle, his arms crossed tightly over his broad chest, his feet planted wide apart. His wings were folded proudly on his back, the golden feathers of the Eagle Clan flowing gracefully from his shoulders to the heels of his black leather boots. His shoulder-length golden-brown hair ruffled in the wind as it blew back from his strong, proud face.

The Clans had ruled the skies of Brydon for as long as man had walked its mountainous terrain. Dearn was a good king, just as his father and grandfather before him. He was a quiet person, reflective, relying on his own instincts rather than debating decisions, as the Clan leaders preferred. His lover for the past year, Tamora read the worry and concern on his face that others may not have seen.

He had barely spoken to her since the night before and had not come to her bed. He had, in fact, not been to her bed in months now, and this worried her more than anything else. He had distanced himself, drawn away from her as well as the others.

Tamora understood why he was so distant. They had found the bodies in the neighboring valley the evening before as they flew in search of a missing family reported to have been seen earlier in the day. The carnage and brutality of the deaths had sent shock then rage through all of them, but most especially Dearn.

The four bodies had been hopelessly mangled, their wings missing. Their bodies were hacked apart, left for the scavengers of the forest to drag away. When Tamora looked at Dearn, she saw the iciness of his golden eyes and watched the flat, unemotional expression take over his face. It was as though a part of him had shut down when he saw how his people had been murdered. He had frightened her.

21

A further search had raised even more fear within all of them. Deserted aeries were found throughout the passes they had checked and entire families had come up missing, their homes ransacked and the evidence of violence, the scent of death, unmistakable on blood-splattered walls. But only those four bodies had been found, despite an intensive search throughout the night by all the warriors in the Fortress. They had been able to find no one else.

"Don't just stand there." His voice was deep, dark with suppressed fury. "What have you learned?"

Tamora took a deep breath. He had sent her out over an hour before to find the information he needed while he met with his closest advisor, Havar. What she had found would do nothing to ease the fury raging through him.

She stepped closer, desperate to touch him but sensing an invisible barrier between him and any comfort she would offer. She hated to admit that barrier had been forming even before the deaths; they had merely strengthened it.

"Most of the Clans are reporting in now. There are missing families or family members among them all. The greatest number of missing seems to be from the Eagle Clan. There are only a few families of the Owl and Crow Clans reporting in. We've heard nothing from the Falcon Clans at all as of yet." She reported the bleak news, knowing the loss of those warriors would be a great handicap to the Clans.

The muscles in Dearn's jaw bunched with the effort to control his anger. His shoulders tensed further and his body seemed to vibrate. She had never seen him like this, though she had been fully aware of his capacity for it.

"The warriors," Dearn hissed, his eyes narrowing as he raised his head to watch the patrols still gliding over the mountain. "They hit the warriors the hardest, thinking that would weaken us."

Tamora fought her trembling at the tone of his voice, and she remembered the suspicion he had whispered to his advisor in the early hours of the morning before she retired to her room. Her wings shuddered in fear.

"Dearn, we aren't certain at this point." She moved closer, touching his arm, desperate to find some way to be close to him once again, to ease a bit of the worry surrounding him. "We've sent several of the Raven and Red Hawk troops to see what they can learn, but they haven't reported back yet. Until we have proof —"

"And what other answer do you think there could be? How much proof is needed, Tamora?" Dearn moved from her touch, his hands gripping the rail that ran along the balcony with knuckles that paled with his fierce hold as he stared down into the courtyard. "What other answer can you come up with? You remember the stories of the past as well as I. To prove their kills, the Vultures and Elitists cut the wings from our backs, taking the disks within them back to their human king. It was the only way to prove the deaths and receive their rewards."

"The Vultures have been dead for centuries, Dearn." She nearly winced at the edge of fear in her own voice. "They no longer exist."

"There is no other answer." Fury lent strength to the fist that cracked against the wood of the railing, nearly splitting it in half and causing Tamora to flinch. "Who else could possibly get into those aeries undetected?" He turned to her briefly, and in his eyes she saw a flame of such vengeance that her breath caught in her chest as he continued. "Only a rogue Clan could do it, and only the Vulture Clan was born so merciless. The Winged Clans do not kill their own, Tamora. Only the Vultures had such a lack of honor and mercy. Gods preserve us, but Cinder has had his revenge once again."

"But they're extinct." Tamora remembered her lessons in history better than Dearn could imagine. She remembered well the stories of blood and death, rapes and dismemberments. Back then, they allowed their women captives to live, to give birth to the seed planted within their bodies. It had been the

Vultures' ultimate revenge against both the warriors and the women they hated.

"Are they?" Dearn turned to her, his amber eyes flashing. "We were told they were all killed. We had only the word of the humans to go by in those days. Our historians, however, recorded there were many of that Clan unaccounted for. There was never confirmation of their extinction, Tamora, because we were betrayed once again."

She saw his certainty that he was right. His eyes blazed with the knowledge; his savage features were tight, giving him the look of an avenging god. All he needed now, Tamora thought, was the flaming sword of Dorin, the god of strength.

"But how could they have been hidden?" she whispered hesitantly. "Someone, somehow, would have seen them."

"I do not know how, but I do know they have returned." Dearn moved back into his bedroom as Tamora stared at him in disbelief.

The Vultures. She could only shake her head as she followed behind him. They had been merciless, totally lacking in any honor or loyalty, even to their own Clans. Their women took no mates, but instead went from man to man. The children were raised in squalor and without benefit of proper care. Many died within the first year of life from neglect.

The stories of the Vultures were steeped in horror, and it was said all Clans had breathed in relief when King Merson, Dearn's ancestor, sent out the order to have them all killed for their crime of aiding the human king in the war against the Clans. Merson had been unable to perform the deed himself, so it had been his decision that the first act of the new human king would be to rid the land of the Vultures, who had been captured and locked into a cavern at the edge of the mountains. That had been a mistake, Tamora thought, for it appeared that somehow, someway, the Vultures had survived and were now seeking vengeance.

"I'll meet with the Clan leaders in about an hour." Dearn turned to her as she re-entered the room. "I want you to find Havar and have him gather them together and meet me in the ballroom. We'll decide what to do then. We must move quickly, before those of our Clans who may be hidden are killed as well."

"Dearn, you need to rest first," she told him, worried at the pale cast of his skin, the edge of weariness that lay over him like a cloak.

Then his eyes met hers, and she saw in them a depth of pain that nearly took her breath.

"Sleep." He sighed wearily. "Gods have mercy, Tamora, every time I close my eyes I hear the screams of my people and see their blood soaking into the ground at my feet. Just do as I ask. I will sleep when I must. Don't worry about me."

"But Dearn—" She reached again to comfort, to soothe the torment she saw in those golden eyes.

He shook his head bitterly, stopping her before the action was completed.

"Just go, Tam. No...do as I ask. If I need you, I will call for you," he ordered, his tone and expression forestalling her objections.

Tamora nodded jerkily and turned to do as he bade. Her last glimpse of him showed him standing tall and silent in the middle of his bedroom, the breeze from the open balcony doors softly ruffling the feathers of his wings.

As she started down the hall, a broad, male hand on her shoulder startled her. Stopping, she stared into the violet and hazel eyes of Dearn's general, Brendar. He looked as tired as Dearn, his sun-weathered skin a bit pale and his mouth pulled into a tight line as he frowned down at her. His Red Hawk wings were folded against his back but were dusted with weariness from the long hours he had spent pulling together the Clan warriors and searching the passes.

"Is he doing okay?" he asked her softly, glancing toward Dearn's door.

Tamora pushed her hands through her hair as she shook her head.

"He hasn't eaten and he hasn't rested, Brendar. I cannot comfort him. I don't know if anyone can."

Brendar sighed roughly, one wing unfurling to curl about her shoulders, and Tamora leaned into the embrace, uncaring that the intimate action was out of character for the man as well as the situation. She was Dearn's lover, but he had not the time to hold her. She needed to be held, even if it was by this terse, confrontational warrior who had always set her teeth and her temper on edge. The same warrior who had comforted her through the earliest hours of the morning with his body and his touch, a betrayal of their king and of themselves.

"What of you?" he whispered into her hair, the warmth of his breath reminding her of his warmth and passion. "Have you rested any?"

"A bit." She breathed in roughly and pushed away from him as she heard a door close farther down the hall. Guilt seared her heart. "I must go. Dearn has asked me to call the Clan leaders together in the ballroom. I fear he intends to go to war on his own."

"He would not." Brendar shook his head violently as he stared at her in disbelief. "He is our king, he knows we will not allow him to do such a thing."

Tamora grimaced and waved her hand toward Dearn's door in ironic invitation.

"In there, he is. Perhaps you should inform him of this, for, I tell you, Dearn is like a beast at this moment, and he will go to war."

* * * * *

As the door closed, Dearn sighed deeply and closed his eyes for a moment. His wings shuddered and he willed them to lie serenely despite his rage. It would not do for his Clans to see his anger or his worry. His fear.

He saw all too clearly in his mind's eye the bodies they had found the night before. The Eagle Clan female had been brutally raped and allowed to bleed to death from her wounds rather than killed swiftly, as the men had been. It was a technique the Vultures had excelled in. They hated the Clans but more importantly, they hated the women of the Clans for their distaste at mating with them. Slovenly and unclean, the Vulture race had been the most undesirable element within the Clans, and no woman outside their Clan would willingly lie with one of them.

The moment he saw how the woman had died he knew he was facing an enemy that had somehow risen from extinction. An enemy that would not be easy to kill, nor would they be easy to track. The Vultures were resourceful and as adept within the sky as any Eagle. Tracking them would require more than just the patrols he had sent out the night before. It would require much more strength than the Clans had needed in centuries to destroy them.

They will die, though, Dearn swore, and this time he would be certain none would survive to return later. When the Vultures were defeated this time, he would be there to ensure each and every one died. Every man, woman or child — it mattered not to him. The evil that infested that breed was too strong, too much a part of their character to allow even one to survive.

He moved swiftly to pull the thick, black warrior's leathers from his clothing chest. If the slovenly slithers wanted to kill and maim then, by the gods, he would make certain it wasn't easy for them. By his blade and the will of Ashrad they would die.

The Clan leaders would protest. They would raise a fit that would likely blow the top from the Fortress and curse him for weeks on end for his decision. But they were his people. He was born a warrior and had trained as a warrior, and he would fight as a warrior. He would go insane sitting safely within walls while his troops battled and died alone, without even the security and confidence of knowing their king was at their side.

Dearn had studied the fighting habits of the Vultures far more than anyone he knew. Even at an early age his hatred of that breed and his fury at King Merson's cowardly decision had tormented him. He had feared even then that they had not died. How does an entire Clan die, even in such an inferno, and there not be a bone to show for it? It wasn't possible, and Dearn had known it. But he would be certain, he swore, that this time they would pay, and they would pay with their lives.

After he finished dressing, he heard the wings howl through the Valley of the Gods, the sound resembling the strangled cries he knew his people had sounded before their deaths. His fist clenched and he could feel his body tightening with the need for action, the need for battle. No, he would not sit here behind the protection of stone and the warriors who would give their lives in his name. His people were dying because his ancestor had refused to see the end to a Clan that had lost the right to call themselves winged warriors.

Dearn vowed to himself and to those whose cries echoed in the valley below that he would not be so weak or so merciful. He would see each and every Vulture and human participant in those deaths with their bones broken, the skin flayed from them by the rocks that would crush the life from their bodies.

They would know fear, they would know terror, and in the centuries to come the humans would learn that the vengeance of the winged warriors would be swift, encompassing and without the weakness or mercy that had been extended centuries before.

Chapter Three

స

Matte watched the patrols flying to and from the Fortress, tracked them and made a mental note of the numbers and the strengths she could see in each. Numbers and strengths far superior to those of the Vulture and human forces massing against them.

The Vulture and Elitist forces had killed many of the warriors. Didn't their screams, their pleas, echo in her dreams each night to remind her? There had been little she could do to aid any of them, but she and her warriors had done what they could, where they could.

The Clan warriors appeared well-trained, flying in close formation with scouts and sharpshooters swooping down to track the ground as the others patrolled above. They were now flying in such large troops that the Vulture leader, Edgar, raged in fury at the inability of his forces to successfully attack them. Fear was slowly starting to inch its way into the ranks of the killing teams he sent out each night.

The forests teemed with Clan warriors, both in the sky and in the trees below. The aeries at the farthest reaches were deserted now, the land silent except for the animal life. Canyons echoed with silence; vast rivers and lakes whispered of their loneliness in the face of the Clans' desertion.

Yet in each area Matte had glimpsed signs of those who hid and watched — and were ready and eager to place an arrow into the heart of any Vulture.

Unfortunately, she, though a Bastard Breed, looked enough like a Vulture to be mistaken for one at a distance. The winged warriors would now be killing anything or anyone remotely resembling a Vulture and asking questions later.

King Dearn wasn't a fool. He was arming his men well with swords, arrows and crossbows and sending out large troops of mixed warriors of each Clan. He was taking no chances. The scouts were patient and disciplined. It was nearly impossible for Matte to catch sight of them, and she knew Edgar and his men had yet to see one. Unfortunately, it might be a while before those scouts could slip back to the Fortress with their reports.

She prayed it would be soon. There wasn't much time left if they were to defeat Edgar's forces with the minimum amount of bloodshed. Not to the mention the fact that she could not keep her betrayal a secret for much longer.

"Do you think he suspects?"

Her lieutenant, Stovar, a Bastard Breed Eagle warrior, crouched beside her, the frown on his rough-hewn face one of concern. His folded wings were darker than a normal Eagle's — his hated Vulture heritage had darkened the russet-and-golden hues, dimming the vibrancy that a full Eagle would display.

Matte could only shake her head. She knew they had left enough messages, enough clues and had warned enough families of the Clans that Dearn should have known well before now what was going on.

The largest troop flew out, and she caught a glimpse of the king's colors. She narrowed her eyes against the glare of the sun, tracking the warriors and their numbers, and as she did she saw one flying well protected by the others.

King Dearn, dressed in warrior's leathers and flying out with a fighting troop of his best warriors. He was magnificent, she thought, studying him intently.

The king was easily discernible among his warriors, his arrogant bearing and superbly conditioned body graceful in the sky. The leathers fit his body snugly, the black vest unencumbered by a tunic beneath it, and his golden-brown hair flew out behind him. He had to be the most amazing specimen of warrior she had ever seen.

"Were we able to get one of our spies within the Fortress?" she asked Stovar as she continued to watch the flight. She had given the order weeks ago to have someone installed in the Fortress who would blend in easily. One who could guard the king's back against any assassins King Alfred or Edgar would try to send against him.

"She got in, but we've not heard from her yet." His voice was low so the sound carried no further than her ears. "It will be difficult to get information out for a while, I'd say. King Dearn appears to be running a tight army. I haven't seen anything but warriors out all day."

"He should know by now." She sighed. "He should have known before this. I was hoping the Call would go out sooner. Too much blood has been shed already."

Though she didn't voice the thought, Matte worried desperately for the infant they had left sleeping in the brush at the base of its parents' cliffside aerie. At present, one of her people was taking care of the babe until a patrol of Clan warriors was sighted. Finding milk to feed it and clothes to keep it dry had not been easy, and Matte knew they would run out of options if that pass wasn't patrolled soon.

The waste and cruelty of those deaths haunted Matte. Despite her close association with blood, death and the mercilessness of the enemy, it still shook her each time she witnessed the damage a diseased mind could accomplish.

"There will be more." Her lieutenant shook his head. "The king's madness is nearly as fierce as the Vultures'. It's as though Edgar and Alfred are feeding off each other's insanity. Our people are growing despondent, Matte. They cannot stand by much longer and witness such atrocities without acting."

Matte lowered her head. She had her own orders, the needs of her own people to consider; she had done all she could. Yet, she knew for her warriors it was not nearly enough.

Their rage and fury over the senseless bloodshed were driving many of them to recklessness in their attempts to sabotage Edgar's plans.

"We will do what we must, Stovar," she whispered. "We cannot back down now. We've gone too far. Dearn has his people in the Fortress; all that is left is to meet with him. I will do that as quickly as I can. Edgar will be forced to release my warriors to my command now. As soon as the danger to them is over, we can move ahead with our own plans."

She felt a frisson of fear at the thought of finally meeting with the Winged Clans' king and putting her proposition to him. Rumors were that Dearn was the most savage and fierce of all the warriors. He would not be an easy man to bargain with.

"As long as you do." Stovar nodded his dark brown head slowly. "You better get back." He nudged her softly as the king's troop disappeared into the mountain. "They'll be looking for you soon. I'll stay and see if Lenora is able to get anything out."

She nodded, aware of the risks of staying too long and allowing any suspicion to arise against her.

"Don't stay too long," she warned him. "I may need you later. I'll send one of the others back to take your place."

He nodded again, his face turned away from her now as he watched the Fortress. She couldn't blame him for longing to sit and stare at it for as long as he could. It was as magnificent as they had always heard it was. Soon, she prayed to the gods, it would welcome her and her people as it had refused to before.

* * * * *

Ralnd's aerie appeared deserted. It was the first thing Dearn noticed as the group he commanded neared the mountain home of his cousin late that afternoon.

The rough wood door stood open like a gaping mouth; the entrance to the cave was dark and forbidding as the winged warriors approached in silence. Dearn's gut clenched with dread.

His greatest fear since finding the murdered Clan members two nights before was that his cousin and family had fallen victim to the assassins as well. He worried when they had not shown up the night of the birthday celebration; it was one of the reasons he went out that night himself in search of the missing. Now, staring at the silent cliff that housed the aerie, Dearn could feel the horror of what he would find crawling up his spine like an evil touch.

The aerie was the same as the five others they had checked since leaving the Fortress. Such silence among the mountain homes of the Clans was ominous on such a warm summer day. The children should have been outside. The wooden shutters should have been thrown wide to catch the cooling breeze that flowed through the mountain passes and admit light to the interior of the caves.

Ralnd's shutters, too, were closed. There was no sign of life and no sounds of children calling from within the dark interior. It sent a shudder of unease skating down his spine.

Dearn gave the signal for his warriors to land on the wide ledge of the aerie. He saw the looks that passed among them and felt the same apprehension he could see on their faces. Nothing looked different about this deserted aerie, but the feel of it was more forbidding than those they had stopped at earlier.

Six of the fourteen landed on the ledge, standing still and silent as their narrowed eyes scanned the cliff faces around them. Dearn signaled the others to patrol the area. There were twelve aeries in this valley, three of the families inhabiting them already reported missing. Ralnd's family made the fourth.

The unnatural silence was the first thing Dearn noticed as he landed beside his men. Even the breeze did not stir. It was so quiet and still they could hear the echo of the river rushing through the canyon more than a mile below.

"Look. Heelmarks." One of the warriors surveying the ledge pointed out the indention along the dirt at the side of the door. The heel of a boot had pressed into the firm soil. It was a mark identical to others they had found on other ledges.

Only humans placed heels on their boots. The winged warriors wore flat-soled leather coverings on their feet. The evidence suggesting human involvement in the disappearances and deaths of the Clan members was mounting up.

Again, trepidation skated along Dearn's spine. Humans did not seek out the Winged Clans. Except for a certain few in the Southern Range, the humans' prejudices and fears kept them in their own valleys, far below the mountains.

Why would humans be attacking the Clans? From history, they should remember how ineffectual they were against the Winged Clan warriors. But the reports he had received from the families escaping from this valley told the story.

The families said they had been attacked by humans accompanied by winged warriors. Alone, humans knew they hadn't a chance against the Clans, but there had been that one time in the past when their weaknesses hadn't mattered. That one time when they allied themselves with the Vultures.

"Damar, you and Palon check the valley," Dearn ordered the warrior who had come searching for his sister Mera. Damar started to protest, but Dearn reinforced the order with a look he knew they were all wary of. Damar thinned his lips and did as he was bidden.

Spreading his white wings, he launched from the ledge and began to search as Dearn moved closer to the open doorway, reluctant to step inside.

"Ralnd?" He called out his cousin's name, fighting the apprehension he could feel gathering in his body. "Ralnd? Mera?"

He entered the darkened aerie. He could feel the rest of the troop at his back, watching the mountain, their wings fluttering in the moaning breeze that suddenly whipped past them, a moan Dearn felt rising in his soul, fighting for release as his eyes adjusted to the dim light.

His blood seemed to congeal in shock as his mind fought to deny the sight before his eyes. He gasped, his hand going to the hilt of his sword and clenching it convulsively.

Years of discipline and training prevented the cry of horror from escaping his throat. At that moment, Dearn knew the restless spirits of his cousin's family sounded their fury in the cry of the whipping winds moving through the cliffs outside their mountain home. He could feel the blood draining from his face, feel his limbs weaken in sickness and despair as he surveyed the carnage. He wanted to fall to his knees and howl in despair, but knew his strength might be all that kept his troop together now. A strength that was a fraction of what he needed to face the anguish spawned by the heart-wrenching evidence of brutality that lay before his eyes.

Dearn waved his men back, unwilling for them to enter the nightmare he was experiencing. Knowing that, should they enter, the precious time he needed to come to terms with this would be lost.

With leaden steps and a silent scream, he moved farther into the blood-caked room. He called out no names this time, uttered not a sound, for he knew there were no ears to hear his call. He wanted to run, to fly from this place and forget he had seen such horrors or that such cruelties could exist. There was no escaping the reality of it, though. There was now, only facing the agony of their deaths and finding those who had committed the atrocities.

Dearn fought his tears as, with each small step, he felt another part of his soul shatter.

The living area was destroyed. The furniture lay in pieces; the dining table was missing two legs and lay on its side. The large cast-iron cooking pot rested against the wall on the opposite end of the room from the large fireplace carved out of the wall. Precious ceramic images of the gods lay shattered — the largest, that of Ashrad, ground into dust, the print of a boot heel clearly defined within it.

Ralnd's children were in the middle of the room. Dearn's wings shuddered; his body trembled as a storm of emotion shook him from within. He prayed for strength, for he did not know if he could bear the sight that lay before him.

There was so much blood. It was splattered on the walls and had poured across the floor in streams of death. He knelt beside the shattered bodies, his hands shaking, his breath shuddering at the sight of the small, brutalized babies.

He blinked, fighting to clear the haze of tears from his eyes. Surely, what he was seeing was not possible. Such savagery could not exist.

Yet, it did. The proof lay in the broken, bloodied bodies of his cousin's children.

"By the gods!" Gregor, the youngest of the troop cried out his horror as he entered the room.

Dearn couldn't move. He could only shake his head as he heard the rest of the warriors cry out. He wanted to turn and somehow help them come to terms with such evil, but how could he? He couldn't come to terms with it himself.

He was aware of them slowly filling the room and the heavy silence descending around him, and he could do nothing to ease the shock and fear he knew filled them. All he could do was stare into the lifeless eyes of his godchildren. The children he had once dreamed might be his. The children he had sworn to protect.

He reached out, his fingers barely brushing Dania's pale, cold face. It was bloodied and bruised, the skin torn and abraded and showing signs of the heavy fist that had smashed it. She was just a babe, barely able to use her wings when last he had seen her; and now here she lay in the dried gore of her own body. Her golden eyes seemed to stare at him accusingly, her sightless gaze a testament to the brutality of her death.

Beside her lay her severed wings, small, delicate, just large enough to support her small body in the air. He touched one golden feather gently and again fought the tears welling from his soul. There, just within the point where they had been cut from her body, the small white disc was missing.

Aaroen and Gable lay beside her, their wings at their feet, those discs gone as well. The stone floor was stained black with their blood, the hideous metallic scent overwhelming where the sticky liquid seeped into the crevices beneath their small bodies.

So tiny, Dearn thought, unable to take his eyes from them despite the panic he could feel mounting in the men behind him. *By the heart of Ashrad, what do I do now?*

His heart raged as his men gathered around him, their low prayers and desperate curses as they gazed upon the destruction striking at his soul. *Dear merciful Ashrad, what do I do?*

Dearn could hear no answer to his broken plea, only the keening moan of the winds outside the aerie.

"Search the aerie." He had to fight to clear the lump of rage from his throat before speaking. Tears tightened his chest as the fury tightened his fists. "Find Ralnd and Mera."

Ralnd and Mera's bodies would be close by; they would not have left their young alone, especially at night. Only after darkness had fallen could anyone or anything have slipped in and invaded their home to cause such destruction. They would be here.

He fought to prepare himself, instinct warning him what he would soon face. *Merciful Sorin, show me the way*, he prayed to the god of strength.

Gregor stumbled from one of the bedrooms. The young man's face was white, his body trembling in shock as he sagged against the doorframe and barely controlled his retching. Dearn shot to his feet and moved quickly to the doorway, pushing past Gregor only to stagger back in mind-numbing shock.

His stomach heaved, his heart felt as though it had exploded within his chest; but he knew it was his ragged cry that had finally been torn from his body.

"Ahhh, gods!" he cried out as he gripped the back of the chair that sat just inside the doorway and fought for breath. His heart tightened in agony as he viewed the scene before him.

Ralnd was bound in another chair in the corner of the bedroom, a dagger lodged in his heart. His face was twisted in lines of rage and horror, his eyes still glazed with the disbelief that must have been there when he died. The disbelief that such horror could have been committed against his family.

It was the sight of Mera's body, however, that dug a trench of sorrow through Dearn's soul. Small, delicate Mera, with her laughing eyes and glorious blond hair, had been so severely abused and beaten that her beautiful face was barely recognizable.

"Mera..." Dearn could barely speak. He could barely breathe, so great was his need to sink to the floor in despair. Ah, gods, he cried out silently, not Mera.

But it was Mera, or at least as much as the twice-cursed demons of the Seven Hells had left of her. He shook his head, seeing the uncountable wounds that would have bled slowly, draining the life from her. There were marks of teeth on her breasts, on her thighs. Bruises in the shape of fingers marred her pale skin, and her thighs were smeared with the dried evidence of the rapes she had suffered.

Her eyes were open, staring in resignation and in pain, staring at him, beseeching him. He could hear death and anguish beating a hollow, ragged pulse within his soul.

"King Dearn." Gregor stood behind him now. "What are we to do? That's Damar's sister, he will be here—"

A howl of rage rent the air. A second later, Dearn moved to block the entrance, to keep the brother from seeing the pathetic remains of the sister he had adored above all others.

He was a second too late. Damar burst in, his momentum carrying him past Dearn's attempt to hold him back. He came to an abrupt stop. Not another sound came from the man, but his full white wings began to shudder and tremble with the excessive emotion traveling through his body.

The White Lance warrior swayed as though in the grip of a fierce, destructive wind. Dearn watched as his fists clenched to halt their betraying tremor, but nothing could still the restless rush of wings at his back.

"Gods have mercy. Sweet, precious Aleda have mercy." The cry echoed through the room as Damar looked from the bed where his sister lay to the chair where her husband sat. He shook his head and blinked, as if trying to convince himself that what he was seeing could not be.

"Merrie?" He whispered his sister's name with brittle hope and moved farther into the room. Broken whimpers of disbelief issued from his throat. His face sagged in lines of despair, his shoulders trembling with the sobs bottled up inside him. Dearn wished he could find some way to comfort the man, but he knew no words would ease the pain such a sight would bring to a loving brother.

Damar stopped at the bed, picking up one of the blood-splattered blankets that had fallen to the floor. His hands shook so badly he could barely hold the material; and still those soft, eerie whimpers of agony escaped from his throat. Gently, he raised the thick cloth, spreading it slowly over his sister's broken body. Tears ran in slow, heartbroken rivulets down his face as he focused on the battered face before him.

"Ah, gods, Merrie." Damar cried out her name, sinking to his knees beside the bed, his hands clenched in the quilt that now covered her. His head fell to the bed mere inches from hers, and as the white-blond hair of the brother mingled with the bloodstained blonde of the sister, his shoulders began to heave with his sobs.

Dearn lowered his head, wishing above all things that he could block out the sight of death and the cries of one of his strongest warriors.

"Who would do this?" Damar's tearful whisper seemed to echo around him. "Who could do this?"

Dearn could only shake his head, steeling himself as his father had taught him so many years ago. Steel defends and strengthens, his father had told him. *Enclose your heart in times of need with the steel of your determination and your strength. In doing this, all things will be bearable.* Dearn wondered now if he had somehow foreseen the dark days coming.

"We'll find out, Damar," he promised, his voice hardening.

Oh, yes, they would find the ones responsible for this, and they would suffer. The guilty party would suffer as only the Clans could make them suffer for their crimes.

"I need to take her home." Damar reached out and gently closed the wide, terrified, dead eyes.

"We will take her home, Damar. Gregor, you and Semar return to the Fortress. Have Havar send another unit out to help bring Ralnd and his family home. I'll await them here." Dearn turned to the young warrior, who now stood outside the door. Gregor could only shake his head, his gaze still on the floor.

"Sire, you should return with us," he whispered, his voice trembling, unable to look up at the carnage before him. "It's not safe here."

Dearn shook his head. He could not leave this place, not until the bodies were prepared and could leave as well. He could not leave the cousin who had been his closest friend, nor the woman who had held as much of his heart as any woman could.

"It's as safe as it can be until the ones responsible are caught," Dearn assured him bleakly. "Go now, Gregor, and watch your backs. I can't afford to lose any more of my warriors."

Gregor nodded and then turned and rushed from the room, calling out to his cousin Semar as he did so. Dearn prayed they would make it safely to the Fortress, and wished now that he had included more men within each troop sent out to investigate the aeries.

"Vultures." The word passed Damar's lips and echoed within Dearn's soul. "I remember the stories. Many of our Spiritmen said they would return, and that they would try to destroy the Clans once again. Now, they've returned." Accusing blue eyes, so like his sister's, turned to Dearn as though seeking affirmation.

"We have no proof of that yet, Damar," Dearn warned him quietly. "Until we do, there is no cause to panic the Clans even further."

"We need no further proof." Damar's usually placid eyes now glittered brightly within his pale face. "You suspect the same. I know you, Dearn, I can tell by the look in your eyes."

"At this moment, my suspicions do not matter." Dearn turned and walked to the door. "Until we know, we will be silent about this, and that's an order, Damar."

"And the humans are fighting with them." Damar ignored Dearn's command to silence. "Just as before, Dearn, they are attempting to destroy the Clans."

"Whoever or whatever is doing this will be brought to justice, Damar, to the justice of the Clans. Until we know for certain who is behind this, we must tread carefully. Panicking our people will not serve justice." Dearn spoke quietly, firmly, refusing to turn back to the horror he was attempting to escape.

"Dearn, will you hide your head and your heart from the truth?" Damar's accusing question followed him to the doorway. "Even now? Even after seeing Mera? You loved her as well as Ralnd did, Dearn, will you not admit the evil that has taken her from us?"

Dearn paused, feeling the rage and grief his warrior felt. Feeling it as deeply, as fiercely as a broken heart could. He took a shuddering breath and fought to retain control, to hold back the grief spreading through his body.

"I hide from nothing, Damar," he whispered, hearing the huskiness of the unshed tears that clogged his throat. "But, by the gods, I swear to you now if I could hide from this horror, then it is something I would surely do."

Dearn exited the bedroom, leaving Mera's brother to watch over her alone. He could no longer bear the sight of what had been done to her. The blanket Damar had placed on her could not cover his memory. Nor could it comfort the aching wound in his heart.

As he walked quickly through the living area, Dearn's life seemed to flash before his eyes. His younger life, the time when he and Ralnd had flown through these passes as boys, whooping and yelling and making a nuisance of themselves. He remembered the time they had snuck into the White Lance range and watched as Mera and her sister Lark bathed in a mountain stream. Both had been besotted with her, but it had been Ralnd Mera loved. She had no desire to be queen of her Clans; she had wanted only to be Ralnd's mate.

Dearn had stood aside, but he had done so jealously and with no small amount of anger at the time. In the years that followed, he had been able to put aside those youthful, turbulent emotions. However, he had never put aside his feelings for Mera.

He stopped on the wide ledge and surveyed the valley below. This had been Mera's dream. This aerie and her life with Ralnd had been all she had dreamed of after first meeting the Eagle warrior. Dearn had stood with Ralnd during the mating ceremony and had sworn to see to the care of his family should he ever meet an unfortunate end. Now, Ralnd and Mera were gone, as was the family Dearn had sworn to care for.

"King Dearn." Lucan, the son of the Red Hawk Clan Chief, approached him quietly, his hazel eyes worried, his voice low so the others inside would not hear him.

"Yes, Lucan?" Dearn answered him as he listened to the winds cry through the valley.

"A child is missing."

Dearn frowned in confusion as he fought to understand what the warrior was telling him. All the children were accounted for; he knew that by the broken bodies inside.

"What do you mean, a child is missing?"

"Mera and Ralnd's new babe is missing."

"The child was to go to Mera's mother three moons ago," Dearn told him tightly. "She was not here with the others?"

"No, Sire." Lucan shook his head. "I was there when a message came to Lady Saran. Mera was going to bring the babe to her during your celebration. She did not send her to her mother, and neither is she within the aerie."

At that moment, the winds howled mournfully, screaming through the valley with the force of a desperate spirit; and Dearn knew that somehow Mera's spirit was trying to reach them, to lead them to the child still missing. He clenched his fists in fury; he didn't want to see another broken child lying before him. Already he had seen too much death, and feared there was much more awaiting him.

Chapter Four

ഔ

Dearn signaled to the two Raven warriors sitting on the top of the cliff across from Ralnd's aerie to keep an eye on the skies around them while he and Lucan checked below for the child. After receiving confirmation from them, he dove silently from the ledge, his wings spread to catch the thermals that flowed through the mountains. Without thought, he banked and headed toward the entrance of the pass. If the child wasn't within the aerie then it had to be close by.

He fell into a crisscross search pattern with Lucan. There was no way the infant could be alive. Vultures threw such small babes from the aerie ledges for sport, to hear the wailing cries as they fell to their deaths.

Dearn crossed Lucan's path for the third time and his eyes surveyed the narrow stretch of bank along the swiftly flowing river. He allowed the grief and pain overwhelming his heart free rein. He could feel the wind drying his face as the tears wet it. For the first time in memory he wept, and the wound that gave birth to those tears he feared would never heal.

He had vowed to rid Brydon of the Vultures. First, he would learn how and where they had managed to hide for the past centuries and why the humans had joined them in this carnage. Then, he would destroy them as quickly and as surely as they should have been destroyed before.

Such evil should not be allowed to exist. The Vulture Clan and the humans who fought with them would die.

As he turned to make another pass, he caught Lucan's signal to land and nodded quickly in assent. He had seen nothing below to investigate, but he knew the warrior would not be satisfied did he not check out whatever he thought he had seen. With a quick signal to the others, flying in a protective pattern around them, he made one last pass of the valley. He wanted to be certain there was nothing or no one still lurking to attack while they were grounded. His force was small, and until the messengers he'd sent returned with additional warriors, they were vulnerable.

There were no signs of life, nothing to mark that anyone was within the area. With a final sweep, Dearn joined Lucan on the riverbank. As his feet touched land, his hand went to his sword and his eyes moved methodically over the landscape.

Lucan was heading for the end of the small stretch of open bank to investigate whatever he had seen. Dearn slowly followed him, cataloging the small signs the humans had left on the soft ground.

He heard a sound, one that wasn't part of the roar of rushing water or the moan of the wind. It was little more than a whimper, a weak, demanding cry from where the open space turned to brush.

Dearn broke into a run even as Lucan moved into the sparse growth. It wasn't possible. The babe couldn't have survived, he told himself as hope soared within his heart. Yet, what else could have made that cry?

Lucan was kneeling in the sand as Dearn reached him, his arms wrapped around a small object as he rocked to and fro, sobbing. It was not a broken, mangled corpse the warrior cradled. The babe cried as a motherless, hungry infant would. Her tiny wings were wrapped around her body for warmth, and she searched desperately for mother's milk against her rescuer's bare muscular arm.

"She was spared." Lucan continued to rock the child as his body heaved. "Thank the gods, she was spared."

The babe whimpered weakly once again, her little rosebud mouth puckering in anger as she protested the arm that lacked the nourishment she needed.

"But how was she spared?" Dearn murmured as he gazed up to the aerie.

The fall was a long one; one that such a small child could not have survived. That meant only one thing. One of the humans within the murdering party had found some measure of mercy in his heart—it was a fact that Vultures had none. It would not save the human, Dearn thought, but his death would be swifter.

His eyes went to the ground and the small nest that had been prepared within the brush for the child. There, evidence of the supplies needed to care for an infant lay—a bottle with a soft leather nipple, several soiled rags and a small, dirt-smeared piece of cloth that had been used to cover him.

"Get the child back to the aerie, Lucan," Dearn ordered softly as he turned and scrutinized the gorge. He looked up, checking the positioning of his men and the protection those positions could afford him should the enemy come upon them. The tracks in the sand indicated there had been many humans, but there were also the tracks of the heelless boots of winged warriors.

"Mera should have food there somewhere," he heard Lucan mutter as the child whimpered once again. "Hang on, little one, and Uncle Luc will see what he can find."

Dearn would have smiled at the sound of the big warrior pacifying the babe, his voice softened to comfort as he tucked her carefully within his vest.

"Take off, Lucan." Dearn turned to him, his order harsh now. "Get that babe to the aerie, I'll be right behind you."

The warrior nodded, his body bracing as he flared his wings, the huge feathered shapes moving fiercely now as he ran, picking up the speed needed to launch his body from the ground.

It wasn't easy. The air currents this low were not as strong as those above, and gaining momentum and speed to take off, though not impossible, took determination. Dearn was right behind him. As the warrior lifted from the ground, Dearn executed the same maneuver and felt the firm draft that flowed along the river take his wings and aid him aloft. He watched the shadows of the cliffs closely, inspecting them for spying eyes and the enemy, who could well be lying in wait. He had an odd feeling in his gut, one that warned him as surely as the harsh moan of the winds had seemed to warn him, that danger was much closer than he could guess.

As he entered the aerie behind Lucan, he heard several men back in the bedroom speaking to Damar, and in their voices he could hear their attempts at comfort. He took a deep breath, looking reluctantly to the children's shrouded bodies still lying in the middle of the room. Someone had covered them with blankets, tucking the edges carefully under. Atop the one enclosing Dania's tiny form was the small blood-splattered doll she had once carried with her everywhere she went. A doll he had given her to mark her last birthday.

In the cool depths of the pantry, Lucan had found a small jar of what appeared to be goat's milk. In another section of the wall he found a bottle and quickly assembled the babe's meal. Intent on watching the little one eat, Dearn was startled by the abrupt arrival of the warriors he had left to patrol the gorge.

"Take cover, Sire," Lorent, a Red Hawk warrior hissed imperatively as several of the larger men fought to surround him, pushing him farther into the aerie as others lifted the heavy door to place it securely within the opening.

"Sire, we sighted Vulture warriors. Dozens of them," a White Lance warrior reported, his face pale. "There are too many to fight and no time to fly."

"Get into the aerie, away from the doors." Dearn moved to the window, easing the shutter open barely enough to see through.

Damar and the warriors who had been in the bedroom with him emerged, their swords drawn.

"Stay back," he commanded them tersely. "We found Mera's babe; we cannot afford a fool's fight for vengeance right now. Stay back, and stay silent, and we may yet come through this undetected."

He looked worriedly at the child, praying it would not begin to fret once again.

"Lucan, take her into Mera's room," Damar suggested. "It's the farthest from the door. If she cries, perhaps she will not be heard. And for the gods' sake, stay away from those windows Ralnd insisted on putting in there."

Lucan moved quickly, though Dearn could see his reluctance to go back into that room.

"Get ready. If they come into the aerie we'll fight. We should be able to hold them off until Semar arrives with extra troops." He peered through the small opening once again. "There's no way in Seven Hells we can fight our way past them."

"Dozens" was a fairly accurate count of the number of warriors now flying through the valley. And, by the blood of Ashrad, he had been right. Vultures.

Their feathers appeared lifeless even beneath the bright sunlight, branding the Seven Hells' demons for what they were. They landed on the opposite aerie ledges, their laughter and jeering voices causing him to grit his teeth in fury.

"Stay silent." He motioned his warriors farther away from the entrance. "Let's see what they do."

They were searching the aeries, and they were being damned careful about it. As the gorge became crowded with large, broad bodies and huge wings, more went into the aeries and searched through them.

"What could they be looking for?" Damar stood beside Dearn, looking through the shutter on that side.

"They could have sighted us in the area —" Dearn's eyes narrowed as he realized he saw Clan colors in the wings of some of the men patrolling the gorge. "By the gods, what are they?"

It was as though someone had taken the colors and diluted them or, in some cases, brightened them. Mixed in with the Vulture warriors were others who should not have been. A breed that should not exist.

Pale cream wings, dark russet, brown and gold wings. Wings so black they were nearly blue diluted with the dull shades of a Vulture. Bright red, russet, and the gold of the Redhawk Clan mixed with black and dark brown.

"The Bastard Breeds. Seven Hells, those warriors are a mix of Clan and Vulture, Sire. How can they exist?" Damar whispered, horrified, his face white and his eyes dilated with shock.

Dearn shook his head, continuing to watch as the aerie ledges filled. He prayed to the gods they would ignore this one, but the gods, apparently, were not on his side.

He drew his sword, his hands moving in a silent signal for his warriors to be ready. He watched carefully as a woman, of all things, moved in front of the small window, her back to him.

"Stay silent, King Dearn, and for the gods' sakes keep your fine feathers within that aerie." Fury and disgust laced the voice that came softly through the window. "The last damned thing I need is the death of a king on my conscience."

Shock held Dearn silent; his men glanced at him, uncertain what to do.

"Who are you?" Dearn whispered. "And why do you aid us?"

"There are forty-eight Vulture warriors—pure-breed, bloodthirsty Vulture warriors—along this valley searching for your aristocratic ass." Anger vibrated in the woman's voice. "You don't heed messages and you ignore warnings, but you better heed this one well. Stay silent, stay hidden, and you may yet live to fly yourself and that babe out of this valley."

Suddenly, a brash, harsh voice called, "Matte, have you found anything?"

"There's nothing here, Edgar. You're chasing shadows again." There was an edge of weariness to the woman's voice now. "Have your men hurry and finish this so I can find my bed."

"Dammit, they were seen heading here." The voice moved off, calling out orders for the warriors to hurry.

"What are you?" Dearn asked as the Vulture moved way. "Why do you carry the colors of the Eagle Clan?"

"And why do you ask so damned many questions?" the woman snapped, her back still turned to him. "Keep quiet, for the gods' sake. There are Vultures all around here."

All around the gorge, in fact, but Dearn noticed that the warriors with Matte all had the multicolored wings that so confused him. He did as she ordered, though the fact that she ordered him rankled. The woman was above her station, he thought. Was she not careful, the day would come when such orders might well give her more trouble than she could handle.

* * * * *

Matte leaned indolently against the side of the aerie yawning. She fought to appear bored, tired and weary of the hunting. If she showed but a breath of any sign of distress she knew Edgar would quickly become suspicious.

So far, she had managed to keep him off guard and unaware of her activities, but the fools within this aerie were testing both her patience and her ability.

"This is insanity, Matte." Stovar stood beside her, propped against the doorframe. "If one of Edgar's warriors lands on this ledge we're doomed."

"They're too lazy to check an aerie they believe we're checking already." Her voice was soft, a tight smile curving her lips as she fought to keep her act up. "We'll fly through this one, my friend. As long as those inside stay well-hidden."

She prayed they did. By the blood of Ashrad, she didn't need this. Only luck had placed her once again in Edgar's company as they flew for their camps. And only fool's luck had caused that Vulture scout to catch sight of the Clan patrol flying toward the gorge.

For a few more minutes she watched as Edgar's men searched in vain for the Clan troops, forcing herself to appear as though she were dozing as she did so. Thankfully, those within the aerie stayed silent.

"Damn you, Matte, wake your men up and let's go." Edgar hovered before the ledge, his black eyes glittering furiously. "Leave one of your men to watch the gorge and we'll head back to camp."

Matte straightened, signaling one of the younger warriors to do as Edgar bid.

"I'm right behind you, Edgar," she assured him mockingly. "Just lead the way."

He flew off and Matte breathed a sigh of relief, then turned to the warrior she had bidden to stay.

"Stay behind us, Beldar," she ordered the scout, her voice low. "I don't want Edgar to know we've disobeyed him, yet neither do you want the fury of those Clan warriors inside on your head."

Beldar nodded, and then Matte paused once again.

"It was nice meeting you, King Dearn." She smiled, imagining his fury as he listened to her voice. "I pray our next meeting will not be under such circumstances."

"Pray instead that I do not get my hands around your neck," he growled from behind the shutters. "For if I manage to do so, I will forget you are a woman and choke the life from you."

Definitely fury, Matte thought, *and not a small amount of wounded male pride.* Perhaps he, too, objected to her brand of respect, just as Edgar did. She was thankful that her own king was not nearly so surly, nor so intent on demanding more than the respect due him.

"I will keep that in mind, Your Highness. The gratitude you have displayed for my day's work warms my heart." She grinned.

She stepped away from the aerie, gave her men their order to fly and was gone as quickly as she had arrived.

* * * * *

Within the aerie, Dearn exchanged glances with his men. Their expressions all contained an edge of confusion and bemusement.

"It would appear we may have found the babe's savior," he remarked, glancing through the crack of the shutter once again. "Do as she says. Stay within and keep away from the door. Our forces should be here soon, and we'll then leave."

"Sire, what were those warriors?" Lucan shook his head "I have never seen such colors before."

"Neither have I, Damar. But one question has been answered in this. The Vultures have definitely returned."

But what, he wondered, would he do about the ones who appeared to be working with, and yet against the Vultures? If his suspicions were true, the Clans were about to face yet another specter of the past. The Bastard Breeds would be the descendants of those children whose Clan mothers had been raped by the Vultures centuries before. The children denied by King Merson and sentenced to death beside their fathers, a death neither the Vultures nor the children had suffered, just as he had suspected.

As Dearn watched them fly into the distance, his eyes held by the departing figure of the woman who commanded warriors, wore a sword and whose voice held the arrogant resonance of one used to command, he wondered at the strange turn events were beginning to take. He had expected no ally within the Vulture camp. Dearn knew he should be pleased, but he found himself confused instead. If the woman meant to betray her Vulture brothers, why then had she and her warriors not sought sanctuary in the Fortress rather than playing spy within the Vulture camp? More questions, and yet still so few answers.

Chapter Five

ഇ

Dearn's reinforcements arrived as the light of Ashrad was setting over the mountain and the three moons of his children were rising in the western sky. Semar had made certain there would be protection enough for the babe and his king. There were nearly a hundred warriors in flight about the gorge.

They brought the baskets to carry Ralnd and his family home, each borne by six warriors using long, thick straps of leather. They were awkward, but they would ensure that Ralnd, Mera and their babes were afforded the ceremony of death that would ease their way into Ashrad's gardens.

Sadly, Dearn believed the ceremonial fires would be burning high soon; the smoke and ash of his people as they ascended to Paradise would fill the skies for days to come.

The sounds of grief-stricken weeping could be heard from the Fortress when they arrived after midnight. Ceremonial fires burned within the courtyard casting a mournful glow on the Clans awaiting them. Dearn could see the tear-drenched faces of the women, the rage and anger of the warriors and the silent and shock-filled faces of the children who stood silently by their parents.

As he landed silently, he watched as Mera and Ralnd's family members rushed to the broken bodies. The weeping, grieving mothers tore at his heart. Damar went to his mother and Ralnd's. Within seconds, the two women were standing before him. The child in his arms whimpered.

"Sire? The child?" Ralnd's mother Marnet questioned Dearn, for it was his decision which family would now care for the babe. Such instances of both parents no longer living were rare within the Clans. Dearn could remember no time when a child had been so orphaned.

Would she go to the Eagle Clan, her father's people? Or should he give the babe to the White Lances, Mera's Clan?

"The child carries the wings of the Eagle Clan," he whispered as he parted the material that once was a warrior's shirt before serving as a blanket to cover the naked infant. "She should go to the Eagle Clan. All orphans shall be given to the Clan whose colors their wings bear, unless decided otherwise by the family members."

With these words, Dearn decided the fate of any child who might survive its parents' deaths. He was aware that the unofficial custom of placing children with their father's Clans would now become law.

"Forgive me, Saran," he told Mera's mother as he handed the child to Marnet. "A child should grow up with those who share its Clan colors."

Marnet raised her hand and touched Dearn's cheek. Her brown eyes swam with tears, her sun-roughened face drawn with lines of pain as she accepted the fragile weight of the child.

"The child will still know his mother's Clan," Marnet said, knowing that none of the Clans ever prevented a child from knowing its full heritage. "You have ruled well in this, Dearn."

Dearn lowered his head, gazing one last time at the babe he had once dreamed would be his as well as Mera's. A youth's dreams, he had long ago realized.

He nodded once, then turned and left the child to the women who must now share one grandchild, where before there had been four.

As he turned he saw Tamora, her violet eyes filled with tears as she watched him. He moved to her quickly, knowing she would have the information he had asked for before he left.

"How many have made it to the Fortress?" He motioned her to follow as he made his way to the palace.

"Less than two-thirds of all the Clans." She nearly ran to catch up with him and laid her hand on his arm. He stared down at her impatiently, wondering why she would stop him. "Dearn, the entire Falcon Clan is missing, and we have less than half of the Owl Clan."

"The entire Clan?" Dearn ran his hand tiredly over his face. The Falcons were some of their fiercest fighters.

"None of them have arrived. The troops we sent out to search for them report their aeries in chaos, just like the others. But no bodies have been found."

Dearn's knees weakened at this news, and he had to force himself to stay upright. As much as he wanted to, now was not the time to collapse.

Just as before, entire Clans were being decimated. Last time, the Dove and Wren Clans had been the fatalities; both Clans decimated to the point that now there were no survivors of those bloodlines left.

"We have less than two-thirds of our fighting force here then?"

He closed his eyes briefly at her nod.

"Dearn, it gets worse," she went on. "Several of the troops we sent out were attacked as well. They swear their attackers were Vultures."

He clenched his fists, his sense of purpose hardening at this further confirmation. That he knew well it was the Vultures didn't make this news easier to take.

"How many were lost?" He stared into the assembled mass of Clan members, suppressing a howl of rage.

"We've lost twelve warriors." Her voice was low, concerned. "The Vulture troops are large, and those who survived report that they are very well-trained."

"Those Seven Hells-cursed bloodwarts are more than just well-trained," General Brendar cursed as he came up behind her. He looked bloody, weary. His wings were frayed along the outer edges; his warrior's leathers carried bloody streaks from having met the Vultures in battle.

"How many, Brendar?" Dearn asked as he led the general away from the crowd.

"It was too damned dark to tell." Brendar cursed raggedly. "They lay low, waiting. They caught us just outside the Falcon range and were on us before we knew they were there."

Dearn gritted his teeth, fighting the well of impotence filling him.

"How many of your men were lost, Brendar?" he asked, knowing the loss of even one more warrior greatly handicapped them and fearing Tamora might not know the final count.

"Only twelve, but 'twas twelve too many." Brendar's expression and voice were grief-filled. "It was damned near a massacre, Sire."

A massacre. Dearn swallowed tightly.

"Their bodies?" he asked, fearing the information.

"Their wings were taken before a troop could return for them," Brendar informed him. "We returned with their bodies just before you flew in."

"Did you see anything odd about the warriors you fought?" he asked imperatively. "Were the colors of their wings unusual in any way?"

"Seven Hells, no." Brendar shook his head furiously. "They were bloody Vultures, Sire, and nothing more. Trust me, I know—I was there."

Dearn took a deep breath, wondering if any of his other troops had encountered the breed of warrior he and his men had seen.

"We, too, met with Vultures in one of the far valleys," he told Brendar as he stared around the courtyard, listening to the wails and sorrow of his people. "Ralnd and his family are dead. Only the youngest child survived."

"Ralnd? Mera?" Brendar shook his head in disbelief.

"Mera was raped and left to bleed out. Her children were beaten to death and their wings cut from their bodies." Dearn fought to keep his rage contained. "But there is more. The Vultures are not alone. They have brought with them the Bastard Breeds that were meant to die alongside them centuries ago. Bastard Breeds who are, for some reason, aiding us."

Brendar blinked. His wearied face seemed to become more lined, his violet-and-hazel eyes darkened in pain. He would have spoken, but at that moment several others interrupted them.

"Sire?" One of his captains rushed to him, leading a short, nervous-looking human behind him. "We've received several reports from the human cities. King Alfred has declared war on the Clans. He's blaming us for the death of his daughter, Princess Allora."

Dearn stared at the captain in disbelief.

"Allora?" He shook his head in confusion, his attention diverted momentarily from the human. "How does he come to charge us with this?"

"He accuses a troop from the Eagle Clan of stealing her from the castle yards. It's said that she then fell, and King Alfred claims she died on impact when she hit the ground. I found this man in the Southern Village. The humans there are still loyal to the Clans and sent for us when the king's men brought the news to their village."

"S-s-s-sire?" the man stuttered as he bobbed his head nervously. "I am Tomas, I want no war —"

"Stop trembling," Dearn told him harshly. "Tell me how such lies have been perpetrated against my people."

"The body of the princess, broken and bloodied, was found outside the Royal City right after she was taken four months ago. There was little left of her to declare her identity except her long golden hair and her royal clothing and jewelry."

"Did any person there see her taken?" Dearn knew that no Eagle or other Clan troop would do such a thing.

"We saw only the body, Sire," Tomas answered weakly. "King Alfred declared war after he said you would not punish those responsible."

Another lie. No human had come to him with these charges.

"You betray your king by coming here," he told Tomas.

The human swallowed tightly.

"There are those of us who believe Alfred killed his daughter," he whispered. "It was he who brought the Vultures in just before that. He is mad, Sire. Many of us wonder at the truth about Queen Demetria's death years ago. It was never explained, and it's well known Alfred has blamed the Clans for decades for every bit of ill fortune he has known."

Dearn could make no sense of this news. Other than in Cayam, where the Clans' trade overtures were ignored, the two races had dealt well with each other. He could not understand this abrupt change.

"This is no reason to declare war. You make no sense to me, human." Dearn snagged the man with an accusing glare and felt satisfaction when he flinched. "The Clans never venture to the lower valleys, and this is well known. How could Alfred accuse us?"

He watched weary cynicism come over Tomas' face.

"The same way he accuses an innocent man of theft and puts him to death, and yet releases one who murders." Tomas shook his head in bitter sadness. "He is mad, Sire, and that madness may destroy us all."

"Where did he find the Vultures?" Dearn fought to hold back his anger. There were too many questions, not enough answers. Surely the human king was not so mad as to declare a war based on such lies.

Tomas shook his head. "They arrived just before the Princess' death, by one of the king's ships. He sent for them, and it was his plan to use them against the Clans even before Allora died. A small group of us have tried to get to the Southern Village with a warning, but Alfred has the passes carefully watched. The four that were sent out before me have not returned nor did they make it to the village."

"And how did you accomplish it?" Dearn asked him suspiciously.

"I do not know." Tomas wrung the cap he held in his hands in fear. "I know I was seen several times, but the group patrolling never stopped me. I don't know why, Sire, I'm only thankful they didn't. Those bastards are merciless, and the killing has only started."

"What of those warriors who carry the mix of Vulture and Clan colors?" Dearn ignored the captain's and the general's looks of shock as he questioned the man. "Who are they?"

"The Bastard Breeds?" The man looked at Dearn as though he should know the answer to this. "They are those whose ancestors were exiled along with the Vultures. The children, Sire, of your Clan women and the Vulture warriors who raped them. The Vultures claim they have returned for vengeance as well, and they are strong, Sire. I would say stronger than the Vultures who command them."

And, so far, they were wreaking their vengeance against the Clans with a high rate of success. Dearn had no choice now but to prepare his people for a war they had nearly lost in the past and might very well lose now. But how, he asked himself, was he to prepare his people for the descendants of those children so cruelly and so savagely turned away? The ones now appearing to be allied with the Vultures, and yet the same ones who had saved his own troop and the fragile life of Mera's youngest babe?

Chapter Six

ಬಿ

The news of the Bastard Breeds sent shockwaves through the Clan leaders who surrounded Dearn. Questions, protestations and outrage that any who carried Clan blood could have anything to do with the Vultures were voiced.

All but Jalon, the leader of the White Lance Spiritmen. As Dearn continued into the Fortress, he noticed Jalon followed closely behind him, silent, reflective. The old man had something on his mind, and he indicated clearly his determination to voice those thoughts.

"Brendar, inform the Clan leaders I'll meet with them momentarily." Dearn turned to his general with the quiet order. "Then you and Tamora ply them with wine and keep them calm, and I'll be in soon to soothe their ruffled feathers."

There was an edge of impatience in his voice that he couldn't filter out. His Clan leaders were becoming worse than old women in their petty bickering and debates over how this situation should be handled.

"Jalon, you wish to speak with me?"

The old man nodded silently, his blue eyes dark and somber, his body tense.

"Come with me then, and we will talk."

Dearn led the way to the small room he used for private meetings. He poured them both wine as Jalon sat. Jalon accepted his with a look of relief, still not speaking, only watching expectantly.

"What do you wish to discuss, Jalon?" Dearn sat behind the dark oldtree wood desk.

"I wish to speak of bastards, Sire," Jalon said, his voice raspy with age, though his eyes were still clear and filled with wisdom.

Dearn frowned. "What can I tell you that you did not hear within the courtyard?"

"I would know if you saw one who is written of in the Cries of Algernon."

He spoke of old writings handed down for centuries, written by the most favored of Ashrad's winged warriors. Dearn shook his head in confusion.

"I have never read the Cries of Algernon, as well you know, Jalon. How would I know if there is a bastard those writings speak of?" He leaned forward, surveying the Spiritman curiously.

"'A warrior, his hair as black as the midnight sky, save the streak of silver it carries. Eyes the color of the White Lance, Wings the hue of all the Clans, like a rainbow of the land's pride. Honor in full measure, a voice that thunders across the land. One who stands tall, and one who yet shall bend his knee to the Clans.'" Jalon seemed to be reciting a verse he had memorized, and Dearn realized he must have done just that.

He shook his head.

"I saw no such warrior, Jalon. There was one—a woman, though—whose voice rankled my pride and set my feathers on edge. But I gather this is not the one you speak of?" He smiled a bit mockingly.

Jalon sighed in regret.

"No, Sire, I speak of no woman. Perhaps he is one who was not with the troops you met."

Dearn studied him for long seconds, wondering if an explanation would be forthcoming. When one was not, he finally spoke.

"What is this warrior, Jalon, that you think he is the one Algernon spoke of?"

"It was written that the bastards would be conceived in violence and sent beneath the sword. But treachery would save them, vengeance would return them and honor would flow from them. That the Black Scourge of death would return, bearing the bastards as a source of strength, yet a strength not theirs to claim. Algernon wrote of them, and he saw this warrior. The bastards have returned, so, surely, this warrior is among them."

The cryptically worded legend left Dearn confused, but he readily admitted that would be no hard task, at the moment. Weariness lay upon his shoulders like the heaviest cloak and dragged from his mind the strength he needed to sort through this. He would have to find his bed and sleep soon, or he would be unable to make the slightest decisions.

"As I said, I saw no such warrior. But the Bastard Breeds do seem to be betraying those they fight with. This gives me hope for a swift end to this war." He sighed. "I know no more than that."

Jalon, his face filled with regret, rose to his feet, lowering his head as he faced his king.

"Thank you for your time, Sire," he said softly. "I know it is full, and your kindness in sharing it with me is much appreciated."

The long silvered hair of the White Lance priest framed the dark, sun-weathered skin that had begun to wrinkle with age. But the man's wisdom and intelligence had not dimmed and gleamed brightly from his deep blue eyes.

"Whenever you need me, Grace, you know I am here." Dearn stood now as well. "I only regret I do not have the information you wanted."

Jalon smiled ruefully.

"You had much information that I wanted, just not the whole of what I needed," he said. "We will talk later, perhaps."

Dearn watched the Spiritman leave the room, still frowning, still wondering at the meaning behind the priest's words.

* * * * *

Jalon was met by two other White Lance priests as he closed the door to the king's meeting chamber.

"The warrior was not there, but the woman was," he murmured as they walked away through the well-lit stone hallway. "He has seen her, and in his voice I hear the truth of Algernon's words."

"Then the bastards have returned." Heaviness weighed in the priest's voice. "Death will come with them, Jalon, this you well know."

"But with them, my friend, comes the hope for the future. The reunion with those we have lost, a land that will feed us as our Clans grow and bring us strength in the coming centuries against those who would rise against us." Jalon nodded. "The legacy of the Bastard Breeds will not be all death, my brother. With them will come victory — and, for our king, a much awaited season of light."

* * * * *

Several hours later, Dearn entered his rooms, aware that the Clan leaders were far from satisfied with his plan of action and still argued fiercely on the best way to handle the war they were now enmeshed in.

He felt they needed more information before sending a full-scale attack force into the human cities. The humans outnumbered the Clans more than five to one, and if they attacked their cities they warred not just with the soldiers but the innocent women and children who had no place in war.

And yet, hadn't the Vultures attacked their women and children? They had come into their homes, destroyed lives and families, and made war on the innocent, the leaders reminded him.

The debate raging within the converted meeting room had given Dearn a headache that drove him from them, seeking relief from their shouting, angry voices.

For now, Dearn wanted his people in the Fortress, safe and secure from the human and Vulture raiding parties, until he could learn the truth of the charges against the Clans. It shouldn't take long. There were humans who traded with the Clans, and the Southern Valley held several human villages that Dearn knew were loyal. Scouts from those villages had already been sent out, surely there would be news soon. He prayed there was, because he didn't know how much more death his people could endure and still retain their own honor. He was quickly approaching his own limit.

He was soul-tired, weary to the bone, and yet he feared closing his eyes. He feared the images he would see as sleep drifted over him, should he allow it now. The image of Mera, her body abused and beaten, the pain and horror in her eyes, the savagery of the attack marked plainly on her body. And Ralnd. He clenched his fists as he sat down slowly on his bed. Gods have mercy on him, but he could feel the rage and the grief that he knew must have torn at his cousin a thousand times stronger than it did him. Indeed, he felt that, of the two of them, his cousin was much luckier. The Vultures had relieved him of the torment of living with that image, while Dearn now suffered from it each second.

It was like an open, bloody wound on his soul, and he wondered if it would ever heal, if the pain would ever ease.

He lowered his head, feeling his hair fall to cover his face and wishing he could hide forever from the reality of what had come to his people. He looked down at his hands, turning them palms up, watching as the muscles there flexed and wishing there was a Vulture or human neck clenched between them. He would wring the life from them, he swore. He would make them pay for the deaths, for the savagery and the pain.

"King Dearn?" A soft voice accompanied a gentle knock on the door.

Dearn raised his head, watching as the young woman entered the room, her hazel eyes gazing into his. He frowned, wondering whose daughter she was. Surely, she had not been raised within the Fortress or he would recognize her.

"Yes?" He rose from his bed, studying the Eagle colors of her wings while the unusual hazel of her eyes threw him back. It was rare for a child born of the Eagle Clan, even when it carried blood mixed with another of the Clans, to have eyes nearly green — most were of a brownish hue. "What can I help you with?"

"Your mother has sent you dinner and wine."

Only then did he notice the tray she carried.

"Place it on the table, then leave me alone," he ordered as he watched her closely. "What is your name, girl?" he finally asked as she moved to do as he bade.

"I am Lenora, Sire." Was that a flash of fear he saw in her eyes? He wondered.

"And from whose Clan have you come?"

She squared her shoulders, much as he had seen a warrior do during questioning.

"I was Clayden's daughter." She whispered the name of a reclusive Eagle warrior who had left the Clans decades before.

"Clayden? Is he well?" Dearn had often wondered at the fate of his father's old friend.

She lowered her head, only shaking it slowly, and he clenched his fists in renewed fury. She looked so tiny standing there, another orphan, another child who was alone in the world, for Clayden had no Clan of his own.

"Thank you for the dinner, Lenora." He fought the bitter bile that rose in his throat at the thought of food.

"Your mother sent a message as well." Her head rose once again, and once again Dearn was halted by those eyes, so unlike the eyes of other Clan members. "She asks that you come to her after you have rested. General Brendar has sent the same message."

Dearn sighed, glancing toward the open balcony doors. The sun had long since risen along the Eastern Range, and he had not slept in two days. He needed rest before he could tackle any more death.

"I will see them later." He nodded, sighing wearily. "You may go now."

Lenora bowed then turned and left the room, drawing the door closed behind her with a snap. What an odd child Clayden had raised, he thought. But he could have expected little else from the old warrior. Clayden had often fought bitterly on behalf of the few women of the Clans who desired to become warriors. He had even trained a few, but the Clan leaders had refused to allow them to join the warrior ranks.

Dearn had not reversed that decision during his reign for the simple reason that he knew no women strong enough to complete the warrior training. The men would have been unable to train one effectively, anyway. How do you raise your fist to a woman and expect her to defend herself? Tamora was the strongest woman he knew, and even the careful secret training he knew she received from Brendar had not changed the soft delicacy of her body. How could she fight as a warrior when she had no hope of attaining a warrior's strength?

Those questions went as quickly as they came to his wearied mind. He sipped the wine that had been sent up, then stripped his warrior's leathers from his body and lay down. If he didn't sleep he would not have the presence of mind to lead. It was one of the first lessons his father taught him. During times of great stress or crisis, a warrior must learn to sleep when he could so he could keep his body and his mind alert.

He slipped quickly into the darkness, fighting the haunting images of blood and death and the sorrow and whispered cries of the children he had found that morning. But nothing could prevent the blood from intruding, the horror from spreading through his nightmares, robbing him of peace, stealing from him the full effect of the rest he needed.

Chapter Seven

Dearn awakened that evening, if not refreshed then at least stronger than he was before sleep. His rest had been haunted by the strident call of his cousin, a demand for vengeance as Ralnd stood at the pass to the Valley of the Gods.

He lay listening to the restless howl of the winds outside his balcony, the fierce blasts of air that careened through the valley, its usual whisper along the cliff walls turned to a strident shriek he could not ignore.

Within an hour he was washed, dressed and striding quickly to the meeting room, where he had sent a message for Brendar to meet him. He couldn't shake the warning he had sensed in those nightmare images. The plea for vengeance had also carried a warning that all might not necessarily be as it would seem.

The general was there when Dearn stepped into the private meeting room, face set in a scowl, hazel and violet eyes dark and brooding as he awaited his king impatiently.

"What have you learned?" Dearn didn't waste time as he took his seat behind the desk and motioned for Brendar to begin. There was none left to waste.

Brendar faced him warily. "They're staying well hidden, but we've had reports there may be anywhere from three hundred to six hundred, not counting the Bastard Breeds. And the human king has called together his forces as well for a march on the Fortress. We're looking at a hell of a battle, Sire."

Brendar's face was lined with weariness, his scowl one of impatience. Dearn's lips thinned at this news. It was much worse than he had suspected.

"Does anyone know why? This foolishness about Allora is too insane to believe. How has Alfred managed to convince his people of it?"

Brendar paused at the harsh tone of his voice. In his eyes, Dearn saw a flash of knowledge that sent a frisson of unease throughout his body.

"Brendar?"

"There were witnesses," Brendar told him slowly. "They swear four Eagle warriors flew in and snatched the princess from the courtyard. They saw her taken; they saw her fall."

Dearn was silent for long moments. Finally, with a wearied breath he came to his feet and moved angrily to a small cabinet. He pulled out an earthenware bottle of wine and two goblets. He filled them quickly, then handed one to his grateful general before going back to his seat. He took a healthy sip of the potent brew before going further.

"Then it's lies." He picked up the conversation where Brendar had stopped. "Or, somehow, the Bastard Breeds are involved." He shook his head, knowing none of his warriors were capable of such an act.

"It's lies. I agree with you, Sire." Brendar breathed roughly. "But several of the witnesses were residents of the Southern Valley in Cayam trading for supplies. They saw it happen. I know one of the men personally, Dearn, and he swears it looked like Eagle warriors. He did say they were dressed like Vulture warriors. I agree with you, it would have had to be the Bastard Breeds. But if they are Clan mixes, I cannot see their honor allowing this."

Dearn shook his head as he gazed into the rich burgundy of his wine with a frown.

"None of our warriors would join the Vultures, not for any reason."

Of this he was certain. The honor and pride of the Clans was as much a part of them as their bloodlines. A Clan warrior

71

would no more commit such an act than a mawbeast could sprout wings and fly.

"I agree with you, but somehow King Alfred has convinced his people it was Eagle warriors. I haven't been able to learn how the deception was pulled off, but I know it was," Brendar assured him.

"Then Allora is truly dead?" Dearn needed to be certain the princess could not possibly be alive before he could plan the coming war. If King Alfred had been tricked himself, then he was not as guilty of starting a needless war against the Clans as it seemed. It was something he needed to know before the Clans began their assault against the Vultures and Elitist forces. They had to know who was innocent and who was guilty.

"I can't confirm it nor deny it." Brendar shrugged with an edge of ire. "According to the men I talked to, it looked like Allora. But they also say there are rumors King Alfred has aligned himself with the Elitists. If this is true, then who knows what the truth actually is?"

Dearn grimaced. The Elitists, followers of the demon god Cinder, were as merciless and bloodthirsty as any Vulture ever born. And their dark hatred for the Clans went back as far as creation itself.

"We have to learn the truth of this, Brendar. We cannot go to the Clans with information we are not certain of." He voiced his earlier thought as a warning. "Have you told anyone else what you have learned?"

Brendar shook his head, but Dearn saw the protest in his eyes.

"How do you believe we should proceed then?" the general asked him. "I don't like keeping my warriors in the dark about any part of this."

Dearn sat silently, weighing the options in his mind. There had to be a way to figure out what was going on for certain. The thought of killing innocent soldiers didn't sit well with him. But he would before he saw more of his own people killed so savagely.

"I want twelve teams prepared," he ordered. "Two-man teams, the best warriors we have, to begin scouting the outer edges of the mountains going into Cayam. The Vultures will be looking for large troops; perhaps we can find a way for a smaller force to get close enough to learn what is going on. I don't want them taking needless chances, but we have to learn the truth of this."

Brendar nodded, and Dearn knew he was already working out the best men for such teams.

"The Clan leaders are camped outside, awaiting you as well. What will you tell them?" The general knew the leaders would argue for a full-force assault on the human city immediately.

"Nothing." Dearn rose to his feet. "I will be on one of those teams."

Shock rendered Brendar speechless for precious moments.

"No, Sire, this I cannot allow," he said furiously, just as Dearn had known he would. "The Vultures would exult at capturing you, then killing you. It would throw the Clans into chaos."

Dearn allowed himself a small, bitter smile. He could not imagine that the chaos running rampant through the Clans now could get any worse.

"Then you better devise a plan for bringing them out of it, should that happen, my friend," Dearn informed him mockingly. "For I will go, and I will do so with or without your help. And, should my death occur, then the crown shall fall to you."

It had been to Brendar's extreme dissatisfaction that, during the battle for the throne in Dearn's youth, he had been chosen to succeed as interim king should Dearn ever become incapacitated or killed. Horror swept over the general's face, the ever-present panic that somehow, someway, ruling the

Clans would fall to him. A fate worse than death, he had often pronounced.

"Sire, this is insanity," he protested yet again. He quickly drained his wine then continued. "There is no way we can pull this off without the Clan leaders knowing."

"Watch me." Dearn smiled tightly.

"You have lost your mind," Brendar burst out, incredulous. "The leaders will not have it."

Dearn watched intently now, taken aback by the ferocity of the objection, the heat and ire in the man's tone.

"Not my mind, Brendar, but family and friends and children who should be playing, not lying in their own blood," he snarled. "I will have my vengeance, and I will have it by my own sword, not the swords and the blood of my men while I sit here protected within this Fortress."

The fury that had been festering inside Dearn threatened at that moment to erupt. He watched understanding slowly filter into the general's expression, but he knew it was something Brendar still did not agree with. It mattered not; it was something he would do, with or without agreement.

"You'll have to give me a day or two to work it out." Resignation filled his general's eyes. He knew Dearn, and he knew the warrior in him would never be satisfied until his sword was covered with the blood of the enemy. The Clan leaders would scream in protest, but Brendar knew it would do them no good.

"Then work it out quickly," Dearn said, though he kept to himself the plans he would soon initiate. "For I will fight, Brendar, and the leaders may as well resign themselves to this fact."

"I imagine you have a plan to get past them then?" Brendar asked, resigned, though the anger still lingered in face and voice. "I hope to hell you do. Because if you don't, then I'm the one who will have to deal with them."

Chapter Eight

๊ꙮ

Dawn was only a short time away, the best time Dearn knew to slip from the forest and fly into the gorge recently deserted by the Eagle Clan leader and his family. If the Vultures were going to ransack the aeries based on the rumors of gold a few human allies had spread, then they would do so as soon as it was light enough.

Dressed in warrior's leathers, his weapons strapped to his body, Dearn awaited the passing of the warriors on patrol at the mouth of the canyon that led into that gap. Those Clan warriors would easily recognize him if they saw him and would insist on accompanying him. For his plan to work, though, he must go alone. A large troop would merely hinder him.

He intended to hide near the Clan leader's aerie, listening closely when the Vultures arrived for any information he could glean on their true numbers and, most importantly, their plans.

"Going somewhere, Highness?"

Tamora's soft, mocking voice made Dearn tense in surprise. Slowly, he turned to her, seeing the dark leather she wore and her weapons.

"Return to the Fortress, Tamora," he ordered her firmly. "War is no place for you."

"It matters not." She shrugged almost insolently. "If I return I will warn the Clan leaders that their king flies alone this morning. I wonder how long it will take before a troop is heading out behind you?"

Dearn studied her for a long moment, considering the stubborn light in her eyes and the manner of her dress. "If they catch us, you'll die painfully, Tamora," he warned her, remembering the sight of Mera's body. "Go back."

"I know that gorge better than you, Dearn. I played there for half my life. You'll need me," she insisted, her voice ringing with determination. "Let me come with you. I promise I'll be careful, and my brothers and Brendar have trained me well. I'll not hinder you."

Dearn knew she had been trained well, though it was something he had not agreed with. He watched her now, seeing her need to join him, seeing some dark emotion in her eyes he could not readily define. She was female and had no business in places of war, yet he also knew her heart, one that longed for warrior status. Her assignment as part of his personal guards he had given in deference to her pleas, but he also knew it was a position she had well deserved. Now, it was one he regretted, for it would place her in an inordinate amount of danger.

"Why are you here?" he finally asked her softly. "This is no place for you, Tamora. Why do you insist on going?"

He watched her gaze shift from his, going instead to the clouded night and the soft luminescence of the three moons, whose gentle light peeked through the soft covering of delicate clouds.

"I want to do more," she finally answered him, her eyes meeting his once again. "I feel helpless, Dearn, serving in the castle and only carrying messages. This is not the job of your personal guards. I want to be with you."

There was a note of desperation in her voice that was at odds with the shimmer of loneliness in her eyes. Dearn knew not what she wanted; he suspected even she didn't truly know.

"Whatever you are trying to prove, this is the wrong way to do it," he told her, again observing the movements of the Clan troops flying overhead. "This is the wrong time, Tamora. Return to the Fortress, and we will talk when I return."

"Will we, Dearn?" A note of mocking laughter colored her voice. "How long have you been promising me that? Surely since before the war began. Before we even knew of the killings. And still we have not talked. The time for talk has passed."

What, Dearn asked himself, did she mean by this? And what was that vein of angered pain he heard in her voice? This was unlike Tamora, and it worried him.

"We will not talk now, either. This must be done right, Tamora. We will be alone, with no warriors to cover us. If we're caught, we'll die. Are you ready to die for whatever it is you seek?" He didn't want her with him; he didn't want her taking the risk.

"We'll be fine." Dearn caught her swift, confident smile. "Ashrad will shine down on us and he'll see us through. Hasn't he always?"

"Ashrad has never been called upon for such a situation, Tam." Frustration growled within his voice and he had little control over it. He must leave soon, and he would leave even if it meant accepting her company. But he would much prefer she return to the Fortress.

"Ashrad is with us, Sire," she promised him softly. "As are Aleda, Durin and Sorin. We have all we need to do what we must."

Dearn sighed deeply, shaking his head.

"I pray you're right," he told her in resignation. "For if they blink, Tamora, my soul will never rest for the damage that will be done to you. Do you really wish to take this risk?"

"I'm ready to fly whenever you are, Sire." She faced him coolly, confidently.

Dearn nodded, checking the location of the Clan troop one last time.

"Get ready, then," he told her softly. "The moment they clear the pass into the Fortress, we fly."

Had she been born male Tamora could have been a great warrior. She had the speed, the stamina, and the heart and honor of a fighter. Her body, delicate and soft, was not made for fighting, but it was perfect for weaving quickly through the huge trees, he thought as they flew toward the outlying aeries that had been abandoned. Before the sun rose on the day, Tamora and Dearn were safely nestled within one of the dark, shadowed cracks of the cliffs.

They hadn't spoken since starting out. Dearn outlined the plan to her quickly before giving the order to fly. He needed to hear the boasting he knew the Vultures could not restrain and, thus, learn how Vultures were made to appear as Eagle warriors, and how the princess had died. He and Tamora would hide within the hidden crevices of the cliffs, wait and watch. Those aeries hadn't been ransacked, so he expected they would be soon. From their vantage point, what they couldn't see they could hear, and the narrowness of the cliff would make it easy to hear any words spoken above a whisper.

"And now we wait," he told her, watching as the sun made its first gentle wash across the sky.

"You seem so certain they will come."

His gaze met hers as she implied a suspicion that he knew more than he had told Brendar.

"They will come." Dearn was certain of it. This valley was known for its riches in gold and silver. The Clans here had mined those minerals for generations. He knew the Vultures would be eager to see if the inhabitants of these aeries had left any treasures behind in their haste to flee to the Fortress. All he had to do was wait and listen.

"Do you think the woman will be there? The one who shielded you at Ralnd's aerie?" she asked him, her voice carrying no further than his ears.

He eyed her carefully, wondering if she had ventured on this flight out of jealousy. But he saw none in her expression. He saw only curiosity, and perhaps a shade of envy.

Tamora was one of those few who had petitioned the Clan leaders years before to allow warrior training for the women of the Clans who desired it. Did she somehow see herself as less than the warrior woman she had heard of?

"I don't know," Dearn finally answered her, ignoring his own hope that the female warrior would be there and he would somehow learn more of her. He didn't understand his obsession with the woman. She had aided him, true. And he suspected it had been she who had saved Mera's babe. But she hadn't saved Mera or her family. She had been there. She had to have been there, he thought. How could she have stood aside and watched such brutality without fighting to stop it? How could anyone, man or woman, human or winged warrior, who possessed any sense of honor not have fought to stop those deaths?

He breathed in deeply, fighting anew the anger, the loss. He wanted to shake the female warrior, demand the answers to these questions. And yet, at the same time, he felt a stirring for her that he didn't quite understand. It went beyond the sexual need he was used to feeling for women.

* * * * *

"Brendar?"

At the sound of Cleome's voice Brendar turned from his conversation with a warrior who had returned earlier from patrol. The sun was just rising on the Fortress, and those in the patrol were tired and eager for their beds; but he had needed a report of activity in the mountains first.

"Yes, my lady?" He turned to her despite the warrior's need to find his bed. "How may I help you?"

Dearn's mother was small, despite her Eagle heritage. Her silvered hair was worn in a braid and twisted into a neat coronet, her weathered face pulled into a frown that emphasized the aging of her skin.

"Have you seen Dearn or Tamora? I can find neither of them this morning." As she neared him, she stared up at him with irritation.

Brendar stiffened. If both Dearn and Tamora were missing then there was only one place they could be. Surely, by the gods, they would not be...

"Have you checked His Highness's rooms?" The words tore his throat.

He would kill them both, he thought, clenching his fists in fury. He would be the first Clan warrior in known history to kill his king. The first ever to shed the blood of a fellow Clan warrior over a woman.

"Well, no—" Cleome broke off as Brendar stalked past her.

He would not have it. If Dearn had dared, if he had even thought to take Tamora to his bed once again, then he would see the man's head severed from his shoulders. Damn him to the Seven Hells, no warrior ever, *ever* in the history of the Clans had ignored the mating signs. Brendar knew for certain that Tamora carried those signs.

As he approached the bedroom door, he gave a moment's thought to knocking, but the anger surging through him was not to be denied. When the latch did not give, he moved back and, putting all his weight behind his powerful leg, broke the flimsy lock and watched in satisfaction as the heavy wooden barrier released and flew back against the opposite wall. He stalked into the room, his hand on the hilt of his sword.

The room was empty. Fury coursed through his body, his feathers ruffling in the surge of emotion as his eyes took stock.

The bed was still made. His teeth clenching, his body tense and filled with determination, Brendar turned on his heel and stalked to the woman's room as he ignored Cleome's worried questions behind him.

The door there was given the same treatment, and he found the same tidiness in this room as had been in Dearn's, but with one exception.

Brendar walked slowly to the bed, his eyes narrowed at the garments tossed on the coverlet and the pair of black leather warrior's gloves that had been left, forgotten, on the edge of the mattress.

He felt the blood drain from his face. Surely, she would not have... Surely, by the gods, Dearn himself would not have done anything so foolish?

"Brendar, what is the meaning of this?" Cleome was angry now as she watched him pick up the gloves. "It is not your place to treat their privacy so."

"By the gods, Lady." Brendar could hear the husky fear that rolled from his chest. "By the gods, but His Highness is a fool."

He turned on his heel, rushing from the room as he ignored her outraged gasp.

"Joaquin, gather a troop!" His frantic order sent warriors running from their rooms, strapping on swords, grabbing their crossbows.

"General Brendar, what's wrong?" One of the warriors gazed at him in confusion, and Brendar knew he must appear crazed.

"I need three troops immediately," he ordered the man. "Get your men together. Our king and Tamora have flown out alone, and by the gods, he has likely gotten his throat slit by now as well as Tam's."

This information was all the men needed. Within minutes three twelve-man troops were assembled and ready to fly.

"He's flown for Tiber's aerie," Brendar informed his men as they launched from the Fortress walls. "Tamora is likely with him, which places them in that much more danger."

How strange, he had thought the morning before when Dearn laughed about the gold likely hidden in Tiber's aerie. There was no gold there and they all knew it. But there had been that strange little human who had been lurking within the Fortress. The one who had come with the humans of the Southern Valley.

Dearn had suspected the man was a spy, Brendar now understood, and he provided "information" that would draw the Vultures to those aeries. This had made no sense at the time. Why do such a thing and have no troop of warriors waiting? It had, foolishly perhaps, never crossed his mind that Dearn intended to be waiting there himself.

His king was suddenly acting quite strangely, and Brendar had had his fill of it. Just as he was quickly getting his fill of Tamora and her denials. Both would stop, and stop quickly, if he could just manage to save both their feathers, he told himself as he shook off his own weariness and prepared to fly.

Chapter Nine

∞

The territory was exactly the way the old writings of Vulture and Bastard Breed lore proclaimed it. The land of the Clans was mountainous, with sheer cliffs and long, deep valleys where the rivers ran wide and clear. Forests carpeted the land, thick and green and teeming with food. Wild orchards dotted the land, fish swam plentifully in the lakes and fortunes in gold, silver and precious gems were there for the taking — if only they could be found.

Edgar stood within the shelter of the deserted aerie, stared out at the sheer, stark cliffs around him and wondered at the oddities of the Clans. To create such huge holds within the hard stone seemed a waste of time. Why go to the trouble to hew into the mountains when there were trees to nest in or another's aerie to steal?

The Vulture Clans would be more than happy to claim the aeries now since the Clans had gone to so much trouble to make them, though. They would claim the aeries and the land and the women who lived here. The warriors of the Clans would have to be destroyed, of course. Edgar didn't want to be bothered by the petty fights that would break out once he captured the ruling Fortress should any Clan warriors survive.

"This is the last aerie in this pass, Edgar." Matte, the female commander of the Bastard Breed Clans, sauntered out onto the ledge behind him. "They left plenty of food and all their belongings. We won't leave empty-handed. But the rumors of gold were blatantly false. There is no gold, nor are there the dallion stones that were rumored to be here."

Not empty-handed, but lacking in wealth as well as the opportunity for the rougher games Edgar had come to love. He had been anticipating finding another female here.

He glanced over his shoulder at Matte, wondering if perhaps he could relieve his lust with her this afternoon. She could throw a better fight at sixteen than any of the weak Clan whores he had taken so far.

"Good. Too bad the bastards left so little, though," he grumped. "We'll wait for Kyder to bring the reinforcements back to haul it all in. We could have a little fun until he gets back." He leered at her, his eyes trained on the slope of her breasts beneath the snug material of her warrior's leathers.

Her dark eyes leveled on him with distaste.

"I don't think so. I never thought inbreeding was a very good idea."

He hated the sneer in her voice. Matte was the product of his father's lust for a Bastard Breed woman. She was a fierce fighter, but with help he knew he could take her. Her mother, Varria, had been strong as well, a leader of Bastard Breed warriors.

Centuries of breeding only within the Bastard Breed Clans had begun producing near-replicas of those Clans from which they had originally sprung. Edgar's father had put a stop to that by giving his warriors leave to rape the Bastard Breed women at will, where before a warrior could be punished for it. He initiated the new policy by raping Varria with the help of several of his warriors and gained Matte nine months later.

Edgar had continued the legacy by taking Matte on her sixteenth birthday while battle raged around them, though no child had come of the encounter. Even now, he remembered how she fought, how she cried and pleaded with him that day. But he took her, regardless. It had been well worth the Bastard Breeds' leader's wrath, though he had been months in healing after Thorne finished with him.

"You don't know what you're missing," he suggested, wondering if those breasts still tasted as good as they looked.

"Oh, I've seen you in action, brother." The scorn was clear now, the disgust not even disguised. "I'm really not missing much."

Whore! Rage slid brightly through Edgar's body at the insult.

"Bastard Breed bitch! You think that Eagle blood in your veins makes you better than me?" he asked her, furious now.

"My blood has little to do with it, brother," she drawled, her voice lowered, a clear indication she had had enough of him. "And whether it were Eagle or Vulture blood, you would still disgust me."

He could force her, and he would have, under other circumstances—should have done so long ago. Only one thing had stopped him. Her Clan would seek vengeance. The damned Bastard Breeds were nearly as bad as full-blooded Clan warriors when it came to their honor and their loyalty to each other. Their word was their bond. Strike one of them, and the entire Clan would strike back. This, Edgar had personal experience with. It was becoming a pain in the backside, dealing with the Bastards, but for the moment he had no other choice. He needed those warriors too badly to risk their defection. They were strong, fierce fighters and though he admitted it to no one, their intensive training had made them better than even the Vulture Clans.

It would have been good for his cause had he been able to bring the entire Clan of Bastard Breeds back to Brydon's main continent, but he couldn't risk it. Only a small force had been allowed for the simple reason that he was uncertain how far they could be trusted to stay true to the cause.

The Vultures would fight to the death against the Clans— that hatred had been bred into them since time began. The Bastard Breeds, on the other hand, were an uncertain lot. Somehow, some way, they had retained a part of that damned honor system that flowed through the blood of the Clans. It couldn't be beaten out of them; it couldn't be bred out of them. Once Clan blood mixed with Vulture, it seemed to weaken the merciless nature bred into the Vultures to begin with. Damned Clan blood mix seemed to create some bond among the members of the Bastard Breeds that he didn't understand. It was a commitment to each other and strength of will that had confused the Vultures for centuries.

He didn't understand it, but he did care to use it toward his own ends. They had given their word to aid in this battle, and he knew they would keep it. He was certain of the Bastard Breeds' hatred for the Clans. How could they not hate them? The Clans had consigned their ancestors to the same fate as the Vultures, ordered to certain death because of the Vulture blood they carried. Edgar thought it was hilarious. Wouldn't King Dearn be surprised when faced with warriors who carried his colors, his lineage, and who hated him as fiercely as any Vulture ever could?

Edgar still had to solve the problem of managing his lust for the dark-haired commander of the Breeds. Each day his blood boiled hotter, and he knew he would have to have her soon.

Matte was nearly as tall as he, with thick, shiny brown hair and golden hazel eyes. Her face was heart-shaped, with high cheekbones and a stubborn chin. She was slender, yet he knew she possessed an amazing amount of strength for a woman. She trained with her Clan religiously and had developed a surprising amount of speed and agility in her curvaceous body. She was conditioned and well-honed, and built to throw a hell of a ride. When this war was over he would master her as he did the other women he desired.

Matte would surrender to him, just as the delicate little morsel Alfred had promised him would surrender. Soon, very soon, his dreams for his own Clan would be realized.

"Disgust you, do I?" he muttered darkly. "Your day will come, woman."

"Whatever." She shrugged indifferently "So, which of the meager belongings here do we take with us?"

Edgar imagined her bloodied, tied to the floor, pleading for her life as he thrust into her. Oh, she would pay, just like the human/Clan bitch that would soon be his would pay for her rejection of him.

"Are you listening to me?" Matte demanded, her voice grating on his nerves.

"I heard ya," he snarled, seeing her eyes narrow suspiciously on him. "But since you already know what to do with everything, I didn't think I had to tell ya again."

He watched as her head tilted and she gave him that superior, brow-arched look of hers.

"You were thinking about her again." Matte snickered with amusement as she propped herself against the doorway and crossed her arms over her full breasts. The smooth curves, now nearly flattened, made his mouth water.

Damn fine curves, he thought. He couldn't wait to sample them again.

"So what if I am?" Edgar figured he had the right. The woman would be his soon enough, and it was his business if he wanted to think about it. Relishing it was his right, and he would do so until the moment he could take her as he was promised.

He turned to face Matte as he leaned against the wall.

"You're such a fool," she mocked him, making him want to slap her.

"I don't want to hear it, Matte," he growled, knowing if he hit her she would likely hit him back. She had more guts than half his men, and it wouldn't do to make an enemy of her right now. "I have my plans, and they'll work. I know they will. Haven't they so far?"

"Tell me, Edgar, what do you think King Alfred will do when all the warriors of these Clans are killed? You think he's just going stand aside and let you take it all? You really think he's going to give us this territory? We'll become outlaws, just as our ancestors were." Mockery, thick and scolding, spewed from her voice as her hazel-and-gold eyes watched him with a glitter of ridicule. *One day,* he promised himself once again. *One day soon.*

Now, though, he only shrugged. He fully expected the human king to try to double-cross him later. That is, if he allowed the human king to live that long.

"He'll kill her long before he ever allows you to have her," Matte assured him with a laugh. "You'll never get a chance to breed with her."

Edgar's fists clenched in fury. He should have known better than to tell her his secret plans, his dreams for their Clan. What had possessed him to trust her?

"I will have her," he swore, hating the knowing smile that twisted her lips. "I will have her, and I will breed with her. She will bring strength to our Clan."

"She will bring a war between you and your men," Matte sneered. "You won't be able to breed with her for fighting over her."

Edgar clenched his fists in fury. *Snide little bitch,* he thought, he would teach her respect when the time was right. He laughed sarcastically, hiding his anger now but promising her silently that the day would come when she would pay for her lack of respect.

"Well, Seven Hells, Matte, I didn't say I wouldn't share her. And while she's busy, you and I could play for a while. Pleasuring me would be a good job for you."

He watched the revulsion cover her face once again. Oh, yes, this one would definitely be his, and soon. He would make it a requirement for bringing the rest of her Clans to Cayam. Not that he had any intention of ever allowing Thorne, that cursed spawn of Algernon, off the island. But he could keep such information to himself for a while.

"What I'll get is the job to drag her dead body out of whichever nest she dies in," Matte spat out. "You mark my words, they'll kill her before she ever conceives. They've proven it with their fun and games with the women they've found so far. That is, if she doesn't kill herself first."

* * * * *

Matte watched Edgar's eyes narrow, the small, thin slits shining with malevolence. Oh, how he wanted to hit her, but he knew the repercussions would be more than he could deal with. Her Clan was small, but it was strong, and he knew it. Too bad he wasn't as smart when it came to this war. It was a fool's battle, and he was too arrogant to see it.

Her father could have left the Vulture Clan to her—she was plenty strong enough to lead it—but his prejudice against the Bastard Breeds went too deep. He could rape one and accept the child created from his perversions, but he had refused to acknowledge her right to lead. Her Bastard Clan blood infected her, he had sworn. A Bastard Breed didn't have what it took to be a true Vulture leader.

In that, Matte knew he was right. The treasonous plans she had helped set in motion proved it. Her loyalty was to her own people, and she would be damned if she would see them destroyed when King Dearn's Clans defeated the human army and Edgar's men.

"Come on, let's finish getting this stuff together," Edgar ordered her as he re-entered the aerie. "We've wasted enough time here. I want to get back to camp and see what the others have found."

Matte followed him in, keeping her face carefully blank. She would follow him as long as it served her purpose to do so, but Edgar was doomed to failure, and she was determined her Clan would not fall alongside him. She gained immeasurable satisfaction from the thought that soon she would look in his eyes and remind him of that night, years ago, when she had sworn she would have her revenge.

She had been staked to the ground, staring up at him and the men who had aided him in her rape; she had cursed him, promising him that the day would come when she would repay him. He had laughed at her. His laughter echoed in the growing twilight as darkness neared, and he reminded her that soon her blood would feed the demons of the night and that she would have no chance at his.

Then he left. Flying away as she screamed at him, pleading with him to release her. He hadn't. He hadn't returned, he hadn't released her, just left her there with the taste of betrayal souring about her as surely as the stench of his body was.

She had survived that night—barely. It had taken her weeks to heal, but in that time her resolve had only hardened. Hardened until it was like a cold weight in her chest that would not find relief until she saw him dead.

* * * * *

As Edward and Matte reentered the aerie, the warrior hidden along the side of the cliff face exchanged a worried glance with his companion. With a quick jerk of his head, Dearn motioned to Tamora, indicating they should leave before anyone else ventured out. There were too many of the enemy, and with the sun's position quickly changing, their shadowed ledge would soon be fully lit.

They were nearly seen several times as the sun slowly illuminated the shallow crevice where they hid. Dearn was more than ready to leave now that a warrior had been sent to bring reinforcements to help carry Tiber's possessions.

He waited until she had dropped into the sky and was gliding effortlessly out of the canyon before he followed her. He glanced behind him often, making certain they weren't sighted or being followed as he winged away.

Dearn regretted his decision to bring Tamora with him. There were more Vultures than he had anticipated, and more had been sent for.

She was a damned good scout. It had been she who sighted the ledge close to the largest aerie and suggested using it until the midday sun was high. She had guessed the Vultures would descend there first. She had been right, but the invaders had stayed there far longer than either had thought they would.

As a pair, they were efficient in what they did, but he also knew the danger they faced if they were captured. There was no way he could protect her if the Vultures managed to take her.

He kept careful watch of the area as they entered the forest once again and landed within the thickly branched tree they had secured the night before. Vultures didn't fly among the trees much—it required them to land, and their broader, heavier bodies made it difficult for them to take off from the ground with any speed.

For the Eagle pair, the nest they had built against the main trunk of the tree was sufficient. The canopy of branches hid them from the Vultures' keen eyes and protected them from the fierce storms that often raged through the valleys.

Dearn landed beside Tamora then moved her quickly to the nest.

"Who is this woman they were talking about, Dearn?" He could feel her shaking with anger as he took his place beside her.

"I don't know." He shook his head, fearing the fate of the unknown woman even as he continued to scan the skies carefully for signs of pursuit. He suspected, though, that he did know who the Vulture was talking about. Only one woman in Brydon could hold such importance to the Vultures—but she was supposed to be dead. The same woman the Clans had been accused of killing.

"We have to find out who they're talking about," Tamora whispered urgently. "If we could find the woman the Vulture mentioned, then perhaps we could learn more about King Alfred's plans."

"Tonight." Dearn disagreed, knowing his headstrong companion was raring to go immediately. "We can't risk it right now, Tamora. We have no idea how many warriors they have, or how they're eluding our own patrols."

"We're faster than they are. They would never catch us."

He would have smiled at her indignant response if he weren't so worried for her welfare.

"I won't take the chance." He shook his head again. "I should have never let you convince me to take you with me to Tiber's aerie as it is."

By the position of the sun, he estimated how long they would be stuck hiding in the tree. He needed to get back to the Fortress and talk to Brendar about the information he had acquired.

Yes, he thought, they would fly to the Fortress after nightfall, and there he would leave her. If they were lucky enough to sight a Clan troop before then they would fly in with them. He had to get Tamora to safety and brief his Clan leaders. If he didn't, the future of the Clans might be dire indeed.

"This is what has come of our people's decision to attempt to wipe out an unpleasant past," Tamora snarled, her body tense. "The Bastard Breeds, the children of the Clans, fighting against their own people—their families—out of fury and bitterness."

It was a reflection of his own inner turmoil.

"They denied the Vulture blood, Tamora." Dearn's feelings were even more ambivalent now than they had been before. The Bastard Breeds fought with the Vultures, yet hadn't they also saved him and his warriors?

"They were children." Tamora swallowed tightly.

"And now their children's children war against us. They rape our women and kill our children," he reminded her. "There is no room in this war now for pity."

"They saved you and your troop, and yet they kill us as well?" He could feel her trying to sift through this contradictory information.

"Perhaps there is more to this than we can see, Dearn," she finally suggested. "Perhaps the Clans have allies that we were unaware of."

Perhaps that was true, and it was a thought he had entertained more than once himself; but until he knew for certain, he couldn't chance providing the Bastard Breeds with any measure of trust. They were the enemy until they proclaimed themselves otherwise, and this he told Tamora firmly, his voice hard with purpose.

She was silent then, but he could tell by the stiffness of her body, the small hitch in her breath, that still she did not understand. One more reason, he thought, why the women of the Clans were not made to fight. Their hearts were soft, their forgiveness nearly always assured. How could a woman such as Tamora ever kill and survive the decision?

Chapter Ten

 හ

"They're getting closer, Dearn." Tamora's voice was low as she watched the Vultures circle the afternoon sky.

Dearn nodded as he watched the patrols grow slowly in number. The first had shown up not long after he and Tamora reached their nest.

He wondered distantly why the Vultures had no fear that Clan forces would see them. A troop of Clan warriors could easily overpower the Vulture force and capture them. Yet, from all appearances, the enemy had no fear of this happening.

"Do you think we were seen earlier?" Tamora didn't sound frightened, but he suspected she was worried.

"I don't know." His voice was low as he watched the circling enemy carefully. "But at this point, I would assume so."

The Vultures had eyesight nearly as keen as that of the Eagle and Falcon Clans. Dearn didn't want to give their hiding place away by making any unnecessary movement if they hadn't yet been detected. The Vultures were definitely searching for something within the forest, though. Their lazy, ever-tightening circles were bringing them closer to where Dearn and Tamora hid.

"It's the same troop from Tiber's aerie," he told her quietly.

"They surely know all the Clans are at the Fortress now," she whispered. "What could they be searching for?"

"Perhaps not all are there," Dearn mused, knowing it was possible that others besides he and Tamora were hiding within the forests. "Or perhaps it isn't the lost Clan members they search for."

The huge wings carrying the Vultures' bodies were extended full-length as they rode the thermals above the forest floor. Dearn could see them searching intently. But what, he wondered, were they searching for?

Within seconds, he had his answer as the six winged warriors dipped closer, and one pointed silently to the tree where he and Tamora were sheltered. Somehow, they had been found.

"Dearn?" Fear now filled Tamora's breathless whisper as she realized their nest had been sighted.

"We're smaller. We're swifter." He reminded her of her earlier words. "We'll move together. We drop from the tree and fly like Seven Hells, Tamora. If we get ahead of them, we can make it out of the forest and get close enough to the Fortress that they will turn around."

Dearn felt the deep breath she took as she prepared for the flight to come. It would be hard, but she had done it during training exercises.

"Stay close to me," he ordered. "If we have to, we'll hug the ground — they can't fly that low for any distance. We can."

Tamora nodded silently and Dearn cursed the Vultures' dumb luck in finding them.

"Ready?"

Tamora nodded tightly as they parted and prepared to fly.

"Go!"

They fell from the tree and using short, powerful strokes of their wings, they propelled themselves below the branches of the trees and through the forest. Dearn could feel Tamora behind him, attuned to her presence and her fear as only a lover could be. They had flown like this for years, maneuvering together during the hunt, or just for play.

Within minutes of their descent, he knew they had been spotted. The circling Vultures began to move lower, remaining overhead but always right behind them. Dearn cursed them silently while he and Tamora dipped and swerved among the trees, fighting to gain enough distance to disappear from their pursuers' range of sight.

If they could reach the forest edge and enter the canyon that led to the Fortress, he knew the Clan forces would spot the Vultures and they would be safe. The trick would be in getting to the forest edge.

Dearn flew quickly for the final turn that led into the canyon. Not much farther and safety would be in their grasp.

As they rounded the turn into a stand of stately old trees, the ambushing humans stepped forward. The net came at them before Dearn could countermove and avoid it. Thick and heavy, it covered his wings and caught Tamora as well. He cursed vilely, fighting the web surrounding them to free Tamora as they fell to the ground.

"Lookie here, we caught us a pair."

His voice thick and filled with deadly amusement, the human soldier walked up to the net and kicked at Tamora. Dearn moved to block her body and caught the sharp toe of the soldier's boot in his ribs, possibly cracking several. His involuntary cry caused laughter to echo around him.

"Kill me now, Dearn." Tamora's whisper was filled with terror as her hand closed over the dagger at his waist. "Don't let them take me."

His heart thundered in despair as he realized there would be no escape. He could take the pain, even death, but he had seen what the Vultures and these human soldiers did to female captives.

He moved his hand to his belt and released the deadly blade. As he prepared to plunge it into her heart, the world around him suddenly darkened. The last sounds he heard were Tamora's terrified screams.

* * * * *

Matte watched the spectacle before her. The capture of the Eagle pair had been smooth and efficient with the help of the Elitist forces in the forest below. Her heart clenched in her throat as the pair was tied securely to the sharp stakes driven into the ground.

They weren't aware of who they had yet, but Matte knew. She would have recognized King Dearn in any manner of dress. The broad shoulders, the arrogant tilt of his head, the unusual coloring of his gold-streaked brown hair would have been hard for him to hide.

By the gods, what was he doing here? She stood aside, watching as the Vultures secured him to the posts, believing they had no more than an Eagle warrior and his mate. Rape the woman as her mate bled to death, watching the act—it was a favored sport among the Elitists and the Vultures. Matte fought the reminder there was another sect, another breed who excelled in this sport.

At the moment, the Eagles were unconscious. Matte prayed as she had never prayed before to the goddess of mercy and strength that they stayed out long enough for her to devise a plan to aid them.

"Matte, by the gods, what do we do?"

Anton stood tensely behind her, his softly spoken words barely reaching her. She took a deep breath, hearing the horror in his voice. It was a reflection of the fear coursing through her veins as well. If Dearn died, then all their plans were for naught.

"Slip away. Find a Clan patrol and lead them this way. I'll see what I can do while you're gone," she ordered. "Take out the Elitist sentries on your way. It would serve Edgar and our own plans well should the Clans capture him."

Hatred swelled inside her for the Vulture leader, who squatted beside the small Eagle woman, his hands even now degrading her body.

She remembered well the brutality of his touch. She remembered the hatred, the fear and impotence of being tied, unable to fight. Taking a deep breath she fought the memories, the sickness that welled inside her whenever he stared down at a woman in lust. It had been her first taste of Vulture cruelty; it was by no means her last.

"No fight to them while they're out like that, Edgar. Just your sort of sport." She hated the jeering tone she was forced to inject into her voice. "At least unconscious she can't scratch you like the other one did."

The White Lance woman's screams still echoed in Matte's dreams, as did those of her children. Gods help her, would she ever find peace from the horrors she had seen committed in this land?

"Oh, I'll wait till she awakens." Edgar snickered, hearing only the derision in her voice for the Eagle woman. "We want her and her mate well aware of the joys to come."

Matte laughed with the rest of them, but she felt the fist that clenched her stomach. She was terrified. What if she failed? What if she could not save the ruling pair of the Winged Clans? If she saved this woman from rape, if she managed to aid King Dearn in escaping with his mate, then surely he would be willing to listen to her, to allow her people to join their fight in exchange for what was taken from them so long ago.

She had to come up with a plan quickly—they wouldn't be out long. She had to save this pair or her people would be doomed.

She moved among the crowd, taking up a position to watch the captives as the others settled beneath the trees with their drink and their jokes. She was often assigned to guard the prisoners. Edgar enjoyed believing it made her miserable, so she was always quick to give him the ammunition to believe it did so.

Keeping a careful eye on the Vultures and their friends, she gave several of her men hasty instructions to protect the king, if nothing else, should she have to make her move before the Clan troop arrived. Then, she slowly brought the woman to careful awareness.

"Do not blink, do not scream, and you may still yet live to see the morrow," Matte whispered quickly, forestalling the low moan the woman would have emitted. "Your mate lives, but his life hinges on your ability to do exactly as I tell you. If you understand this, do no more than lift the finger that should wear the ring of your mate."

The left ring finger moved only slightly, just enough to convince Matte she heard.

"If they touch you, do not flinch. Do not scream; do not cry. For now, you are safe as long as you are unconscious. One of my men is going for a Clan troop, to lead them back here. But he must have time to reach them."

Matte moved around the woman, checking her ties, smacking at her face, calling back to Edgar in anger that he had allowed the humans to hit her too hard.

"She may die before awakening."

She could tell this bothered him. Edgar found no enjoyment in raping a woman who could not fight the ropes he placed on her.

It was working. Her carefully timed attempts to awaken the woman convinced Edgar his victim was still out cold. He would have to stay convinced, else they were all doomed.

Cold fear pooled in the pit of her stomach as time dragged by. Surely, the warrior she had sent out would be back soon. They had little time left, and Edgar would soon grow impatient. Lust was riding him hard and he could decide to take the woman whether she awakened or not.

Finally, blessedly, the signal came. Now, it was all in the wait and the timing. Gathering her courage, Matte steeled herself to approach the man who haunted her dreams, and who held her future in his hands.

* * * * *

Dearn returned to consciousness slowly, aware of the thundering ache in his head and the fact that he was securely bound. Hands and feet tingled from the ropes tied around them.

Careful to keep his awakened status hidden, he opened his eyes just the slightest bit, aware that his long lashes still hid the tiny crack. He glanced around as far as possible, searching for Tamora. His heart jerked when he sighted her, and rage threatened the fragile hold he had on his control.

She was bound, spread grotesquely and tied to stakes secured into the ground. She hadn't yet been stripped, but he could tell she had been severely beaten.

"Don't move, warrior, don't even breathe funny. They're just waiting on you to awaken before they begin raping her." The female voice spoke from behind him. "Now..." soft as a breeze, the voice continued, "I'll assume she's your mate, which means to save her you have to do whatever I tell you to do."

The voice moved closer as rough hands checked the ties at his feet, behind his back, at his hands.

"I'm going to get pretty painful here in a minute; so just play dead a little while longer and we may yet manage to save both your feathers."

Merely painful didn't describe it. Had he not been prepared for it, Dearn knew he would have betrayed himself when the first kick nailed him in the back.

From his head to his feet he was kicked, pushed and prodded as the female voice jeered him. Thankfully, she didn't take long to prove her point to the loud, mocking voices behind her.

With a grunt of disgust, the long form of the female Vulture sat down in front of him. Peeking through his lashes, he watched the tight smile she gave him.

"Good boy," she whispered, and Dearn wondered at the note of relief he heard in her soft voice. "Now, before I leave, I'm going to loosen your ropes and slip you a dagger. But don't do anything. If you want to save that mate of yours, then you'll wait. Do you understand me? She knows what is coming. She, too, is prepared. You must be as well. Are you?"

He blinked his eyes once.

"They'll get pretty rough with her. They like to play before they actually start raping their women." A brief flash of sympathy appeared in her soft hazel eyes. "No matter how hard she cries, don't move until you hear me yell the warning that Clan troops are sighted. There's one due not far from here soon, if my plan works." She smiled softly. "We have to move fast, but they are headed this way. Do you think you can wait? Can you hear her cry and still pretend to be dead?"

Dearn blinked again and prayed he could keep his word.

"Very good." Her expression turned hard, her brown eyes going flat and cold as she checked the ropes, secretly releasing the knots as she did so. "Then let's get the game started."

"He's not coming around anytime soon." She rose to her feet as she delivered a kick to his shins. "Dumb bastard. Edgar, I think you may have killed him."

"Damn. That's too bad." The man she called Edgar sounded sarcastic and mocking. "Guess you'll have to get your jollies somewhere else, won't you, bitch?"

A round of male laughter accompanied his words.

"Yeah, maybe I ought to start with you."

Dearn was surprised by the silence that followed her sneering dare. Knowing how these men treated their women, he wouldn't have expected them to back down from her.

"Hell, Matte, don't go I' your feathers ruffled." The voice of the one she called Edgar came back in an amused response. "You always have to take everything so damned seriously."

"And you have to take everything so damned foolishly," Matte snapped as she moved closer to the group of men. "If you guys intend to play, then you better get to it. I want to be out of here soon, with or without you. It's been too long since a Clan patrol was spotted — one has to be along soon."

"Yeah, and ol' Dale will warn us when one's sighted. Then, all we have to do is gag those two 'til they're gone." Edgar laughed. "Don't worry, Matte, we'll take care not to get caught."

"Get to it, Edgar, or I'll head back alone. Then you'll be a soldier shy should you have to fight."

Dearn was surprised when the men began moving, heading toward Tamora. *Sweet Aleda,* he prayed, *give me the strength to follow that woman's orders.*

Tamora's scream tore through his head as the one called Edgar ripped her shirt from her body. Evidently, she, too, had been awake.

Cold laughter echoed through the group as her pants were quickly cut away, her screams and pleas ignored as they called out to one another, assigning numbers to decide who would take her first.

Dearn clenched his fists around the dagger when he saw them touch her. Their hands grasped her breasts, kneading, pinching what he knew was tender skin. Her cries and pleas became a litany, a prayer as she begged them to stop.

For what seemed like forever they pawed her, laughing as she cried and fought against the bonds that secured her to the ground, helpless against them. They pulled her long hair, pinched her breasts and described in graphic detail what they planned to do to her. Dearn kept still, quiet, the dagger clenched in his hands until he could feel the hilt digging into his skin. They were hurting her, torturing her, and he did nothing. He fought from second to second not to jump to his feet and plunge the dagger into each of their hearts as he questioned his decision to trust the Vulture woman a thousand times.

He silently cursed as one man rose and began to loosen his trousers, and still the woman had not called out; he cursed her to the deepest pits of the Seven Hells. As he kicked the bonds from his feet and hands, the alarm finally went up.

"Clan troops, you fools. Pull your pants up and fly."

Her cry caused chaos to erupt. Dearn jumped to his feet. The Vultures scattered around the clearing as a Clan cry went out and the war horn sounded, calling any other available warriors to the forest floor. The beating of his heart was only overshadowed by the sound of wings beating in the air as he ran for Tamora, ready to defend her against any Vulture stupid enough to try to touch her again.

He need not have worried. As he pulled her protectively into his arms, his wings flaring to enclose her, the Vultures were running, fighting to gain enough speed to aid their wings in hurling them into the air. When the Clan troops landed, there were only three of the six Vultures left to defeat, and they cowered before the forces now surrounding them. There was no sign of the female warrior or the large Vulture who was apparently the leader.

Dearn released Tamora as Brendar neared them. He would have given her his shirt, but before he could shrug from it, the general had wrapped his own around her. He turned to his men, who were now restraining the remaining Vultures.

"Take care of her," Dearn ordered. He didn't give Brendar time to acknowledge before he was running through the clearing and gaining the speed to allow his wings to lift his body from the ground.

Within minutes he was airborne, ignoring aching ribs and bruised muscles as he searched for the missing Vulture leader and the female with him. He glanced down at the clearing, noting absently the protective manner in which Brendar's wings were wrapped around Tamora before he started to scour the area for the escapees.

At first he had assumed she was a Vulture woman, until he saw the unusual flash of coloration in her wings, the dark brown of her hair, the hazel of her eyes. The same Bastard Breed who had saved them in Ralnd's aerie.

Why had she aided him? As he unsuccessfully searched, his fury grew. Damn her to the Seven Hells, why had she helped them and then run at the first chance to join her demon leader?

* * * * *

Matte watched the Clan king scour the area from a hidden thicket of prickly vine. He was magnificent. Too bad he was mated as well, she thought, tamping down her awakening lust for the warrior.

"Damn you, Matte, why didn't you sight them sooner?" Edgar whispered to her from the shadows of the thicket.

"Hey, ol' Dale was watching for Clan troops. I saw no reason why I shouldn't enjoy the show." She shrugged, careful to keep her expression hidden, her voice bland.

"Bastard humans," he cursed the guards they had set up. "I'll have them skinned alive for this."

"Good luck. Looks to me like the Clans will take care of that for you." She nodded toward the humans being dragged through the forest. "They just captured them."

They watched the Clan warriors gathering. They were unable to hear what was said, but Matte knew the lives of the captured Vultures and those humans were over. She was thankful none of her men had been captured as well.

Chapter Eleven

ଚ

The fleeing Vulture leader and his Bastard Breed companion were nowhere to be found. Dearn searched, his eyes narrowed, focused on the concealing foliage below. They hadn't flown far, else he could still have seen them in the skies. They had to have taken refuge, either in the forest or the nearby aeries.

With a quick gesture he sent pairs of warriors to search the aeries, but he sensed it was in vain. The pair had somehow escaped amid the confusion of the Clan warriors' arriving and the Vultures being taken captive.

Dearn gritted his teeth, a furious curse welling in his throat. He had thought for certain he would have her this time. That he would somehow capture her and get the answers he needed.

He floated on the currents of air, watching the ground, searching and hoping he would catch sight of her. Long minutes later, he realized the futility of his actions.

He returned to the clearing, intent on gathering the troop and continuing the search farther into the forested gorges in the area. His blood was running hot, his muscles trembling with the need for battle and the realization that the Vultures were so confident they would attempt to rape a Clan woman in the open during the light of day.

With the humans aiding them, watching from the forest floor to send out a warning of advancing patrols, they had every right to be confident. Cinder-cursed Elitist humans, with their hatred and merciless hearts.

Yet it seemed even more apparent that within the enemy's camp there was an ally to be found. The woman was a question Dearn had to have answered.

He freely admitted his own arrogance had led him and Tamora into more jeopardy than he could have gotten them out of on his own. He had not just endangered himself and Tamora, though; he had endangered the whole of the Clans on this fool's mission.

"Brendar, get the troop ready to fly. I want those bastards caught."

Dearn landed, shouting to his general as the warriors continued to secure the clearing. Brendar's bare shoulders tensed. He still stood protectively beside Tamora, and Dearn watched pure rage wash over his expression a second before he gained control of himself.

"We need to get Tamora to the Fortress, Sire, instead of chasing after those who escaped," Brendar replied between clenched teeth.

Dearn paused in surprise, and then pinned him with a glare as he considered reminding him who gave the orders.

"She has multiple injuries and her right wing could be broken. She'll need assistance flying in." Brendar refused to back down, but there was a noticeable lessening of the general's commanding tone. "We can't leave her alone."

Dearn swung to look at Tamora, frowning as she turned from him quickly. He clenched his fist and fought the mingled guilt and wrath inside his body. He should have thought of Tamora instead of forcing Brendar to point it out.

"You're right." He ran his fingers through his hair in frustration. "We'll head for the Fortress and question the bastards we have."

"Very well, Sire." Brendar nodded stiffly, his face still set in lines of anger. "You were lucky we heard her screams. Another few minutes and we would have been out of range.

We had nearly decided your intelligence was such that you would not have been in this area after all."

The insulting reference to his lack of common sense was delivered smoothly, with a cool, bland voice. Dearn stared at his general for long moments before he decided to let the remark go. He admitted his responsibility for Tamora's being there. He should have merely turned back, rather than allowing the independent woman to fly with him. In his own, silent defense he had not expected such an attack.

"Yes, we were very lucky indeed."

But how lucky would they have been without the Bastard Breed woman's help? A traitor within the Vultures was the answer they needed if they were going to defeat the enemy quickly.

So why, if the Bastard Breeds were betraying the Vultures they originally fought with, hadn't they made a move to contact him? It was only logical, Dearn thought, and it was a move he would have made well before now, had he been in their position. Their safety could not be assured within the Vulture camps, and, eventually, their enemies would learn of their betrayal, so why stay silent? So many questions and yet so few answers.

He turned to the three Vultures they had captured as they were prepared for flight. At the Fortress he would gain the answers he needed from them. No creature, no matter how vile, could resist the effects of the Elixir of Truth, a special brew prepared by the White Lance priests that prevented any lies that might come to an enemy's lips. It soothed and cajoled the mind when truth was given, but sent fire licking through the body when it met falsehood.

"I'm ready," Tamora snapped at one of the soldiers, her voice hard and angry.

Dearn took a deep, silent breath as he waved the others away and approached her, noticing that Brendar moved away with the greatest reluctance. Guilt ate at him as he watched her feathers shudder with her attempts to control her emotions.

Somehow, she had managed to salvage her breeches. Her shirt was torn, so she wore the general's instead. It was wrapped closely about her, the long sleeves covering her hands as she clutched the hastily buttoned collar closer to her throat. The attached back that ran beneath her wings was twisted, as was the piece behind her neck. The buttons that held each were out of line, but secure.

"Tamora." Her body jerked despite his soft tone. "Forgive me for allowing this."

"It wasn't your fault." She shook her head, keeping her back to him. "It was mine."

"Tamora—"

"I should have not forced you to allow me to fly with you to the aerie," she whispered tearfully. "I could have gotten us both killed—then how would the Clans survive?"

He sighed roughly.

"This was not your fault, Tam," he insisted. He wanted to rail at her for trying to take the blame. He was her king—he could have found a way to force her back to the Fortress and still carry out his own plans. Seven Hells, he could have handled this in a much safer manner all the way around.

"I can't discuss this now, Dearn." Her wings shook as she shuddered with shock.

"Later. After you've rested, then we will talk. And we *will* talk, Tamora. You will not deny me then." His words came out rough and raspy.

She nodded shakily then flinched as he wrapped his arms around her waist.

"You will let Brendar fly you to the Fortress now." He hardened his tone as she began to push away from him. "You're not able to fly on your own, and we both know it."

Hesitantly, she obeyed, going slowly into the other warrior's arms, and then he saw why she had been so careful to hide her face from him.

Livid bruises and bloody scratches marred her perfect face. One beautiful violet eye was swollen shut, and her lips were split and still slowly seeping blood.

"They will pay for this. I swear to you, Tamora, they will all pay," Dearn whispered as Brendar pulled her closer. He stepped out of the way of the troop members who were gliding down to lift the general into the air so he could catch the wind with less effort.

Chapter Twelve

ശ

The flight back to the Fortress was quick. The troop sought the wind currents that blew into the valleys and directed Dearn and Brendar to them, allowing them to glide faster into the haven of the mountain home.

"The Clan leaders will need to see you now. I'll take care of Tamora." The general's expression was combative as Dearn started to take Tamora's arm.

"I don't need help walking into the damned place," she snapped sullenly as she jerked from Brendar's grip. Dearn watched the display in surprise.

"You barely look strong enough to breathe on your own," Brendar snapped. "Stop being so Seven Hells stubborn."

"If I did need help, I would be certain to ask any besides you, Brendar of the Red Hawk." She jerked her arm from him once again and limped rather shakily toward the Fortress entrance.

"Brendar." Dearn halted the warrior when he would have forced her back to him. "Let her go, if she prefers. I'll take care of her later."

He arched a brow as Brendar spun back around, clearly ready to speak, then reined the words back with effort. Dearn had a feeling those words would have blasted him.

"Do you have a better idea?" he asked softly.

Brendar clenched his fists and his fight for control surprised Dearn.

"I have no better idea on how to deal with such a damned stubborn woman than I do about how to deal with my king, who places his own life in a position such as the one you did today," the man finally spat out. "Your decision was based on emotion and a need for vengeance, and you drew Tamora in where she should not have been. Your judgment in this was weak, Sire."

The auburn and red-gold of the general's wings twitched with his fury. It was rare to see Brendar in such a rage. In fact, Dearn thought, this might be the first he had ever seen the emotion in the man.

"In this, Brendar, I will agree." He nodded, amazed to see such heights of emotion from his normally coolheaded commander. "And I promise you that such will not happen again. But it was more than productive otherwise. Come along, and I will brief you as I speak with the Clan leaders."

He turned to walk into the Fortress.

"What about Tamora?" The words seemed to be pushed from between clenched teeth.

Dearn stopped, turning back as he frowned.

"I will send someone to help her bathe and a healer to treat her wounds. I want to speak with the Clan leaders and then deal with the bastards I sent to the dungeons. Do you have any objection to my stated course of action?"

He prayed not. The general was testing his patience as it was.

There was no voiced answer, but the unabated twitching of the upper feathers of the general's wings for long moments was a telling sign.

"No, Sire." The words were respectful even if the tone wasn't, Dearn consoled himself. But this attitude of Brendar's was beginning to become seriously irritating.

"Very well then, let's take care of the garbage we brought in."

Dearn headed for the Fortress once again, thankful that his general was holding his tongue despite the need in his eyes to argue further.

* * * * *

The dungeons had not been used in over one hundred years. The stone chambers were dark and cold, their only light coming from the lanterns hung on the walls.

Strong steel chains had been attached to steel stakes driven into the stone floor. The three captured Vultures were attached to those chains by leg cuffs.

As Dearn approached, he felt frigid hatred well within his soul. These men had raped and brutalized countless women of the Clans before leaving them to die slow, agonizing deaths. They had murdered helpless children and sent terror stampeding throughout the Clans with the carnage they had left behind.

They would pay for this with their lives. Whether their deaths were quick and merciful or protracted and brutal would be up to them. Giving them such a choice went against his own need to repay them in kind for their brutalities, but at this point Dearn knew the information they could provide was more important than his need for vengeance.

He raised his hand as he and his men came within the circle of light around the captives. The guards stepped back and the Vultures watched them suspiciously. *Oh, yes,* Dearn thought as he saw fear glitter in their eyes, *be afraid.*

"Whaddya want?" the largest of the three growled as he strained against the irons holding him down. "Are ya ready to set us free now?"

"I hardly think so." Dearn didn't bother to hide his contempt as he crossed his arms over his chest and surveyed them closely. "I think you are aware you'll never leave this place alive."

He never took his eyes from them as he spoke. He wanted them to know, to anticipate the passing of their lives.

"Then why are you here?" the largest asked him. "Why not just kill us and be done with it?"

"Did you just kill and be done with it?" Dearn was still amazed that his fury was so contained. "I could kill you now, and no one would question my decision. Or, I could have your wings broken and give you to the men gathered in the courtyard for them to take vengeance for what you did to their families."

Their faces slowly paled and their eyes at last grew wide with their fear.

"I can show you mercy," he continued. "Or I can repay you in kind for your deeds. The choice is yours."

Sweat began to drip from the faces of the captives; their growing terror was a small measure of satisfaction for him.

"We choose mercy." Once again it was the largest of the three who spoke.

"Mercy comes with a price." Dearn motioned behind him.

Jalon, Clan leader and spiritual priest of the White Lance Clan, stepped forward, bearing in his hands a tray holding three crude wooden cups.

"You will drink from these cups, which hold the Elixir of Truth. When I've finished questioning you, you will then be killed, quickly and mercifully."

Tears slowly streaked their filthy faces as their eyes went to the tray. Dearn observed, his heart cold and untouched by the sobbing of the cowards before him.

If they knew anything about the Clans they warred against, they would know the significance of the Elixir of Truth. It was given only when death was a certainty, and there were no rewards for the truth a man might willingly give. The Clans were gentle in their way of life and how they dealt with others, but their fury at the needless, senseless cruelties of the

Vultures would assure these merciless warriors that there would be no mercy, no forgiveness.

Jalon placed the tray on the floor within reach of the three men. They stared down at the crude cups, their black eyes awash with both hatred and cowardice.

"Drink from the cups, and when you tell me the truths I seek then will I ensure your deaths are quick and merciful. Otherwise, I will allow the Clansmen who wait outside to torture the truth from your filthy mouths," the priest instructed them.

And he would, Dearn knew. The people awaited his decision now, praying to Ashrad that their priests and king would deliver the Vultures into the hands of the families whose children had died by their sword or beneath their corrupt bodies. Dearn swallowed past the bile he tasted that any mercy should be granted to such foul creatures.

The larger of the warriors stared up at him, tears still leaking down his dirty face.

"We drink this and you'll kill us swiftly? No torture?"

He needed the reassurance, and in his eyes Dearn saw the certainty of betrayal. He smiled mirthlessly that these cold-hearted creatures could look to him and judge him by their own code.

"I am king of the Clans." He watched the shock cover their faces. "Ah, yes. You knew not the man you held, nor did you know whose woman you would have raped. But I know." Dearn leaned closer, his lips curving into a snarl as his guts boiled. "I know the pleasure you would have gained had you known who you held. I know the death that would have awaited the woman; I know the cruelties you would have inflicted. I have seen with my own eyes the results of your crimes and you deserve no mercy. You deserve naught but to have your skin peeled from your bodies in thin strips, your bare flesh left to sear beneath the heat of the sun."

His fists clenched spasmodically and he fought to contain, to control the need to slit their throats with the dagger strapped to his thigh.

The Vulture warriors swallowed tightly.

"Drink the Cinder-cursed elixir or, by my sword, I swear to you, I will have just that done to you and it will be done before the first rays of Ashrad's glory brightens the skies on the morrow."

Control. *Gods grant me the strength to control this fury,* Dearn prayed, unwilling to stop the jerking of his wings, the clenching of his hand on his dagger, the ferocity that trembled along his body.

He prayed they refused to drink the elixir. It could not be forced on them; it could not be poured down their throats as they cried out in denial. The gods had commanded when they first gave the Clans the secret to this weapon to sort through the truth or lies of the humans that it must be taken with free will.

The Vultures looked one to the other. Then the largest, obviously the one the other two looked to for guidance, nodded shakily.

As they picked up their cups with trembling hands, Dearn struggled over his decision. To give mercy to such monsters went against all he knew, yet only in doing so would he find the answers he needed. He would have to find some way to be content with the trade.

So he waited, his body taut as he ignored the Spiritmen behind him, the heavy hand of Jalon on his shoulder. Were these, he wondered, among those who forced their way into Ralnd's home? Had their spies brought to them the rumor that the Lady Mera held the king's heart as well as his cousin's?

"Sire, we can do this alone," Jalon whispered to him, his raspy voice filled with pity.

How many others knew? Dearn wondered. Gods help him, had Ralnd known as well?

"No, Jalon. I will question these worthless animals myself. I would know all they know. I would know of the deceit of the humans, the treachery of the Vultures and anything else these miserable slithers know."

Dearn took comfort with a small smile as the pain of the Elixir of Truth began to wash through the bodies of the rancid creatures.

"Cinder's blood, you swore mercy." The larger warrior clenched his muscles as he fought the fire racing through his veins.

"Relax. Allow the blood of the gods to travel through you. It only brings pain to those who would hide the truth, to those who fight the truth lest the gods have their vengeance and their knowledge." Jalon moved closer—in this, he had supremacy. Dearn could not interfere. "In moments, the pain will leave, and you will be merely warm. But I warn you now. Refuse to answer the chosen King of the Clans, and the pain will return tenfold. Try to lie, to evade or to hide that which you know he would have need of, and the gods will reach inside you and tear your heart from your chest."

Long moments later, the Vultures were slumped against the damp wall of their cell, watching Dearn with hope-filled eyes as the pain lessened and relief eased through their bodies. He bent his knees, bringing his face level with theirs so he could see clearly into the Seven Hells black of their eyes.

"Sire, I caution you." Jalon stepped beside him now. "The questioning must conform to the commands of the gods."

Dearn narrowed his eyes, watching the prisoners with a tight smile.

"Then I cannot question them about Mera and Ralnd or the babes they killed?" He smiled as the largest jumped, fighting the elixir, fighting the knowledge he had.

As the Spiritman gazed down at his king in disapproval, the Vulture began to speak. Dearn questioned him and the others for hours. The knowledge they held sickened him.

The rumors that often spread through families had been betrayed by those they trusted, innocently enough, but it had been betrayed. The Vultures had known each place to strike that would weaken him personally and, in turn, weaken the Clans. They knew his family, his friends and the locations of their aeries.

When Dearn could handle no more, he asked them of the Bastard Breeds.

"Worthless. Hate the Clans for their rejection. Hate them for the exile, the sentence of death." And on and on the information went.

"And what of the woman that Edgar, your leader, has claimed for his own?" Dearn finally demanded. "Who is the one the human king holds in payment for his service?"

"The Princess Allora," the first warrior answered him.

"The Princess is dead," Dearn reminded him. "Remember? Her body was dropped from the sky by the Eagle Clan warriors."

"No." One of the Vultures shook his head violently. "A young girl Edgar raped and killed. She looked like the princess. Alfred had her dressed as the princess and ordered a couple of the Bastard Breeds to drop her from the sky. Matte was furious, but Edgar knows she'll obey. The lives of her people are in his hands."

"And who is this Matte? Is she the commander of the Bastards?"

"She commands Thorne's warriors here. Thorne could not leave the other lands—the battles there required him and there was no room on the ships to bring all the people. The Bats are fierce—he could not leave his people."

Shock rippled through the room.

"The Bats do not exist. You lie."

"No, Sire." There was no pain in the Vulture, only truth. "The Bats are there, held by the expanse of water between the continents. They feed on us, war with us. But, soon they will starve, for when the war is finished Alfred will send ships for the Vultures and Thorne will be left. The Bastards alone will serve as the food of the demons, and Vultures will be free."

* * * * *

Jalon could not contain his shudder of fear, of sympathy for the Bastard Breed warriors. But the name of Thorne was all he needed to hear. He knew that neither Bats nor Alfred would hold that warrior in exile when ships arrived. The Cries of Algernon had foretold this, as well as the name of the one who would come.

"And what will Edgar do next?" Dearn asked. "What are his plans that you know of?"

"We attack the Southern Valley. The women and girls there will be raped and killed. Their men forced to watch as they die. We will punish them all. The Fortress will be ours. Alfred will have the gold and the vengeance of Cinder; Edgar will have the Clans and the women. It will all be ours."

"And when will this attack take place?" Dearn's voice was riddled with fury and anguish.

"When the three moons ride high in the sky. Middle night, while the gods are forced to watch, impotent to stop the death of their loved ones. Then we will strike."

Jalon could only shake his head. The Vultures' hatred of Ashrad was as deep and as long as creation. They sought to wound him when he could do naught but shed light on their atrocities.

He listened as King Dearn finished the questioning, watching as his king fought to control the tremors of his body, of his wings, and the sickness his face said the information had brought to his stomach.

Dearn was a kind, thoughtful ruler. He abhorred the death and the pain his people were suffering. Each death, each mark on the skin of one of his people was a personal wound to his soul, and Jalon knew he was finding it difficult to maintain the mercy his father had always taught him.

"Sire. Enough." Jalon laid a restraining hand on his king's shoulder once again as he watched the dagger slowly slip from its sheath. "Go. Do you what you must to halt their plans. We will finish this."

* * * * *

The winds howled around the Fortress, moaning eerily over the enclosing walls as it brushed through the valley and down along the mountain ranges. Tamora stood on the balcony that overlooked the sheer cliff and let the wind whip through her hair and over her feathers. The rough caress caused her face to ache and her swollen lips to sting, yet she was hesitant to enter the bedroom and face Dearn.

He had nearly been killed because of her stubborn recklessness. Her overconfidence in her abilities had slowed him down and been the reason for their capture.

Had she not blackmailed her king, then the conflicting emotions and loyalties raging through her would not be a problem. She would have been at peace, in some ways, despite the war waging around the Clans. Instead, she was now beset by desires and needs that tormented her, taunted her with the uselessness of everything. She had faced death, and in doing so, realized that part of the estrangement from Dearn's bed was as much her fault as his. Just as she now knew that her presence in Brendar's bed long nights before had been more than just wandering lust.

"Tamora."

Dearn's voice was cool and controlled as he called her back into the room. She tensed at the sound of it. How could she face him now? How could she face him, or Brendar later, after the betrayal of her body and her loyalty with the general, the betrayal her willful nature had led to?

But she did. She turned hesitantly and left the windswept balcony to reenter her bedroom, her head lowered, her heart beating sluggishly in her chest as she faced the man who was her lover. Or, at least, the man who had once been her lover. He had not been to her bed in so long that she wondered who, or what, she was to him now.

Dearn had left her in the care of several maids earlier with a terse order to bathe before the Healer saw her. He told her he would return after her wounds were seen to. And he had returned, true to his word. She wished he had continued on his way and just left her in peace.

He, too, had bathed and changed. Instead of the lighter breeches and shirts he wore about the castle, however, he was dressed once again in the soft leather worn for hunting.

"You're going out again?" she asked him, knowing that he needed to rest. He was weary; she could see it in his face. He had been sleeping erratically, trying to take care of everyone and everything but himself.

"I'm flying out with a troop to the Southern Valley. The Vultures are attacking there tonight." His voice was soft, but his lips twisted into a snarl that reminded her of a howler, a four-legged, furry, sharp-toothed, too-intelligent predator that stalked the mountains and canyons of the Clans' lands. The creature was a fierce fighter, a careful tracker and an animal loyal to its own; and it wore much the same expression when foolishly challenged. Tamora shivered at the resemblance.

"You need to rest first." She crossed her arms under her breasts. "I know you haven't slept, Dearn. You can't benefit anyone without rest."

A small smile tipped his beautiful lips, and he watched her with his amazing golden eyes. Gods save her, where were the lust and affection that hint of a smile had once caused to rage inside her?

Once, she would have gone to him, kissed him, pleaded with him to stay. She would have wrapped her arms around him, using her body to tempt him to bed; yet it wouldn't be sleep they would have sought. Now, she wasn't certain what to do. They were changing, and that change frightened her. It had begun months before, and she had not noticed it until now. How, she wondered, could she have missed such a break in her life? How could she not have understood when she made such a disastrous mistake as the one she had in a fit of temper, with Brendar?

She shivered at the memory of that night. Brendar's wings caressing her, mating with hers, the scent of midnight and rain surrounding them. Pleasure unlike any she had ever known. With a man who would never allow her the freedom she needed to be herself. He would hem her in, possess her. She wrapped her arms around herself, wondering why this thought did not terrify her as it once had.

"What happened today was not your fault, Tamora." Dearn went swiftly to the point, and she nearly smiled. How like him to not waste time when he had something on his mind.

"Had it not been for me..." she began.

"Had it not been for you, I would have still been seen, most likely sooner. I would have been dead, Tamora, with no hope. Thanks to you, and the one who betrayed her people, we escaped with only bruises. Perhaps you should think on that."

He watched her with arrogant self-assurance. His eyes narrowed, his lips thinned now. Tamora shook her head. There was no arguing with this man. When had she ever won an argument with him? He was so supremely assured that he was always right, that he knew always what was best for everyone.

She smothered the anger this thought brought, for she knew he wasn't entirely aware of that about himself; and he was always looking for ways to improve the lives of those he loved. Dearn was a most caring, dedicated king. But, she thought, sometimes he was also a very forceful king.

"You will not have those thoughts anymore. Do you understand me?" Purpose hardened his voice, proving her point to her own mind, at least.

"I understand you, Dearn." Though it hurt, she forced herself to smile.

He, however, frowned, studying her intently as she stared back.

"Something is different about you, Tamora." He shook his head in confusion.

She looked away, unable to voice her bewilderment. The day had brought more than terror. It had made her aware of the changes within herself, and not just Dearn's lack of affection toward her.

"I'm just tired." She turned from him and pulled her robe closer about her body, rubbing the material covering her arms. "It's been a very eventful day."

She tilted her mouth mockingly as she voiced the understatement.

"Perhaps soon this war will come to an end." He sighed roughly, and she could envision him running his fingers absently through his hair as he always did.

"Yes, perhaps soon." She echoed his sentiments as she stared through the open doors to the balcony.

"I must leave. Tamora, will you not even look at me?" The irritation in his voice forced her to turn reluctantly again to face him. "I will return by dawn." He frowned at her and she wondered at the reason for the intense look he now gave her. "We will talk again tomorrow."

She nodded.

"Tomorrow," she agreed. "Be careful, Dearn. It could be a trap."

The woman who had aided them that afternoon had been too eager to help, to her way of thinking. The whispered warning while she checked the ropes binding her had surprised Tamora. Vultures were not known for being merciful. The female Bastard Breed was up to something, and that worried her.

"I will." Dearn nodded quickly, hesitating as he stepped toward her only to frown, turn on his heel and leave.

His mind was now on his mission, not on the woman he was leaving behind. She shivered as the door closed behind him and released a ragged sigh. Too much was changing too quickly, for all of them.

* * * * *

Tamora couldn't have been more wrong. As Dearn left the bedroom his thoughts were on nothing but her and his sudden realization of how quickly their relationship had changed since the war began. What had once been an affectionate, warm affair had suddenly cooled, and Dearn could not place the blame on Tamora alone. His own passions had begun to dissipate well before the first Clan member was found dead.

"Is she all right?" Brendar joined him as he entered the main hall, and together they left the castle.

Dearn frowned at the other man's continuing obstinate look. Brendar was angry over Tamora, and he couldn't understand why.

"She's fine."

The Red Hawk general was noted for his easygoing nature, his quick smile and his playful attitude toward life and women. Until this war, Dearn couldn't remember ever seeing him upset, and yet lately he seemed constantly upset.

"She was not fine earlier." Brendar seemed to stomp beside him.

"I assure you, she is fine now." Dearn cast him a hard look. He grew weary of his general questioning him constantly over Tamora. "Do you not believe me, check on her yourself when we return."

Dearn shook his head. There was a puzzle here, and he was determined to get to the bottom of it—as soon as he could catch a spare moment in between battles.

As Dearn exited the castle to meet with the troop he was leading to the Southern Valley, he was assaulted by the screams and pleas of the three Vultures as they were dragged from the depths of the dungeon into the steadily darkening expanse of the courtyard. They were led to the wall that overlooked the deep gorge and sheer cliffs that supported the Fortress. Their wings hung limply upon their backs, broken before the condemned were brought to their execution.

Contrary to their fears, Dearn had not broken his word and given them over to the Clans for retribution. Their screams, however, grew in volume as they realized the nature of their true punishment.

Impassively, Dearn watched as they were hauled onto the wall and gagged.

"For their crimes against the People of the Clans," Jalon called out to those assembled within the courtyard, "and for their having taken the Elixir of Truth and answering all questions put to them, King Dearn has granted mercy to these three. Their death, rather than by our hands, shall come from the mountain they betrayed. The Fortress is our haven, our home, so unto the stones do we commit their lives."

The gags were removed and the prisoners quickly flung from the wall to the deep valley below. Dearn watched, the accusations of the men echoing in his head. Had he betrayed his people in giving their enemies mercy? He felt as if he had. They should have been given to the families whose children and grandchildren they had destroyed.

The deaths were swift instead, the prisoners' only torture the brief space of time as they hurled to the bone-shattering floor of the gorge. Within moments, the troop assigned to witness confirmed that the monsters lay broken and unmoving below.

A cheer went up from the courtyard. These deaths in no way assuaged the crimes the Vultures had committed, but they ensured that there were three less to ever commit such crimes again.

He raised his eyes to the darkening sky and prayed that soon he would find a way to resolve the war, before his people had any more reason to cry out for vengeance.

"Sire, the troop is ready now," Brendar informed him, his tone still harsh, his voice low as the Clans within the courtyard continued to cheer and cry.

Dearn turned to look at the younger man. Brendar had risen quickly within the ranks of the King's Troops. At thirty years, he excelled in matters of logic, swordsmanship, hunting and war games. There were few who could best him. Brendar was as fierce a fighter as the Red Hawk Clan had, and he was eager now to fly and meet their foes in combat.

Dearn nodded.

The troop of twenty-four warriors was assembled at the wall. There were warriors of each Clan — the best, eager to deliver their own brand of justice to the Vultures.

"Do you think the information was true, Sire?" Brendar asked him as they made their way to the rest of the group.

"I believe it to be true, Brendar. The Elixir of Truth has yet to fail us." Dearn nodded. "Advise your men that the Vultures will have human sentries and scouts hidden within the forest. Twelve warriors will fly with me directly into the village, twelve others will spread out and find as many of the human conspirators as possible. I want them all this time."

The humans who farmed the Southern Valley would be attacked mainly because of their loyalty to the Clans. The White Lance Clan usually protected the small village; the humans who lived there shared none of the prejudices against the Clans held by the humans in the lower valley of Cayam.

"We'll take them all, Sire," Brendar swore as they and the group jumped onto the wall.

"They have a head start on us," Dearn announced as he turned to face the gorge and felt the winds whipping through his hair. "We fly hard, and we fly fast. Stay in formation and don't break until ordered to do so."

A resounding chorus of agreement echoed among the warriors.

"May the blessings of Durin be at our backs, the strength of Sorin in our arms and the mercy of Aleda in our hearts. We fly!" With the simple warrior's prayer, Dearn led his men into the first face-to-face battle against the creatures the Seven Hells had spawned at the dawn of time. He spread his wings, feeling the wind sweep through them as he turned his back to its strength. Lifting them high, he let the currents of air lift him quickly from the wall and send him sailing along the gorge leading to the Southern Range.

Within minutes, the other warriors were in formation behind him. They rode the wind, bodies angling to curve around the treacherous passages. The quickest route to their destination was also the most dangerous.

As Dearn moved with the currents he gloried in the flight, his wings alternately extended to glide or pulling in to allow greater speed. The Winged Clans did not take their gifts for granted. The gods had given them wings to fly and the brains to survive, and they would use both to defeat the Vultures.

Midnight was but minutes past when the troop moved into position to enter the sheltered village. Already, they could hear the screams of the women, the sounds of the huge alarm bell echoing as the villagers signaled for help. Help they must believe would never arrive in time, for it was well-known that the Clanhold of the White Lance was all but deserted, its members safely inside the Fortress.

The aid they needed had arrived in time, though. Dearn felt the thrill of the hunt when the signal came that the sentries had been spotted. Whether those left to watch for the Clan troop signaled the attackers now or not wouldn't matter; they would all be captured.

Unsheathing his sword, he sent a silent signal. Dropping from the sky the warriors landed on the backs of the attacking Vultures, and to Dearn it felt as though he had flown into a rock. He grunted as he slammed into the warrior he had chosen as his target.

Tall and hefty, the Vulture went to his knees as Dearn rolled quickly to his feet. Unfortunately, he didn't stay there long. Within seconds he was standing straight and grinning at Dearn with an expression of satisfaction and amusement on his hard, sneering face.

"A challenge, to be sure," he snorted with dark amusement; he stood several inches taller than Dearn. "You picked the wrong Vulture to tangle with, son."

Dearn braced then pivoted to block the sword aimed for his gut. The blow to his own blade sent a shock from his hand to his shoulder, an indication that this fight would not be an easy one. The clash of steel against steel rang as the Clan warriors attacked the bigger, obviously stronger Vultures. Stronger, but never swifter or surer, Dearn reminded himself silently as he alternately blocked or sidestepped the sword being wielded against him.

He advanced on the larger man, deftly avoiding a blow intended to sever his head. He cut a bloody stripe across the distended abdomen of the Vulture.

"Bloody whoreson!" the Vulture shrieked, barely blocking Dearn's sword as it moved to slice across his throat with the next swing.

The returning blow nearly knocked the weapon from Dearn's hands, forcing him back as he fought to block or evade each of his enemy's thrusts. From the corner of his eye, he saw his men fighting the same desperate battle. The Vultures' huge, muscular arms gave them an advantage — but not enough of an advantage, he assured himself as his opponent moved back to raise his sword for one last deadly blow. As his midsection once again became exposed, Dearn thrust his sword high and deep into the Vulture's undefended chest.

For a second, he was horrified by the ease of taking another life, no matter how evil. Dearn's gaze flew to the Vulture's, his eyes widening at the shock in the larger warrior's expression and the blood that began to spill slowly across his own hands. He stood still as the Vulture's sword fell slowly to the ground and the body began to follow at a dreamlike speed. His stomach clenched as he moved his sword arm back and heard the sucking, grasping sound of the soft flesh as the steel pulled free.

"Whoreson." The dying Vulture gasped one last time as he fell to the ground, his eyes staring sightlessly across the bloodied clearing.

His awareness heightened by danger, a slight shadowing at Dearn's side sent him pivoting, barely ducking the sword aimed at his head. He blocked the strike then bent and killed the attacker. He tore his sword free, raised it above his head and brought the hilt down on the nape of a third who seemed to be in danger of getting the best of another Clan warrior.

Blood poured, moans filled the air, the grunts and fury of battle washed over his mind, and Dearn felt the strength of the gods fill his heart as he watched the Vultures falling. His warriors fought strongly, their blades moving with deadly efficiency. Daggers were used to weaken and to wound while swords defended and maimed.

It seemed the battle was hours—days—long. Dearn felt as though an eternity had filled the night, an eternity drenched with blood and the savage lust for vengeance.

Slowly, the battle waned. The dead and wounded lay about the feet of the Clan warriors. Moans filled the air— broken curses and vile prayers to Cinder from the mouths of the Vultures, vanquished, and knowing death hovered but a short distance away.

Dearn looked around at the battered yet triumphant Clan warriors and felt a glow of pride over their victory. They had known no war in their lifetimes, had fought no true battles other than in the intense training sessions he insisted on. Yet, they had triumphed over an enemy more experienced in blood and death. It was exhilarating.

In the eyes of his men, he could see their knowledge of this as well. No matter how intensive the training, there was nothing that could have prepared them for this. This was not an execution blessed by a White Lance priest. This was a bloodletting. A kill-or-be-killed battle that only by the grace of the gods had they won. And they had won. Dearn felt the blood pulsing through his body at this knowledge. They had triumphed against the larger, battle-hardened Vulture warriors. He wanted to scream his victory into the night sky, hold his sword up in thankfulness to the three gods of Brydon who rode high in the night sky overlooking the battle.

Instead, he bowed his head and whispered his thanks to the sentinels in the sky.

"Do we take prisoners, Sire?" Brendar's bronze face was shadowed in fierce angles as he nodded toward the village where the wounded Vultures were being secured.

"We question them, then we kill them." No mercy save that of a quick death, as the goddess Aleda had whispered in the ears of the Clans when she gave them heart, Dearn thought as he looked around the center of the small village.

The women and children were huddled together in a nearby yard, crying now in relief that they had been rescued from the horror they had seen coming.

"What about the human sentries?" Brendar asked him. "Should we leave one as a messenger?"

Dearn surveyed the faces of the Vultures once again. He owed the woman Matte a life debt, if she was here. Her life alone would be spared. But he didn't see her face or the multi-hued colors of her wings.

"Kill them all, but question them first about the Princess Allora," he ordered.

"Allora?" Brendar frowned. "But the human spy we spoke to reported she was dead."

"Not according to those Vultures we killed at the Fortress." Dearn ignored Brendar's look of surprise. "See what you can find out about it."

"If she lives, she could become a pawn," Brendar said slowly. "Leverage against King Alfred."

"Exactly." Dearn allowed his lips to curl into a smile of cold satisfaction.

As he turned back to the general, he caught a faint movement in the shadowed forest. He narrowed his eyes, recognizing the figure trying to remain invisible.

"Question them." He motioned to the prisoners. "There's something I need to see to."

Matte was waiting for him in the forest, and she would have more information than the captives. It was about time she decided to make her appearance and to place her demands before him. He wasn't fool enough to expect she had betrayed her Vulture brothers for nothing. He would reward her, and the other Bastard Breeds, within reason. But first—first, he would show this warrior woman that the King of the Winged Clans was no fledgling to be trifled with, as she so obviously thought he was.

Chapter Thirteen

ഇ

Matte watched Dearn break away from the group of Clan warriors and advance toward her. She had hidden on the side of the hill—close enough to interfere should death's wings fly too close to him yet far enough away that, should she not be needed, the Vulture warriors would not know she was there.

She knew he would search for her. After the attack on his mate he would have been watching, waiting for her. Any weakness within the Vulture camp would have to be explored, and Matte knew by watching King Dearn that he would exploit any weakness he could find.

So, she waited for him, propped against the trunk of an oldtree, studying him as his long legs ate the distance between the village and her position above it.

Gods, he's a sight, she thought, admiring his broad shoulders, lean hips and muscular legs. His body was superbly conditioned, powerful and broad and innately graceful. She loved watching him move.

He showed no hint there was any need for hurry, carefully giving the appearance that he was looking for nothing in particular. But Matte had seen his face, and the hard determination in his expression was clearly visible in the light of the three moons.

He would ask difficult questions, but he would be fair, she believed. Surely, he would understand there were limits beyond which she couldn't yet go. Hadn't they helped? Hadn't they saved his mate? Hadn't they rescued what members of the Clans they could?

* * * * *

Dearn entered the darkened forest well aware he could be walking into a carefully executed trap. He had waved Brendar's concern aside when he walked away, but until he could learn who this woman was and why she was betraying her own Clan, he wouldn't feel safe with her.

The light of the three moons of Brydon—the two gods, Durin, god of honor, and Sorin, the god of strength, and the benevolent goddess of mercy Aleda—barely illuminated the sheltered area of the thickly forested mountain. He had seen the woman's dim shape, barely shifting within the darkness, just beyond the tree line at the bottom of a hill that sloped into the mountain.

Dearn felt a flare of excitement at finally meeting this warrior woman face-to-face; she who had dared to strike him, to speak to him with a tone of complete authority while he lay bound and helpless. He wondered rather distantly what this said about him, as a man and a warrior, that such a woman could inspire his interest.

"'Bout time you got here." She stepped from behind a sheltering tree as he cautiously passed the point where his men could no longer see him. "Much longer, and I would have been forced to give up on you."

Her voice was husky and filled him with visions of dark, heated nights. Pitched low and filled with humor. The sound of it caused his body to harden, his thighs to tense in a building need. Arousal washed through him, uncomfortable, unwanted. He should not want this woman, but already his body had overruled his head. But this would not, could not, deter him from forcing the information he needed from her if he had to. Before she had time to do more than gasp in surprise, he had her by the neck, her back against the tree, his hand tightening as she went for her dagger.

"Pull the blade, and I'll rip your throat out," he whispered savagely, watching her eyes widen at his tone.

Slowly, she dropped her hand from the hilt of the dagger and lifted both to shoulder level.

He glared down at her, seeing the arrogant slant of her straight nose, the high cheekbones and her hazel-and-green eyes. His body was pressed tightly against hers, and he saw the same surprise in her eyes that he felt as he hardened even more.

"I could have my revenge easily this night," he whispered, leaning close, taking in the flicker of emotion in her gaze that was neither fear nor reckless courage but an intriguing combination of both.

"By raping me?" Her voice was a harsh rasp as she spoke, despite the grip that left her little air to breath. "You would not be the first, Sire. Nor, I expect, will you be the last."

Weary resignation colored her tone, and Dearn knew that, should he attempt to take her, she would not fight. She wanted something of him, but more than that, she accepted his right to the rage that coursed through him like an angry demon.

He took a deep, furious breath, then loosened his grip as he laid his forehead softly against hers, still staring into the dilated depths of her eyes.

"Clan warriors do not rape, nor do they kill without provocation," he assured her in a whisper. "What of the Bastard Breeds?"

"Honor is honor, Sire," she whispered back. "The blood of the Eagle Clan flows through my veins, and in my heart their honor is true."

He could feel her along his body — warm, tense. So very soft. An intriguing combination of hardened warrior and giving woman. Her muscles were firm, tight with the need for action, but her breasts were soft, her skin silken. It was enough to still a measure of his rage, but not all.

"Yet you fly with the Cinder-loving demons who have killed my people," he growled, his tone accusing.

"I have saved a babe lying silent and unnoticed in her cradle. I warned whole Clans before the Vultures made it to their aeries. And my men have saved more from the rapes than there have been those who died from them." She was confident, yet clearly saddened by the deaths she could do nothing to prevent.

A weary breath escaped Dearn's chest and he loosened his hand further, though his fingers lingered, wondering at the incredible softness of her throat, the soft woman's scent that beckoned.

As much as it pained him to do so, he finally released her fully and moved back from her, watching as her hand rose, her fingers touching her skin lightly where he had held her.

"There will be no bruising." He pushed his fingers through his hair in frustration. He hadn't wanted to release her. "The first lesson a warrior learns is the proper manner in which to assert his strength."

Her head tilted and a small smile crossed her lips.

"My brother's father was a great believer in such lessons," she said with wry amusement as she stepped tentatively from the tree. "Most often they were painfully enforced."

"Much the same as my father. What of your own father, then? Did he not enforce such training?" Dearn was clearly confused by her choice of words.

"My father was a Cinder-spawned bastard," she gritted out. "There was nothing of honor or courage in him."

Dearn let the information settle between them. He would have more questions later as to the Clan concepts of the Bastard Breeds, but for now, there were other matters that must be attended to.

"I wondered if you would come alone," she finally said as he continued to study her without speaking. "You seemed in no hurry to do so."

He grunted.

"I have been a bit busy," he told her with an edge of sarcasm as he glanced back toward the village. "Vultures to round up, humans to save. This takes a bit of time."

He took in detail now, where before he had been too preoccupied to do so.

His mockery, he noticed, had little effect on her—she merely nodded then leaned comfortably against the trunk of the nearest tree. Her casual stance emphasized her slender, though curvaceous, body. One leather-shod ankle crossed the other; long, shapely legs were encased in the light leather of a warrior's garb, clothing that emphasized rather than detracted from those extraordinary limbs.

A dark leather vest covered her breasts, lacing up the front and leaving a tantalizing strip of skin bare beneath the laces. Her arms were bare as well, and glowed with a rich summer color. At her hips, she wore a wide black belt; her sword was strapped to it and tied to the loop on the garter at her knee to keep it in position during flight. One dagger was strapped to her forearm and another, longer one, to the thigh opposite her sword. Never had Dearn seen a woman dressed so. And never had he known one to inspire the sudden desire in him that she did.

He was confused by his hunger to hold her, to feel the softness of her lips, to taste her mouth and her fragrant skin. The full flesh of her breasts beneath the laces of that vest cried out for freedom. He watched their heavy rise and fall, his fingers itching to set them free. It was not common for him to feel such instant, overriding lust. It baffled him that he would feel it for this woman. She could still turn out to be his enemy, and yet Dearn wanted nothing more than to place her against that tree once again, wrap his wings around her and take her until his lusts were sated. A dangerous reaction, in light of the present circumstances.

"The Vultures allow their women to fight?" He shook his head, struggling to get past his desires. "Women should not be expected to go to war."

Amusement flashed in her oddly-colored eyes, though the smile that shaped her lips was derisive.

"I've had to fight all my life, Your Highness. I was born in war, raped during battle and have lost more than my share of brothers, sisters and cousins in that land your ancestor consigned us to. Why should I not be expected to go to war here as well?"

The savagery in her tone had his head tilting so he could decipher her expression in the golden glow of the three moons. What he saw there had little to do with respect or fear. She was meeting him as an equal—an odd turn for Dearn, who had never had a woman face him in that manner.

"You should fear me more. I could have you killed now, and none would question me for it," he finally announced, wondering at the flash of anger he felt at her attitude. Just as he wondered at the pure rage he had felt as she so succinctly described her life.

Raped in battle? Gods grant her mercy, and when he recalled the descriptions the captured Vultures had given of her homeland his guts clenched in fury. That a woman should live such a life, forced to fight to survive, raped by demons so vile even Cinder forsook them—it made him sick.

Dearn finally understood why he had been so bothered by her appearance and manner before. This woman was not just any Bastard Breed woman—her diluted bloodline ran with that of the Eagle Clan. It explained her regal bearing, her fierce determination. There was no missing the unusual coloring of her eyes and hair, or the golden threads of color that wove through the dull black of her wings. Even in the diffused light of the three moons, he could see the distinct markings.

"Yeah, I'm a Bastard Breed." She understood with uncanny accuracy what was going through his mind as his eyes went over her. "Bet you've never seen another like me."

Dearn was silent for long moments as he processed this information. Once again he had found the truth to replace the old lies.

The written records his father had possessed stated the children born from the rapes by the Vultures were killed along with the last surviving Vultures. A cruel attempt to wipe away the horrific memories of the Vulture's cruelties had resulted, supposedly, in the deaths of more innocents. Instead, the children clearly had survived.

"We were told the children were destroyed," he informed her, feeling more at ease now with his trust of her, yet still oddly off-balance because of her inner strength.

"Just banished across the seas with the rest of the garbage." She shrugged her slender shoulders, but there was an edge of bitterness to her words. "I am Matte, commander of the Bastard Breed forces. I assume you are Dearn, king of the Winged Clans."

It was no question—this woman knew well whom she spoke to.

"I am King Dearn." He nodded nonetheless. "Though I am confused at how easily you knew who I was at the Eagle aeries."

"I made it my business to learn of you." She shrugged. "That was a foolish maneuver, going to those aeries with so few warriors to guard your back. Had I not been with Edgar's troop that day the outcome might have been much different."

"Ahh." Dearn nodded. "Did I remember to thank you for that day?"

She smiled quickly at his ironic tone—a flash of teeth and a rueful shake of her head.

"Now that we have that out of the way..." She straightened yet still leaned against the tree. "Did you kill the captives you took in the forest today?"

The change of subject was not something he wished at the moment.

"Of course." He wondered if she had expected otherwise.

She shook her head slowly, rubbing her forehead. There was a sense of sadness, of futility in the movement.

"Poor fools," she whispered, a note of bitter sadness in her voice. "The tales Edgar spun them of gold and riches and seizing their homeland infected their brains. We were unable to convince them when the ships came that it was a fool's battle."

"So I gathered." Dearn crossed his arms over his chest as he watched her take a breath then raise her head to meet his gaze. "I heard quite an amazing tale from them, of the land beyond the seas, and of warriors who carried Clan blood and fought at their sides against a demon thought buried in myth. How much of this is true?"

"I would say all of it." Her lips twisted at the acknowledgment as she took a weary sigh. "We survived by fighting together there. How we survive here is another matter, though. In that land, there were no innocents who were so cruelly slaughtered, other than our own children. There, it was band together or die alone. We did what necessity dictated."

There was a short pause. She stared at him, her eyes shadowed not just by the night but also by her memories.

"Have you ever seen a Bat, Highness?" She stared into the sky, her expression bleak.

"Nay, none of those demons inhabit this land, Matte." He tilted his head as he watched her.

"They are the most beautiful creatures you could ever hope to see." She looked at him, her face reflecting the irony of what she said, her hand clenched on the hilt of her sword. "Glorious in their beauty and perfect form. Yet, they are so vile, so viciously evil, there are no words to describe…" She shook her head. "Most of my people are still there. Awaiting us. Awaiting rescue."

This was much as the Vulture warriors had stated.

"Did they tell you anything useful before their deaths?" she asked when he said nothing, her posture now wary. "I know those in the clearing know nothing—Edgar is being more careful now whom he sends out in the raids."

Dearn watched her thoughtfully as he rested one hand on the hilt of his sword. There was something, evidently, that she had particularly needed him to learn from the captives.

"They told us of this attack, and that King Alfred sent boats across the seas to fetch the Vultures to fight this battle with him. We knew Alfred was behind it, yet we have not determined why." He wondered if she would give him the information she wanted him to know herself.

She blew out an angry breath then clenched her teeth before turning away, her hand gripping the hard wood of the tree she stopped beside.

Her knuckles paled with the force of her grip, indicating the importance of what he should have learned.

"They knew more," she snapped, spinning back to him. "Surely, they knew about more than just this attack? Was there nothing more that they told you?"

Dearn wondered how long it would take her to tell him. He glanced back to the valley, gauging the headway his warriors had made in securing the village, and knew he had little time for playing games.

"They told a mad tale about a girl who died, yet still lives." He questioned the story, uncertain that the warriors had been told the truth themselves. The Truth Elixir was reliable, but what men believed was not necessarily true.

Satisfaction seemed to shimmer around Matte's body as her eyes widened. Evidently, this information had been reliable.

"Did they tell you the name of this woman, and where she is now?" Matte's voice became demanding, despite its softness.

"Alfred's daughter is dead. He would not have thought up such a mad scheme for his only child and heir," Dearn argued, calculating as he probed.

"There is where you are wrong." She moved away from the tree to confront him, her body trembling with anger. "Alfred has a new heir. A male child who will claim his throne by the fact that he is the son Alfred has dreamed of for so long. Allora is alive, and she could be the pawn you need to weaken his army and to win the war. But there are very few who know that this woman still lives."

"Her broken body was seen by more than one human. How could Alfred have pulled this off?"

"The girl he used resembled the princess well," Matte explained. "She was little more than a child and was killed without remorse. King Alfred needed the humans to follow his mad plan, though, and Allora's murder by the Clans would ensure this."

"Why?" Dearn growled. "Why would Alfred want to destroy the Clans? And why use his daughter to do so?"

"For the same reason he promised his daughter to Edgar, the Vultures' leader, once the Clans are destroyed. Because he is mad. There is a demon inside that king that frightens even me. He is not rational."

"Even madness has a cause." Dearn knew there had to be more to this than Alfred's insanity.

"I can make no sense of his reasoning." She shrugged. "Edgar believes this woman will strengthen his Clan and that Alfred will give him the mountains when the Clans are destroyed. He has refused to heed the warnings of the king's deceits. He will gain neither the woman nor the mountains."

"Why is Allora so important to Edgar?" Dearn frowned, wondering at the motives of the Vulture.

"I am not certain why he believes her to be so important." She spoke slowly, frowning as she gazed into the night sky. "The woman is unusual, but, still, only a woman." She shrugged again, as though confused by the Vulture's reasoning.

Dearn watched her more intently as he sensed her reluctance to say more about the subject than she had. But he also felt that pushing her on it would not get the answers he needed.

"What made Alfred and Edgar think they could succeed with this plan?" He caught her arm as she began to turn from him. "Alfred alone should have known we would fight back. Madness is no excuse for what he has done, or for his belief that he could succeed."

"The plan was for them to have killed more of the Clan members by now." Matte sighed wearily, though she shivered as his fingers gripped her flesh. "They would have succeeded, too, had it not been for Edgar's 'games' with the women. That, and the fact that many times the aeries were empty before they arrived." She said it with mocking satisfaction. "Many of the people you believe to be dead are merely still hiding."

Dearn released her as she pulled against his grip. Her skin was soft, warm. He would have her in his arms if he thought she would allow it.

"Why would they still hide when they know they can find safety within the Fortress?" This revelation confused him. There wasn't a Clan member alive who didn't know they could find shelter within the King's Fortress.

"Because they have children and would be easily spotted by the Vultures and humans looking for them. They will make it there, when they can. You seem to forget how far away the Fortress is on foot."

Dearn saw her point. Flying with babes was much trickier than flying alone.

She turned from him and again stared up into the star-studded sky. The three moons were in diagonal alignment across the sky; the golden orbs reflected an eerie light back to the forest below, shading everything in a ghostly glow.

"My men and I have saved as many as we could without risking death ourselves, but it won't last much longer. There are only so many you can save before you're suspected. Something will have to be done soon," she informed him.

"We found the babe," he told her softly, thinking of Mera's child.

"Gods! Those little ones." Dearn heard her voice catch in horror as she whispered the words. "I was nearly caught taking that babe out, but I would have saved them all and risked it if I had been able to."

The pain in her voice knifed at Dearn's soul. Ralnd and his family had been killed, all but the youngest. This woman had risked herself to save a babe but had not attempted to warn the Clans of what was coming.

"Why didn't you tell us?" Fury ripped through him as the image of those shattered lives rose like a storm of sorrow before his eyes. "You could have done something."

She spun around, anger tightening her expression, glittering in her eyes. "How many warnings do you fools need?" she spat into his face. "Three of your Falcon warriors were killed by Vultures and placed at your doorstep before the edict for removing the discs was issued. We managed to sneak a note into the pocket of one of the men's vests, and still you weren't warned?"

The three young Falcon men found at the base of the Fortress had not been warriors, only reckless, wild youths. Their deaths were assumed to have been by misadventure, as had been known to happen. Their bodies had not been searched before burial.

"My men risked exposure to warn you countless times. They did everything but breech the Fortress, and still a blind eye was turned. We did all we could, King Dearn, and still escape with our lives." She let her words sink in, her anger washing over him with the force of a windstorm.

Events of the months before came back to haunt Dearn. The instances of Clan members being dived at by unknown assailants, aeries torn apart while families were absent. The blame had all been placed on the delinquent youths of the Clans and ignored. Restlessness often drove the young. When they were caught they were dealt with, but unless violence occurred little was done about it.

He slowly backed away from her, turning to stare down at the village.

"Why did you not fly to the Fortress? You could have revealed yourselves. If nothing else, one of your men could have come alone and spoken to me."

He turned back to her, spearing her with his anger. They had not done enough. His people had been massacred. Entire families tortured and murdered.

Her gaze met his, and in it, Dearn read her fears.

"How could we be certain of our reception?" she whispered. "Was it not your ancestor who ordered the deaths of ours? I could not send my men to you, not knowing for certain how they would be received. We did all we could and still maintain our safety." She sighed. "There are so few of us left, Dearn. We are the last hope of our own people, who await our return across the seas. There are only so many risks we can take without assurance of safety."

The bitterness and pain in her voice touched a chord inside Dearn that he was hesitant to look at too closely. Tenderness built that he didn't want to admit to having for this woman.

"Join the Clans now, then." He turned back to her with the offer, gripping her arm. "Fight alongside us."

She pressed her lips together, her expression trembling between pain and desperate desire. He could see the need in her to do as he asked, to fly with him. A need he felt to the very depths of his own soul.

"Who, then, will save a babe hidden quietly in a corner?" she asked him with an edge of sadness, her head lowering as she took a steadying breath. "No. Not until Edgar's men are dead."

There were over three hundred Vultures in Edgar's Clan, Dearn now knew. She had picked a fight for herself that he was afraid she would lose.

"How many of your people are there?" He needed to make plans and prepare his warriors to defend her and those who followed her, should the need arise.

"We are only sixty," Matte answered him. "You can identify us by the red insignia on our vests." She touched the red triangle at her left breast. "We are all Bastard Breeds. We are required to wear this emblem so none of us ever forgets it." Heartache laced her voice and glittered in the depth of her eyes.

Without his consciously willing it the tip of Dearn's wing caressed her bare arm in sympathy. With that touch, Dearn felt a strange shudder move through his own body. How soft her skin felt, how warm and beckoning beneath the sensitive, nerve-rich contact feathers of his inner wings. So soft and tempting. The tiny feathers on the underside of the wings, normally tucked beneath the flight feathers, were the few that had sensation. The extrusion of the fragile extensions of the contact feathers was rare, and they were very receptive. Dearn could remember no time when his had been so sensitive.

"Your people will be protected." Dearn pulled his wing back, realizing the intimate gesture was lost on Matte. "Do you know where Edgar is now?"

If he was accessible, then Dearn had every intention of finding and killing him immediately.

"He is with King Alfred, preparing the human soldiers to march on the Fortress, which they plan to do in two days' time. He's taken himself out of the raids after nearly being captured this morning. But King Alfred promised to supply him all the human women he needs to toy with." The disgust and pain in her voice told well the horror those women faced.

"Are they at Alfred's castle?"

"No." She gave him a curious look. "They are several miles away, in the mountains. Do you need the location?"

"I know the location." He shook his head, half-formed plans coming together as he asked the questions. "How many guards are there at the castle, and how many are Vulture sentries?"

"Two sentries, though both are my men. There are no human guards left there, because the sentries would be able to warn them in time for a contingent to fly back to the castle in case of trouble."

Dearn stared into the woman's clear eyes, noting the edge of hope he could see in her face, the battle-weary tint of pale skin around her full lips. She was tired, and yet here she was with him instead of resting, as she needed to do.

He wanted to believe her, he realized. Brendar and the Clan leaders would call him a Seven Hells' fool for it, but he was going to trust her.

"Betray me, Matte, and I'll make certain you regret it," he told her, realizing there would be no way to hide his plans from her. He needed her help too damned much.

"I won't betray you, Dearn." There was sincerity in her words. "But I seek payment in return for the help my men and I will give you, and the risks we will take on your behalf."

Dearn viewed her without speaking, thankful that the mercenary gleam in her eye didn't hide the more ominous plans he had feared.

"And that payment is?" he asked her softly.

"A home for me and my men, and those who will follow from the other continent. The Bastard Breeds only, Dearn. We deserve the land the Vultures once claimed," she demanded. "We were denounced unfairly, and we have the honor of the

Clans despite King Merson's fears we would not. We want to come home."

There was the passion and the fire she had kept hidden from him. As she spoke, her voice deepened and raw, stark need echoed in her tone.

A windswept, though fertile, plain on the outskirts of the Western Range had once been home to the Vultures. It was uninhabited now, the aeries there having fallen into disrepair because of the lack of occupation.

"It's yours." Dearn nodded, seeing her breast rise and fall quickly in relief. "In return for your aid, you shall have that land."

"Then you have our loyalty. This was discussed among all the Bastard Breeds before our leaving the other continent. But you must also promise to help us find a way to bring the rest home as well."

There is no give in her, Dearn thought. She wouldn't be satisfied with her own safety and the safety of those who were now on the main continent. She wanted assurances that all her people would be included. The voice, the carriage of a commander—he nearly shook his head at the sight of such a strong woman. She would be a worthy mate for any man.

"You have my promise. The moment the Clans are safe and King Alfred is dead, then I will arrange payment myself for ships to be sent for your people," he told her.

She licked her lips nervously, a trembling curve of a thankful smile on those lush curves. Finally, her body relaxed enough that he could tell she had been holding herself in a high state of tension during the negotiations. He wanted to kiss those lips. He had to forcefully restrain himself from doing so.

"Tell your men to expect us at the castle," he told her as he turned to leave, knowing that if he did not do so quickly the impulse to taste her might well overpower him. "I think it's time someone rescued the princess."

With that, Dearn left the forest and returned to the matter of the executions awaiting him below. More blood to stain his hands and his soul, he thought, and seven less monsters to prey upon his people.

Chapter Fourteen

ဢ

Dearn stared into the darkened water in the rock basin of the bathing room. The blood of the Vultures he had killed mixed with the blood from his own wounds, yet still, his skin appeared darker, reddened, stained with death.

He tossed the washcloth on the ledge chiseled into the stone above the basin and closed his eyes in defeat. He wondered if he would ever feel clean again.

"King Dearn."

Behind him, his assistant's voice was soft, almost consoling. He turned, and in the older man's pale blue eyes he saw the knowledge he had been attempting to hide from himself.

"It will never go away, will it, Havar?" He studied his hands, the rough, reddened skin, the nicks and abrasions of battle. And the stain of death. He met the sympathetic gaze once again.

"It has been so very many centuries since the Clans have seen war," Havar finally sighed. "We cherish our peace, and nurture it as well as we do our children. It is only natural that a Clan warrior should suffer with the stain of death when he must take a life. It assures him his honor, and his heart, are still alive and well."

Dearn shook his head, still feeling the heaviness within that heart, and walked around the old man to leave the room.

"You could cease fighting yourself, Highness," Havar suggested as he followed. "The Clan leaders are in rare fury over your decision to lead your own warriors into battle.

Perhaps you should maintain more distance. This, too, would ease the pain."

"And ask my warriors to do what I will not do myself?" Dearn argued, disgust edging through him and shading his voice. "What king does such a thing, Havar?"

"King Merson did not join the battles that raged through the Clan lands at the time of the first war, Highness," Havar reminded him. "He is known as our greatest king."

Dearn clenched his teeth at the reference to his ancestor.

"King Merson sentenced children to die, the children of our own Clans, because of the nature of their birth. They were sent across the seas, left to fight for positions among the Vultures. They fight, Havar, just for survival against an evil so black even Cinder would not claim it."

He was thinking of the Bats and the tales of their evil.

Through the centuries, no one had thought to question the decision King Merson had made. The outcasts were the children of the Vultures, created in violence and death, and the blood they carried had condemned them. Merson's own daughter had birthed one and then had taken her life because of the shame.

Dearn remembered feeling a spark of discontent at the time he read the account, a brief flare of regret for the children whose lives were abandoned. Children found guilty before any crime had been committed.

The Spiritmen had fought bitterly over the decision, suggesting any number of ways to deal with the situation. But Merson would have none of it. The children would die along with their fathers.

But they hadn't died.

"And centuries from now, those who come after you may look back in fury that you allowed the ancestors of those children back into Clan lands," Havar suggested, interrupting his thoughts. "It is not ours to question the past, Highness.

Right what you can, and lead as your heart guides you. But don't let your honor and your caring nature lead you into self-recrimination."

Dearn studied his advisor, wondering what was on the old man's mind. Havar stood, as patient as always, his face round and lined with sun, weather and age, his eyes sharp and focused. He wore the traditional clothing of an older warrior — soft cotton pants and a loose white shirt beneath the dark leather of his vest. His silver hair was long and tied back at his nape, just as he had worn it as a warrior. He was the wisest man Dearn knew and had been one of the strongest warriors he had ever known.

"Do you believe the decision to be a reckless one?" He knew the Clan leaders were outraged over his decision to give the land of the Vultures to the Bastard Breeds, should they serve the Clans in this new war. Their arguments, their anger confused him. The leader he had met had honor — he had seen it in her eyes, heard it in her voice as it resonated inside him. Clan blood ran swift and true within them, and still the Clans wanted to deny them.

"Highness, I merely caution you to curb your anger." Havar smiled, his voice as patient as the expression on his face. "Your leaders react to you. They see the defensive anger raging in your eyes, and they immediately become defensive as well. It is our nature. Patience, strength and confidence will aid you in the face of their bickering, where anger will merely inflame them."

This Dearn had already known. He ran his fingers through his hair roughly as he remembered his father counseling him in the same manner when first he had taken his initiation to the throne. He understood that a ruling body must work together if anything was ever to be achieved. But when able-bodied warriors turned their backs on the battles raging around them, he felt the sickness of betrayal inside his soul.

"They seem like children, hiding here within the Fortress, intent on debating each course of action to the tiniest detail while others are dying."

"It has been the way of the Clans since the beginning, has it not?" Havar's voice was steady, calm, but in it Dearn sensed a suggestion. A solution to the matter he had been thinking on for days.

"The Clans are changing, and with this war, much more will change around us," he whispered, turning away from Havar. "Perhaps it's time other things changed as well."

"And what changes would those be, Highness?" Havar asked him softly, knowingly.

Dearn turned to him, seeing in this man the father he had lost so many years ago. Havar had been his father's closest friend, and had taken the advisory position after the old king's death.

"You know the changes I require, Havar." He held the older man's eyes with his as he grasped the resolve to push ahead with the plans they had discussed years before. "I leave you in charge of this. When I return from Cayam with the Princess Allora, I will expect an appraisal of the proposal. I want a ruling council intact and ready to serve at a moment's notice. The Clan leaders will then be free to command their warriors once again."

What he had in mind would infuriate the Clan leaders and force them to make a decision he knew they did not wish to make. A council comprised of twelve men beyond fighting age and three Spiritmen to aid them would become Dearn's advisors. With them would lie the responsibilities of overseeing the Clans during this war, and the choice of a new king should Dearn be killed in battle. It would free his Clan leaders to fight instead of bicker, and his general to aid him in his strategy for war without the fear of being forced onto the throne should Dearn meet an enemy's sword.

Satisfaction gleamed in the old man's eyes, and Dearn knew his decision would put into effect a plan that not just he but his father before him had thought long and hard about. Until now, there had had been no way to justify the need for change.

"I shall have everything prepared, but I will require your written permission to put it before the Clan leaders," Havar informed him.

Easily done. Dearn went to his writing desk to write the letter that would be given to the leaders. It was short and lacked the finer qualities of introduction and explanation he would have normally included. He considered diplomacy a wasted effort at this point. There were too many considerations, and time was stretched to where he could borrow no more.

He handed the letter to his advisor, watching as Havar's lips edged into a grin.

"They will protest." The old warrior nodded. "But I know their honor is fierce. They will give up the fight without too much bickering."

"Don't be so certain of that." Dearn gave a weary sigh. "They were still arguing over the benefits of kidnapping the princess when I became fed up with them and left."

"And still were they arguing over it when I came up." Havar chuckled. "The fire of battle rages in them, but so do their worries for their Clans. With you flying each day, wearied and bloodied from battle, they fret incessantly over you. You are our king—this will not change even with the formation of a council."

"Perhaps they will find a way to relieve their fury in other areas then." Dearn shrugged, unconcerned. "I need them leading their warriors, not haggling like old women over my safety."

Havar chuckled once more over this image as he tucked the letter securely within his leather vest.

"I will send your dinner up. Shower, Highness, and rest for a while. Tomorrow's journey will be a long one, and filled with dangers. I will send Tamora to you as well."

"No, just dinner." Dearn couldn't explain his lack of desire for Tamora, even to himself, so he ignored his advisor's questioning look. "Have Brendar come when they bring my meal. I want to discuss the flight with him and finalize the plans before I rest."

"Tamora has worried greatly over you, Dearn." Havar was not as inclined to disregard the subject.

Dearn sighed heavily and shook his head.

"Tamora needs her rest, and I have much to do. I will speak to her before I leave on the morrow. But, for now, there are other things that require my attention."

"As you say, then." Havar bowed. "I will take my leave of you and see about preparing the council as you wish. Brendar shall be up shortly."

Dearn watched as the older man hurried from the room. As the door closed, he breathed another weary sigh and glanced with longing toward his bed.

Soon he would rest, he promised himself. He would fight to ignore the images of blood running in slow rivulets down his sword, washing onto his hands and staining his body. He would try to sleep, as he knew he must do soon or else lose that edge he needed to stay alert.

As he relaxed, he thought of Matte and wondered again at a woman who fought as well as his own men and yet still seemed to look at him as only a woman could. He would have thought that fighting and leading warriors would require a hard, bitterly determined woman. Yet that did not seem to be the case. Matte appeared as soft as any woman and as tough and determined as a warrior. Her eyes held only the bitterness of battle, not the hard, cold depths he would have expected.

He remembered her body flattened against the tree, the slender length of her limbs pressing against his own and the desire that had flared. He had almost kissed her. The lack of logic in that bemused him, even now. He had needed to either release her or force himself on her, as the demons in her previous life had surely done.

Gods, she was too small for the battles she fought, the weight of decisions that rested on her seemingly fragile shoulders. But despite her slenderness—the feel of small bones and soft, supple skin—there was a force in her that surprised him. She was no weakling, and had she wanted to, she could have given him a Seven Hells' fight when he threw her against that tree.

Before returning to the castle in the early hours of the morning, Dearn had questioned those humans living within the Southern Valley, where many from Cayam had also taken refuge. They had told tales of the Bastard Breeds leader that had confirmed his own impressions of her. They attached honor to her name, despite the fact she fought with the Vultures. No human woman had been dragged to the beds of her men, no children had fallen beneath their swords, no unarmed men had taken a thrashing from their fists. The Vultures committed the atrocities against the people while the Bastard Breeds worked behind them to interfere with their devastation.

The humans themselves had not seen it like that—they hated the Bastard Breeds as much as they did the Vultures. But Dearn had seen the truth of it.

A farmer's daughter had been dragged to the barn by several Vulture warriors, and within seconds two of the Bastard Breed warriors had swooped in, swearing Clan warriors were flying close. They had taken off immediately, fleeing from discovery. Dearn knew, though, that there were no Clan warriors flying in that area at that time. There had been no Clan troops patrolling at all then, before he had known of the Vultures' return.

The accounts differed in the details, varied as to the time frame or the Bastard Breed warriors involved, but the men

Dearn had talked to all agreed that none of the rapes or murders had been committed by Matte's people.

Now, how the hell had she managed to pull this off? he wondered. The Vulture leader, Edgar, was reputed to be hard as stone and intolerant of any warrior who didn't follow his example. The humans following him, for the most part, were Elitists, the bloodthirsty followers of the demon god Cinder. Their motivation for warring against the Clans was easier to understand than King Alfred's.

The Elitists and the Clans had been enemies since time began. It was well known that the Clans enjoyed the favor of the three moon gods, as well as their father, the sun god and the father of life, who dwelt in the paradise of Ashrad. Once, it was told, there were four moons that lit up the night skies of Brydon. Each moon was the glory and the home of a god. Cinder was careless of his, often leaving it to come to Brydon and stir up trouble between humans and the Winged Clans. Though stirring trouble among the humans, even now, was a sorrowfully easy task to accomplish.

As legend had it, Cinder gathered the humans who would follow him and set them to rid the land of the Winged Clans because he was jealous of the favor the Clans received from his father, Ashrad. Cinder's jealousy had been well known by the Clans, and his efforts were observed with a worried eye.

There was one who refused to allow the slaughter to continue. Algernon, the fiercest warrior of that time and the strongest in all the Clans, prepared to fly to the sun god and carry the tales of atrocities and death to Ashrad's feet. Algernon had known that a fiery death would come to him as he neared Ashrad's throne, but at his death the god would allow him entrance into Valodin and would hear his pleas for the people of the Clans.

When Ashrad learned of his son's dark deeds, he cast him from the gardens of Valodin and sent him to the fiery depths of the Seven Hells, where he could rule the merciless hearts of the men who followed him in his evil. Those who had given

Cinder homage were bound together and, with the fierce heat of the sun, their flesh stripped, their bones melded together. Thus were the Screaming Gates of the Seven Hells created. The hatred of those malevolent spirits kept Cinder forever confined to his wasteland.

The fourth moon was sent flying through the heavens, cast out of Brydon's skies so no reminder would be left of the son who had betrayed his father and the people his father loved. It was told that the great fiery mound that resided within Cinder's Pit on the edges of the Western and Northern mountains was the remnants of that once-glorious moon.

Cinder's human followers were called the Elitists and, even now, thousands of years later, so far beyond creation that the old stories were called fables, they still carried the designation and practiced in Cinder's name.

Dearn sighed wearily as he stretched out on his bed and awaited the meal Havar had promised to send up. There was so much loss, so much pain and anger running through the Clans right now. He had his hands full trying to bring an end to this bloody war without taking needless lives and pacify his people as well.

With all the Clans' members now ensconced within the Fortress, and confusion and fear running wild among them, it was all Dearn could do to keep the peace within the mountain. He couldn't lead his men and comfort his people at the same time.

I need a queen, he thought distantly. A strong, determined woman who could lead both warriors and Clansmen alike. A woman who could fight by his side or ease a child's tears, whichever was needed.

Slowly, his eyes closed, weariness washing over him as sleep stole through his body. A queen. His last conscious image was not one of blood or death but of hazel eyes and dark brown hair, and a woman who wore warrior's leathers and whose lips begged for his kiss.

Chapter Fifteen

ဆ

The Clan leaders were waiting when Dearn and Brendar exited the castle the next morning. They didn't speak; they merely watched their king in silence as he gathered his men and outlined their plan once again.

Dearn knew that Havar had immediately begun selecting the men for the Council of Twelve, as well as the three Spiritmen from the White Lance Clans that would advise them.

"You've angered the Clan leaders," Brendar murmured.

"Perhaps not." He saw confusion and, in some, even a bit of relief. Several had gone so far as to join the flight to rescue the imprisoned Princess Allora.

"The Clans are confused by your decisions but I, for one, am thankful that the burden of ruling will not fall to me should your foolhardiness end in your death," Brendar said. "I still agree with the leaders—you should stay here within the Fortress."

"My warriors coddle me worse than the women do," Dearn muttered. "Stop fluttering around me, Brendar. I was a warrior before I was a king. I will lead as I see the need to lead. My men are more confident and more assured when I'm in the sky with you, even you see this."

It was a fact. Dearn's influence was stronger, fiercer when he was with them. They drew from their king's confidence and strength. It had been this way even before the war. Dearn was a natural leader and knew how to make his men fight with all they had when other leaders and their troops would fall behind.

He stepped aside now as they neared the large flat stone in the center of the warriors' courtyard. There would be four troops of twelve warriors, one to secure the area around Cayam and cover Dearn's retreat, the second to fly with him into the city and guard him as he took the woman from the castle. The third troop knew where to find the women and children of the commanders of the human army—it would be their task to kidnap these women and children and bring them to the Fortress. The fourth troop would shield their return.

All were trusting in the information the Bastard Breeds had given them, but they were prepared for betrayal. Dearn could do nothing less, with the lives of entire Clans at stake. The Princess Allora could be a bargaining chip in their favor, despite Alfred's supposed disavowal of her. If nothing else, the humans would see their king's lies for what they were.

"Do any of you have any questions?" Brendar finally asked.

The warriors shook their heads as they adjusted their weapons, their wings fluttering in preparation for flight.

"May Ashrad shine on us in favor then." Brendar repeated the prayer of the warriors before Dearn led the way to the Fortress walls where they would launch.

As he stood atop the wall, he looked out over the crowd assembled to see them off. There was Tamora, her brow creased in a frown, her face still pale and bruised. Her eyes weren't on him, though, but on the general who stood beside him. Brendar's frequent anger toward him and Tamora's often confused looks toward the general—definitely, something he needed to think on.

But later. Much later.

* * * * *

The royal castle was quiet now that King Alfred's forces had marched out. The shouts and laughter and sounds of heady excitement had slowly filtered away and no longer invaded the tower room that had been Princess Allora's prison for so many months.

Allora stood at one of the large windows and watched the last of her father's army leave the castle grounds. Leading the procession of men had been a tall, commanding figure with hair the color of a summer sweetnut, brown and streaked with strands of sunlight, and a body fit and honed for battle.

She whispered Canton's name, feeling her heart clench at the thought of never seeing him alive again. She had lived through her unjust imprisonment, each day praying he would learn the truth. How, though, would he learn the truth if he was dead? He would never know he was leading his men to war for a lie, and that the king he swore loyalty to planned his death.

She touched the warm glass of the windowpane and a sigh escaped her lips. She didn't see the beauty in her face that Canton had told her was there. The slightly tilted eyes, a light blue in color and framed with thick white-blond lashes, didn't look all that extraordinary. Her thick blonde hair was braided, showing high cheekbones, emphasizing her full lips. She touched them, remembering the kiss Canton had bestowed there during one of their last meetings. Her first kiss, and it appeared it was destined to be her last. Which was no more than her father intended, she knew.

His cruel words that morning haunted her still, the pain in her soul a reminder of the cruelty of men.

Dirty Winged Clans. Their women tempt and tease and drive a man mad with desire, never realizing they can never hope to hold their faithless hearts, he had raged as he stood over her. *I will rid this world of them, Allora, just as I fought to rid you of your deformity, the poison in your heart. I have failed with you as I did with your mother, but I will not fail again. They will all die!*

Allora battled the tears rising behind her closed eyes and, not for the first time, prayed for a miracle. Surely, the gods that protected them all would send one to save them now.

"How could it have come to this?" she whispered as her fingers touched the reflection of the tears shimmering in her eyes.

"We knew it would come to this, Princess." The gentle voice of her maid reminded Allora that she was not alone. "It was only a matter of time, as you have always been aware."

Mary had been her mother's maid. After Demetria's death and the appearance of Allora's deformity, Mary had been brought to her. Allora knew her father would kill the maid as well. He would not want to leave a witness to the fact that he had murdered his child.

"It's insanity," Allora whispered. "The workings of a crazed mind."

"His mind has always been crazed." Mary sounded tired. "What he cannot own, he will kill. Joining forces with the Elitists in this war was but a final step for him."

"As he will one day kill me."

Allora knew that day was quickly approaching. Her father had grown progressively more insane in the past few years. His rages and mad ramblings became louder and more vicious. But it was only after he joined with the Elitists that his heart had hardened completely against her.

His main complaint was her resemblance to her mother, and the terrible deformity Allora had inherited from her. He blamed the Winged Clans for his wife's death, his daughter's deformity and, until recently, his inability to sire a male child.

The male child had been born several months before, at the expense of his mother's life. She was a woman given to him by the Elitists, selected to carry a son for their chosen king. Since that day, Alfred's discontent with his daughter and her appearance increased, while he became more frightened that somehow, someway, the Clans would learn of her existence.

She had often wondered if her life would be different if they did know. There could be few punishments worse than the imprisonment inflicted on her now.

Her father often proclaimed that she would be his downfall. He had bleakly informed her that it would never be possible for her to lead his people. Never could she allow anyone to know of her deformity or the curse placed on her. Even Canton had been unaware of the terrible secret she carried.

"Yes, he will one day kill you, just as he was responsible for your mother's death." Mary's bleak acceptance of her charge's fate made it all the more real to Allora.

Mary had warned her when they were imprisoned that it was but a step to the death they had always known would come to her. Allora's mother, Demetria, had thought her own death by her husband's hand would save the life of her child. She could not have known that the deformity she herself bore had been passed on. Allora wondered if her mother would have fought harder to escape her prison had she known what was to come.

She trembled with fear. She was barely eighteen years old and already she faced death. Still, she preferred that to the alternative she had overheard the night before.

"Did you hear the Vultures talking last night?" Allora whispered, trembling as she remembered the gloating, confident voices that had drifted through her window. "He intends to give me to that Edgar when the battle is done. He will kill Canton, Mary, and give me to that monster, if he does not kill me himself."

Allora clenched her fists as she fought the terror those words brought her. Each night she heard the Vultures talking from their post above her room, and she knew the cruel nature of the one they spoke of. Even more horrifying was the thought of Canton's death.

"Alfred will kill you first, Allora," Mary told her softly, resignation filling her voice. "His madness is such that he will never allow you to leave this castle again. Nor will he allow another to have you."

Allora heard what the older woman did not say. That Alfred would allow no other to have what he himself lusted for.

She contained the shudder that brought, but the unspoken words lingered between them.

"If only we had been able to get a message to Canton," Allora said as she stared out into the emptiness of the castle yards. "He would have saved us, Mary, and stopped this madness of Father's. But, now, he will be killed because I failed."

Her father had thwarted each attempt Allora had made to get a message to the general. She had only stopped when he began killing the messengers she managed to send.

"Canton will take care of himself," Mary assured her. "He will know of his danger by now. He's a smart lad—I doubt he believes all that your father tells him."

"But how can he save himself?" Allora shook her head. "There are so many of the Vultures, Mary. What chance does he have?"

"He will save himself by the wits the gods gave him," Mary promised. "Now, come away from the windows, child; the sun is nearing and you must be careful."

Her father's choice of her prison room had been deliberate. Her mother's sensitivity to the harsh afternoon sun had been passed along to her daughter.

She had known when the key turned in the lock of the tower room door that the late afternoons would be miserable. The harsh rays of the sun brightened each corner of the small space and fill it with a suffocating heat.

Now, she turned her back to the window and allowed her maid to draw her toward the far side of the room, where Mary would shelter her with her own body.

The sound of crashing glass stunned Allora and brought a cry of fear from Mary. Turning, she had only a quick glimpse of looming shadows before hard male hands jerked her from her feet and she was rushed toward the gaping hole where the window had once been. She cried out, clutching the muscular arm wrapped around her waist and fighting mind-numbing terror as her captor bore her to the window ledge.

Allora had a moment of realization before the one holding her threw himself from the ledge. She had hoped a miracle would occur; instead, death had made its timely appearance.

As the stones of the courtyard loomed closer, she felt peace suffuse her. Death was preferable to the hands of the monster her father had promised her to. Had she lived, she could have never faced the eternal pain of seeing her beloved Canton killed.

It seemed, though, that death would be cheated. Within seconds of disaster the downward plummet halted, and suddenly she was rising. The air flowed through her hair, rushed over her thinly clad body and, for a brief second, stole her breath. She could feel wind rushing over her small stubs of wings, ruffling the few immature feathers that grew there and sending a surge of pleasure through her unlike any she had ever known.

Gods, was this what it was like to fly? To touch the sky? To feel the wind rushing over the body, through the hair, past the wings? She wanted to cry out, to scream a protest for the injustice of her deformed body. This was what she had been meant for, to be one with the sky and the wind.

She was flying. Allora turned her head and looked into the savage features of the warrior who carried her into the sky, and she felt a moment's gratitude. This was no Vulture, but one of the proud warriors of the Winged Clans who was giving her a taste of what she had been born for.

Despite the knowledge that he would likely drop her at any moment, Allora still closed her eyes and allowed her own arms to extend in pleasure. She smiled in exultation as her head lifted to the wind. She breathed the scents of the sky and the dew-kissed, clean smell of the warrior carrying her. When she closed her eyes, she imagined that she was alone, flying high and free of the pain her life offered.

* * * * *

Dearn glanced down at the young captive. He had been shocked to realize when he'd first snatched her that the humps on her back weren't some terrible deformity. The unbound protrusions were actually the beginnings of wings. Unfortunately, it appeared they had been bound for the greater part of her life and never given the chance to grow properly.

It appeared the deaths among the Winged Clans had been going on far longer than he had thought. There was no way a child could have been stolen from one of the Clans and news of it not travel to every aerie within the mountains. Her parents must have been killed and the child stolen. Yet even that explanation made little sense. Someone within the Clans would have noticed at the yearly meeting had any family gone unaccounted for.

As he carried her across the sky he felt her relax as instinct took over and she became an extension of him. Her body moved with his, her legs stiffening and extending out along his, her arms outstretched as though they would somehow make up for her lack of wings. There was a smile of utter joy on her face, and he could feel the small shudders of her tiny wings against his breast, fighting to mimic the actions of flight and freedom.

Holding her carefully, Dearn shifted until those crippled wings were free. They struggled to do as Ashrad had commanded them and carry their owner into independence and grace.

Pity filled Dearn's heart. He could not imagine what it would be like to be denied flight. To know you had been meant to be one with the sky and the wind and yet forbidden that simple privilege. There could be no pain greater than that of lack of flight, he thought.

The binding of her wings, forever stealing from her the right to soar, was another crime to charge against the human king. That man would pay dearly for what he had done to the Clans—and to this child, as well. Such a creature should have been killed long ago, to save the innocent from the cruelties he could inflict upon them.

Still, Dearn now understood why Alfred had kept her locked away. She was Princess Allora—of this, he had no doubt. Her mother must have been of the Clans, and her father had carefully hidden it during her lifetime. He would have had to hide it, or else all the Clans would have sought retribution before now.

The only question left in his mind was the identity of her mother. There had been no women missing from the Clans that he knew of, no children stolen. And Dearn knew no woman would willingly give her child to a human. It was a crime punishable by death, but also a crime unheard of except within those long-ago Vulture Clans.

This discovery changed his plans, and those the Clan leaders had agreed to before he left. This woman could not be used against the king, nor could she be allowed to stand with her father and share his death. As a member of the Clans, vengeance would now be sought for her, not against her.

* * * * *

From her vantage point in the forests surrounding Cayam, Matte watched the flight of the troop of warriors who had snatched Princess Allora and her maid from their prison. Where she stood, it was easy to see that Dearn had been the one to carry the girl from the tower room and fly quickly back toward the mountain.

His action surprised her. For some reason, she had expected him to allow his troops to take care of this matter, not to involve himself directly. Then she wondered why she should be surprised.

The King of the Winged Clans flew daily, and Matte knew from the reports she received that he often flew nightly, as well, with his own troop of men. He was seen as often as the fierce Red Hawk General of the Clans. She wondered when he found time to sleep then decided it was best not think about when the King of the Clans found his bed, or what he did there.

There were three troops of Clan warriors waiting outside Cayam as well as her own people Matte had hidden within the area. She could take no chances Dearn would not succeed.

She had sensed he was a strong, fair ruler, and the tales she had heard over the months verified this, but she still could not override that instinctive distrust of any man not of her own Clan.

"They made it!" Beside her, Stovar muttered the satisfied exclamation. "We must hurry to our place now, Matte. We can't let Edgar know we were anywhere near the castle."

He was right, Matte thought, taking one last look at the retreating flight of the commanding King of the Winged Clans. As much as she enjoyed the sight, it was time for them to go.

"Be certain the others follow quickly," she ordered the warrior who had accompanied her and Stovar. "I want everyone where they belong when Edgar learns of this."

The warrior took off, the soft red highlights within his nearly black wings reflecting in the bright light of the sun overhead. Dark would be falling soon, and there would be no way Edgar or King Alfred's forces could go in search of those who had taken Allora. If the warriors flew through the night, as Matte was certain they would, there would be no danger to them.

"Was the human spy in place?" she questioned Stovar softly a moment before her wings lifted.

She caught his nod and allowed a breath of relief to escape her chest. Everything was proceeding just as they had planned before leaving for Cayam. Soon, she promised herself, soon, the battle would be over, and they could take control of the lands that were promised to them. Soon, all her people would return home.

Chapter Sixteen

∞

"You have never flown?" The warrior's voice in her ear caused Allora to jump. For the briefest moment she had allowed herself to believe she flew alone.

"N-n-no," she stammered, tensing in his arms. The knowledge that this man likely considered himself her enemy tore through her consciousness. He wouldn't care that her father had bound her wings from the day they began to emerge, not long after her mother's death. That the wind had never touched them until this day.

"Will it hurt?" She hated the fear she heard in her voice.

"Will what hurt?" He seemed confused by her question. "Your wings are too small, little one, to hold your weight. I could not allow you to attempt flight alone."

Now confused herself, she glanced over her shoulder, seeing the puzzled frown on his face, the question in the sun-kissed golden-brown eyes.

"I do not mean flight." She trembled, and she hated that as well. She had no courage, and how she needed it!

"What, then, do you mean?" He glanced down at her then back ahead of them as his wings tilted and their bodies shifted, bearing them farther above the ground.

Then it seemed they flew faster, yet his wings did not seem to move with as much effort.

"I mean falling," she finally said after swallowing. The terror rising inside her threatened to strangle her. "Will there be much pain?"

Her arms were no longer outstretched; rather, she gripped the strong forearm that held her snugly to his side. She was squeezing it so tightly, she realized, that her nails must surely be biting into his skin.

"Why would you fall? I have trained for many years, Princess, with those who weigh much more than you and never have I dropped any. Why should I drop you?" There was the lightest vein of perplexed amusement in his voice. As though he had not expected her question.

Allora looked back once again. She met the golden-brown eyes and wondered at his expression.

"Is that not why you have taken me? So that I may die in vengeance for those of your people my father killed?"

The warrior frowned, his eyes traveling from her back to the sky in front.

"Were you human alone, then you would have stood in judgment, but likely you would not have died unless proof was brought that you were a part of those deaths," he told her in a voice edged with weariness. "But no, Princess Allora, I would not drop you from the sky, no matter your heritage."

This was an answer she would not have expected. It was a well-known fact that the Winged Clans killed all those children born outside the bloodlines, wasn't it? Did her father not say that his own ancestor had been ordered by the Clans to kill all those of human/Clan, Vulture/Clan birth?

"Do the winged warriors no longer kill the children born outside their Clans? Those sired by human or Vulture?" She voiced her fear, wondering if perhaps he had forgotten this law.

Despite the strain on her neck, she continued to look behind her, saw his expression harden and his gaze turn bleak.

"Once, very, very long ago, such an order went out," he finally admitted, so softly she had to strain to hear him. "That order was given in rage and in fear, and it is one that was rescinded long ago. And never, at any time, have mixed-blood children born of humans been killed by the Clans. Not then, and most especially not now. Death was ordered for those children born of violence and blood, Allora, sired by the Vultures and the Elitists on Clan women helpless to halt their acts of violation."

Allora took a deep, fortifying breath.

"Then you would not have killed me had my mother returned to her Clan with me?" She felt the beginnings of rage at yet another lie revealed.

The warrior shook his head, as though struggling within himself over some matter. She could see his jaw bunch as he gritted his teeth.

"I am sorry. I've angered you." She turned away, closing her eyes, terrified now that he would surely kill her for speaking so to him. Perhaps the Clans would not have killed her, but surely they did not want her.

"We will speak of this later, Princess," he said gently. "You have not angered me, but often the foolishness of past mistakes, both those of my Clans and of the humans, does anger me."

Allora merely nodded.

"Would you please ease your nails a bit from my skin, my lady? I swear the pain is more piercing than that of the talons of the sly-footed stalker."

There was an edge of amusement now to his voice. Immediately, she released the hard grip, a smile tipping her own lips as she thought of the small, furry little animal whose claws were long and sharp enough that they could scale the tallest tree.

Her mind was marginally at ease now. She knew not where they were taking her, nor why they wanted her, but she knew she would not meet her death in the journey there. Of course, this caused a new fear to arise. If they had not taken her to kill in revenge for the deaths of their people, why then had they done so?

The flight that had begun comfortably enough soon turned to agony. The cold night air of the mountains bit through the thin material of her gown and chilled her skin. Soon, Allora felt frozen. Her bare feet had ceased to know any warmth long before, and her face and ears were numb from the cold wind. This was little, though, compared to the pressure on her waist and stomach. The arm gripping became a band of steel that bit into her, making breathing difficult.

She had endured pain for years. The binding of her wings was a torment unlike any she had ever imagined. The constant piercing throb of the disfigured wings, wrapped tightly within the material the Elitists' priests swore would halt the growth, was like fire and ice and bone being shattered inch by inch.

But the pain of the binding eased when the cloth no longer encased her wings. She had not worn it in four months and had become used to the end of the tenderness there. Now she was being racked by another pain, and despite the knowledge she had endured worse, this new one was nearly unbearable.

She clenched her teeth for what seemed like ages. She fought the tears, the need to beg that he ease his grip. Then she feared easing that grip would surely result in her death.

Night had fully fallen, and the three moons of Brydon were but slivers of light within the sky when she could bear the agony no more.

"Dear sir," she finally gasped as tears began to fall from her eyes. "Please, by the gods, it hurts."

She felt him start in surprise as she pulled at his arm, seeking some small amount of relief.

"Sweet Aleda!" he called out to the warriors who flew on either side.

She didn't understand the order, could hear no more over her own struggles to breathe as the pain in her chest and stomach became excruciating.

"Endure for only moments more, Princess," he entreated. "By the gods, forgive me for not thinking."

Allora hated the sobs that tore through her body, but it hurt. It hurt worse than anything she had ever known and she would surely, gladly, face a fall if he would just release her.

Then they were tilting, his body angled, taking a small measure of the pressure from her cramped midsection, and she inhaled roughly.

"Only moments more," he assured her again, his wings dipping as he banked.

Before them was a dark, gaping hole in the side of a mountain. Distantly, Allora remembered the tales Mary had told her of the aeries and knew that soon she would see one, as she had never thought she would.

The jolt when the warrior landed on the ledge took her breath again. She felt her feet touch the ground but would have crumpled to the stone ledge had he not kept his grip on her and eased her into the wide room of the aerie.

He picked her up in his arms then and moved through the darkened cavern with the ease of one whose eyes were long accustomed to a lack of light.

"The aeries have been mostly ransacked, but perhaps there is something here we can use," he muttered as he set her down on the broken end of a padded couch.

Within seconds the room was filled with warriors. In the darkness, Allora could not make out the individual colors of their wings, but she was well aware of the stolen looks they cast her and, for many, the angered expressions on their faces. Those malevolent looks would have been impossible to miss.

"Sire, we hadn't much further to go. Surely, she can make it. We are not close enough to the Fortress yet to consider ourselves safe." The warrior who protested stood aside from the others, and his voice was caustic.

An instant later, with a shock, she realized he had referred to the other as "Sire."

"Her ribs are likely bruised to the point she can no longer tolerate being held, Marden." The king's voice was firm and brooked no further argument. "I cannot fly with both arms burdened in case we're attacked. So, we must solve this problem before going further."

He turned to another.

"Come with me, Semar. We will see if we can find something to harness her to one of us and make the flight easier on her."

A warrior standing behind her moved in the king's direction, casting a long look back at Allora as he did so. As they left the main room and entered what must have been another room inside the aerie, she saw a brief flare of muted light. The soft glow spoke of dallion stones, the energized crystals the Clans used for light. It was a resource her father often grew furious over, for the Clans refused to sell them or trade for them.

There was a hushed discussion from that back room, and Allora wondered at their conversation. She would have glanced back had the other warriors not blocked the doorway. She lowered her head instead, clasping her hands tightly in her lap as she fought her shivers and her fear.

As a particularly hard chill shook her, nearly rattling her teeth with its force, she heard an exclamation of disgust from the warrior who had seemed to hate her the most. The same one who had protested landing at the aerie.

"Here." He swooped toward her.

She flinched, barely managing to stifle a whimper of fear as something heavy and warm landed on her shoulders.

"Settle down, Princess. I do not kill women, no matter their crimes or those of their fathers," he snarled. "It is merely a coat. We need you alive, not dying of chill."

It was, indeed, a coat. Soft and thick, and incredibly warm from the body heat of the warrior who had worn it.

"Th-th-thank you." She couldn't say more for the shudder that racked her at that moment. Then, embarrassingly, she heard the harsh rumble of her stomach. The warrior growled in response, causing Allora to hunch her shoulders in misery. It seemed there was no part of her body that could refrain from making its misery known.

"Ease off, Marden." Another warrior approached her, once again from behind, then knelt beside her as he extended a small parcel in his outstretched hand. "Here, Princess, it is not much, merely a snack my mate sent along with me. She swears I cannot leave our aerie without food to accompany me."

It was much more than a snack. The scent was overwhelmingly delicious, making her mouth water and her stomach rumble once again.

"Take it." He moved the food closer to her, unwrapping it with one hand and allowing the delicate aroma to tempt her. Two thick slices of fresh-baked bread, filled with the aroma of spicy venison.

Hesitantly, Allora reach out, her fingers sinking into the lighter-than-light freshness of the bread, gripping it as her eyes rose hesitantly to meet the warrior's.

"Take it," he whispered, smiling softly. "My mate would skin me alive did she know I let you go hungry. And I have more, I promise you. As do the others, for their mates are the same in regards to their stomachs."

Allora looked around and, sure enough, the warriors were pulling their snacks from the leather satchels strapped to their sides.

"And here is a bit of wine. I warn you, though, my mate waters it excessively." A wine pouch was handed to her from her other side, again by a warrior who had stood behind her.

Allora's stomach protested alarmingly at her continued denial of the appetizing aromas wafting within reach.

"Eat, Princess, or our mates will de-feather us." The warrior who had handed her the wine chuckled. "You will see, our people are kind, and only prone to ill humor when their own stomachs are empty." He gestured to the one who had tossed the jacket over her shoulders. He was propped against the far wall, eating.

Allora brought the sandwich to her mouth slowly, her teeth sinking into the bread, melting through the tender meat. She would have closed her eyes in ecstasy were she not being watched.

"Do you like it?" The previous owner of the food watched her anxiously. "My mate will want to know, and I don't want to face the consequences should I tell her I forgot to ask."

Allora swallowed, then smiled, fighting the tears she could feel growing in her eyes.

"You may tell your mate it is food fit only for the table of the gods and not for unworthy humans," she whispered in gratitude. "I greatly appreciate your generosity in sharing such fine fare with me."

She then gave her full concentration to the food, warmth slowly replacing the chill as a sense of peace descended with each sip of the wine.

* * * * *

Dearn observed the exchange, knowing those warriors who stood behind her had seen the pitiful winglets rising from her shoulders. It was they who were gentle with her, and they who plied her with food and wine.

The warrior who had given up the warmth of his jacket sat now against cold stone, eating his own food, drinking his wine. Dearn felt a small smile on his lips as a slight shudder, nearly undetectable, shook the man's torso.

They had come prepared for the cold, yet they had not thought to come prepared for a woman who would not be dressed as warmly. Thankfully, the Vultures had left the clothing of this aerie undisturbed. It was thrown from one end of the bedroom to the other and several pieces were marred with dirty tracks, but that would not affect the warmth of the garments in the least.

Sighing wearily, he continued to gaze at her. She was the image of a younger Mera. There was no doubt she came from the blood of the White Lance—the wings on her back were proof of that. But her features, those exceptional eyes. He shook his head. How could it be?

As Dearn watched the princess eat, he pulled his own food from the pack at his side and bit into it. He had no mate, but his mother had been ever vigilant and made certain he was supplied.

It took only minutes for the warriors to eat, and Dearn was thankful to see that the Princess was hungry enough that she ate just as quickly.

"Now that we have all taken our rest, we should continue." He stepped into the room. "Princess, I have found you clothing, if you will step in here and dress appropriately."

He kept his voice light, comforting. She was terrified. He could see it in the small shudders of those wings, which the cold would never affect.

She came quickly to her feet, clutching the coat around her shoulders.

"I found you a coat as well, my lady," he assured her.

Timidly, Allora extended the heavily padded coat back to its owner.

"I thank you, Marden, for the use of such a fine coat." Her voice was filled with sincerity, and a deep appreciation for the small acts of kindness she was receiving.

Marden came to his feet and accepted the garment. The warrior sighed deeply then bowed slowly from his waist.

"I thank you, Princess, for keeping it warm while I ate. I never could eat while burdened with such a heavy coat." He smiled at her—a small smile, but Dearn noticed it was one that showed the small woman the warrior bore her no ill will.

He shrugged the coat back on.

"Come along, Allora, before you freeze in this night air." Dearn beckoned her through the aerie. "We will dress you warmly, then prepare you for flight. I promise you, we will be certain you will receive no more bruises."

He and Semar had cut wide strips from a thick quilt that they would use to bind her to him while they finished the flight to the Fortress with her. It would allow her to experience flight in a facsimile of freedom that should bring her joy, as the clothing they had found would keep her comfortable and warm.

They needed to hurry, though. They had tarried too long, and were they not careful they would be caught by the light of morning before entering the pass into the Fortress. The Vultures would then easily sight them, and the Princess's life could become jeopardized. Dearn knew they could not take that chance.

Chapter Seventeen

၈

Dearn landed with his slight burden within the courtyard of the Fortress, relieved to have the journey at its end. He stood, holding Allora carefully as one of his warriors rushed to remove the bindings that had held her in place through the last part of the flight.

Dawn was moments away; the early-morning darkness was lit, though, by the multitude of candles and torches being held by the Clan members gathered for the warriors' return. Hundreds of them had turned out for the arrival of the human princess after hearing the call announcing them from the furthermost points of the passage into the Valley of the Gods. Their fury lay thick and hot in the air; their eyes glared accusingly at the small woman in his arms.

This was lost on his young captive, though, as she turned to stare up at him with eyes the color of the White Lance Clan, a blue as clear and as deep any mountain lake. Eyes the color of Mera's. A face as gentle and as sweet as that of the woman who had held Dearn's heart for so long.

It was with bittersweet regret that he saw all this, and he wondered again at the absence of that flash of overriding agony he would have expected to feel at the resemblance. Had he not loved Mera as much as he had once thought?

For a moment he recalled Mera's accusation that his love for her had been a product of his competition with Ralnd. That they played so fiercely to outdo one another Dearn's pride could not accept that Ralnd had succeeded somewhere he could not. Namely, in acquiring her devotion.

"By the gods!" Saran pulled her hand back, reaching out desperately to her husband, who enfolded her as well.

Dearn understood her shock. No babe of the Clans was ever treated so cruelly. They were loved dearly, receiving an overabundance of touching and affection all through their lives. He had seen how Allora acted in the aerie. Each small kindness had made her uncertain how to act, how to feel. This woman was still, in fact, a child, isolated from family and warmth, knowing not how to reach out, or how to accept something so slight as the embrace of a mother's wings.

"She is my niece."

He heard Saran's entreaty to her husband and saw the need she had to enfold the girl in the protective shelter of her wings.

"We will let her rest first, Saran." Dearn touched the older woman's shoulder gently, knowing this blow so soon after Mera's death might be more than she could bear. "Let her rest and get used to her freedom, and she will be less frightened."

"Freedom?" The old woman's breathless whisper caused him to turn his head and be pierced by faded brown eyes sharpened with disbelief. "You expect us to believe you will set free and not kill us? Why, then, did you take us? Do you think we are unaware of your Clan Justice?"

Dearn studied her without expression. Clan Justice was punishment given to enemies, where they were thrown from the Fortress walls to the valley floor to be smashed on the rocks below. Only the most heinous crimes were dealt with in such a manner.

"To thwart King Alfred and, hopefully, produce a bit of courage when his army attacks," he told her coldly. "Were she a Bastard Breed, she would be brought before the Clans along with her father for trial. But even Bastard Breeds have honor, old woman. And this child will not be tried for her father's crimes, nor will they be held against her. She will be protected here within the Fortress until her grandfather arrives

He would have smiled then, but the loss of Ralnd and his family was still too recent. So he concentrated on the Princess—her life and his own responsibilities to her—instead.

There was such a look of satisfaction and of thanks in her eyes that Dearn felt humbled. He wanted to shake the feeling off, to cast away any tenderness for this child of the demon king. Yet, how could he, when this child was also part of his Clans? When she had been abused the whole of her young life because she carried the wings of her mother on her back? Her rescue would do more than give them an edge against King Alfred; it would also prove to her father's people beyond a shadow of a doubt that their king was mad.

"What will you do with her now, Sire?" Mera's brother, Damar, walked slowly from the front of the crowd, his arms crossed tightly over his chest as he cast a caustic look at the warrior who moved away with the strips of cloth that had made the girl's journey easier. "Will you beat her, or throw her from the sky and watch her fall to her death? Perhaps we can tie her down and rape her as our women were raped?"

"Aye, what punishment, then, shall she be given?" a young woman called out, and Dearn recognized her as the daughter of another Clanswoman who had been killed.

"She will make a becoming addition to the rocks in the valley when she and her father line it together," a man said who had lost his wife and all his children in an attack.

Dearn watched as sadness filled Allora's eyes. There was no fear, only resignation. She expected to die. He could see it in her proud face, in her gentle, if sorrowful, smile.

Then she turned her head so she could face the crowd, her back straightening, her chin rising, ready to face the executioner. She confronted the fury of the approaching warrior and the Clans behind him.

A gasp went up and Dearn watched as Damar halted in shock, his eyes widening. He stepped back, like a man who had taken a hit in the stomach and had yet to catch his wind.

Dearn understood the feeling. He had felt much the same way the moment he realized he held a woman of his own kind instead of the human he had thought to find.

"What manner of Cinder's sorcery is this?" Damar cried, seeing her resemblance to his sister as a young girl. Allora could have been his sister.

"Her wings have been bound, Damar."

Dearn turned Allora around, revealing the small, barely formed wings growing on her back. She wailed, struggling against him to hide from the hundreds of eyes that were suddenly focused on her deformity. He held her firmly, though, gripping her arms as he ignored her soft plea.

"Please don't."

She was of the Clans, and the people must see it. They had to see the malice, the cruelty of the human king toward his own daughter. Any man who would treat his own child so would surely lie and deceive his people and lead them into a battle based on that deception. He wanted them to see, and to understand why he fought so hard to end the war not with an annihilation of the humans but just that of the Vultures, and the Elitists who aided them.

At that moment, Brendar landed, and in his arms he carried the old woman who had been held in the room with the princess.

"Take your hands off her!" The woman fought, fear making her voice hoarse and filling it with tears. "It wasn't her fault. Don't you hurt her!"

"Silence, old woman." Dearn turned to her quickly, his voice hard and commanding. "I would know why the human king has bound the wings of one of my Clan members. From where was this child taken?"

"From her mother!" the maid cried out. "She is the child of the angel Demetria, of your White Lance, and King Alfred. A Bastard Breed, I believe you call them." She sneered at the age-old insult.

Chaos erupted. Protestations and strangl[ed] disbelief echoed through the courtyard. Demetri[a] echoed through Dearn's head along with the n[...] should have known.

It had happened nearly thirty years [...] disappearance of the teenager during a flight fro[m] the Fortress had caused the Clans to live in [...] children for years. They had searched for the chi[ld] yet had found no trace of her either in the mount[ains] the human cities.

"Demetria's child?"

Saran, Damar's mother, approached the girl [...] turned Allora back around and tightened his gr[ip] as she shrank back from the trembling hand [...] touch her face.

"Demetria was my sister," Saran whispere[d] ruffled. "She was my sister."

And so the reason for Allora's resemblan[ce] explained.

"Stop this!" Allora tried to avoid Saran['s] stared around the courtyard with wide, unfo[cused] hands tightened on the front of her gown, and [...] Dearn felt the shiver of the tiny wings.

"Allora." His voice was soft as he tried to [...] "Calm down, little one. No harm will come to [you within these] walls."

"Let her alone!" The old woman finally [...] free of Brendar's clutches and rushed to her [...] not been touched other than to have her wing[s...] was a small child. Give her peace. She has kn[own no love but] mine, no caring but mine."

The old woman pulled Allora into her [...] rubbing her back gently as she sheltered the [...] woman with her body.

to take her home. You may stay or go as you please, since you serve her."

As he spoke, he watched her eyes round in shock.

"Then Alfred lied once again." Her voice sounded strangled, her eyes filled with tears. "You do not kill the Bastard Breeds?"

"The past is a harsh taskmaster, madam." He sighed. "The princess will live in freedom from this day forward. If we can find a way to defeat her father before he destroys us all."

He beckoned to Tamora.

"Take her into the Fortress and place her in Mother's wing," he ordered. "I want someone outside the door at all times, and someone on the balcony, as well. She's distraught, and I don't want to take chances."

Tamora nodded. The balconies overlooked the cliff, and the fall to the river below was a long one.

"Come along, Princess." Her voice was soothing as she led the two women from the courtyard. Whatever crimes the humans had committed, they weren't the fault of the princess. Dearn knew Tamora would hold nothing but sympathy in her heart for the cruelty committed upon the other woman by her own father.

"Damar, send a message to your grandfather. Inform him that Demetria's daughter is here, and the circumstances," Dearn commanded, weariness plain in his voice even to his own ears as Allora disappeared into the Fortress. "He will want to make arrangements for her as soon as possible."

"King Dearn, how could this have happened?" Damar was still in shock.

"I have no answers for you, Damar, only more questions of my own," Dearn answered, gripping the younger man's shoulder in a show of comfort. "All we can do now is be the family she never had. That part will be easy. The rest Allora will have to come to terms with herself."

Chapter Eighteen

ဢ

Dearn motioned for Brendar, Saran's husband, Creidon, Tobian, the Raven Clan leader, and Havar to follow him. His body ached for his bed but this had to be finished first.

"Brendar, did the women and children of the human soldiers arrive safely?" he asked.

"They arrived hours ago, Sire," Brendar informed him. "We were getting worried about you."

"We were forced to put in at an aerie." Dearn shrugged. "The princess was not dressed for flight." He would have said more, but Allora's uncle by marriage cut in on the discussion as they entered the office.

"Dearn, there is no way Allora can be used against the humans now. A new plan must be made."

"I'm aware of that, Creidon." Dearn moved to the liquor cabinet and extracted a bottle of wine and enough glasses for the men joining him. "New plans will be made. Perhaps the wives and children of his captains will be enough."

"Not according to what we heard," Tobian informed him with a weary sigh. They were all tired. "From what my men have reported, they will do us little good. Those men blindly follow Canton, Alfred's general, and he had no family to kidnap."

"What man has no family?" Brendar stared at the Raven leader in surprise.

"A very lonely man." Tobian shook his head. "We have no leverage against him now."

"The blind following the crazed and desperate." Brendar accepted the glass and sipped gratefully. "I don't believe King Alfred will be swayed by his own daughter, let alone the wives and children of his captains. On top of that, we have a commander with loyalty to no one but his king. We're in a hell of a situation here."

"And if his men, his people, learn that his daughter is also of the Clans?" Creidon protested. "What will they think then? Will they be so quick to follow him when they learn of his lies?"

"They will require proof." Brendar shook his head. "They have all seen Allora, but with no sign of her wings, as they were bound. You will have to show them. Show her."

"That puts her at too much of a risk," Dearn argued. "She is fragile—you've seen that for yourself. Her captivity was designed to break her spirit, her will. When he sees we have her, he will not care if she lives or dies."

"He planned to give her to the leader of the Vulture Clan if they defeated us," Tobian reminded them. "He doesn't care if she lives or dies."

"There must be something else we can do. Some way we can pull the teeth of the beast marching toward us," Creidon argued fiercely. "King Alfred and his paltry Clan of Vultures must be stopped before they reach the pass into the Fortress, Dearn."

Dearn knew this, just as he knew that if the Clans flew against the humans now they would be victorious. The wholesale slaughter of human lives, however, was something he wanted to avoid.

"I agree they must be stopped at all costs." He walked to the balcony's glass doors. "We have a week to decide how it must be done. I hesitate to give the order that will result in such a high loss of lives—both human and Clan lives."

"There is no other way, Dearn," Brendar argued. "I understand your hesitation, but they can't be allowed to reach the pass. Once there, the Vultures will have no trouble getting into the Fortress. If they reach that point, then the humans will kill our women and our children before we can stop them."

"You are talking about more than a thousand men," Tobian protested. "Nearly all of the male humans in the valleys."

"There are more. There always are," Creidon snapped. "They breed like rats. In a few years, their numbers will revive once again. Just think what will happen if they somehow convince the humans from the other provinces to march against us, as well. What chance, then, will we have?"

Dearn was quiet as he looked out over the valley. He now understood many of the lessons his father had taught him, and why he had placed such emphasis on preparation—and patience.

"Dearn, the humans acquire their rulers differently than we do. They don't make them prove their leadership qualities and decision-making talents, as you had to do before taking the throne. They are born into it, or take it by right of strength. You cannot reason with humans because they know only one voice, and that is the voice of their king." Brendar's voice was filled with disgust.

"Such bitterness." Havar commented at this point. "I wonder if the human men feel the same? Or do they fight out of fear that the same end will come to their children that they believe came to King Alfred's daughter?"

The voice of wisdom, Dearn thought as he turned back toward them.

"It would seem to me that you would do better speaking to the wives and children you have taken and learning the weaknesses of their men, instead of lamenting the ones that do not reside with the king or his commander," Havar continued. "They are not the ones who will fight the war. It is the lowly soldiers whose lives will be lost."

Dearn listened to them argue. As always, he inserted few of his own thoughts, but let the ideas that flowed around him hold center stage as he considered each one. Whichever decision was made here tonight would be the plan they followed on the morrow. He had to listen closely, and listen wisely, if he was to choose the best path for the warriors to take.

"And when that fails? When they follow their king like lambs to the slaughter—what then, old man?" Tobian snarled. "They will be at the pass and have easy access into the Fortress and to our own families."

Havar regarded them all, his blue eyes faded with age, yet Dearn saw the warrior he had been so long ago.

"So, we kill them all," the old man stated mockingly. "Start with those women and children you have locked in the same dungeon where we held the Vultures. Kill them now. Why wait? Leave their rotting bodies at the entrance of the pass. That will convince the humans of our determination to vanquish them once and for all."

Varying degrees of horror were now reflected on the men's faces. And while shock and surprise was the root of the others' reaction, anger fueled Dearn's.

"The women and children are being held in the dungeons?" He pinned each of them in turn with glare. "Why in Seven Hells are they in the dungeons?"

Silence reigned for long moments as the men faced a rare sight—the fury of their king.

"They are captives," Brendar pointed out. "Where else would we put them?"

Dearn closed his eyes briefly, pinching the bridge of his nose with his thumb and forefinger as he fought for that patience his father had spent so much time teaching him.

"Are you all children?" He opened his eyes, shaking his head. "Do you believe this a game where the innocent are nothing more than your pawns? Will you now sink as low as those we fight, and destroy those weaker than yourselves?"

There was no answer forthcoming, but their shamed looks caused disappointment to gather and pool within his heart.

"Havar, please send someone to prepare the rooms we will need for our guests." He stressed the word, hoping to impress upon them the conduct that would be practiced where the human captives were concerned. "We will go to the dungeons and release them and have them brought up."

"Very good, Sire." Havar nodded his head approvingly as he left the room.

Silence reigned after the door closed behind him, and Dearn studied his now-silent aides.

"You will all accompany me and extend your apologies for their treatment," he said at last.

"Sire, the Clans will not accept the humans being treated so well," Brendar objected. "The wrath running through them is strong right now. We should be careful how we step."

"I shall step as I always have, in Clan pride," Dearn snapped, his outrage flaring at the veiled warning in his general's words. "You will aid me in settling these people into the Fortress. Then all of you will accompany me to the courtyard, where we will inform our people why those humans are here and why they will not be mistreated. Our laws were created for a reason, Brendar, and I'll be damned if they will be broken just because it suits my people at the time."

Therefore, thine enemy, weakened and vanquished, shall surely be given mercy.

The child of the enemy is innocent until the child raises the sword against thee as well.

Those laws were part of what governed the Clans and war. He would not be the one to break them.

"You're right." Creidon sighed as he rose wearily to his feet and motioned to the others. "We have our laws for a reason, and we will obey them."

Dearn led the way through the castle, then into the stairwell that led to the farthest reaches of the mountain depths. There, with no access but those of the steep, drafty stairs, the dungeons lay.

He heard the children crying before they reached the level of the dungeons. The sound echoed in the stairwell, biting at his heart, and he could tell it affected not just him. The others slowed, their heads hanging lower with each step.

Finally, they reached the huge cavern that housed the individual cells. Dearn stood within the damp space and turned to face his men. He could not speak for his anger as he listened to the children crying, the women crooning gently to them.

Several guards stood within the cavern as well. Their faces seemed carved from stone, but Dearn saw the disgust in their eyes.

"You disagree with the humans' living quarters?" he asked one Eagle warrior, his voice soft, emotionless.

For a moment, the soldier refused to speak, and he knew it was because they assumed it had been his decision to place the humans there.

"Forgive me, Sire," he finally hissed through clenched teeth, his voice shaking with his emotion. "This is no place for women and children."

"Where do you place prisoners, then?" Dearn persisted, his voice still quiet, though vibrating with fury.

A fury the guard assumed was directed at him.

"I care not where prisoners are placed." The warrior stared over Dearn's shoulder, refusing to look him in the eye. "My cousin died by the bastard humans' hands. But that is no fault of the babes who lie in there now. The gods will not be pleased in this, Sire."

Dearn glanced at the other guards and saw varying degrees of agreement.

"Why, then, did you not come to me?" He allowed his own anger to show at last. "Do you so willingly accept such injustices that you will not bring them to light?"

Surprise reflected in the warrior's eyes.

"Are you human soldiers, blindly following your commander? Where is the spirit of the Clans that flows through your veins? If you disagreed with General Brendar's orders, why did you not do something?"

Feet shuffled, heads ducked. Shamed faces were hidden from his wrath. All but one—the guard brave enough to reveal his indignation.

"I would have soon," the warrior said. "Until I could, I provided them with blankets for the babes and have tried to assure them of their safety."

Dearn turned in time to catch Brendar's look of amazement, and of resignation. He had known he was in the wrong and had known that eventually he would be brought to task for the decision.

"Give me the keys." Dearn held his hand out imperiously. The ring of iron keys was dropped quickly into his palm. "We will escort our guests to the main section of the castle, where they will be assigned their rooms. They will be fed and provided every comfort." His next words were directed to his Clan leaders. "I expect there will be no repeat of such circumstances again."

He did not wait for them to agree but turned his back on them and opened the cell door. There, huddled in a corner, the women and young children stared back at him in terror. Children began to scream and huddle closer to their mothers, and Dearn's heart clenched as he heard echoing in their voices the screams of the children of the Clans as they were murdered.

"What do you want?" One young woman no more than seventeen years old confronted him. Her long red hair cascaded in tangled waves about her pale face as she stood in front of what must be her mother and sister.

"Sienna, please, do not anger him." The mother's fear clogged her voice.

"You will not harm us." The young woman fought her tears as she faced him. "My father will skin you alive if you harm us."

She shook as though chilled, and the pale flecks of her freckles stood out harshly against her white skin as her sister cried behind her.

"Come out of here." His voice was harsh, clogged with emotion and a grudging respect for the girl's courage. "You will not be harmed, I swear this to you by the grace of Ashrad. Come, you will be taken to your rooms and given food and drink."

Shock now molded the girl's face, but the others still huddled together fearfully, as though unable to believe this act of kindness.

Dearn could not stand the sight of the cowering children or their cries any longer. He turned and strode from the dungeon, leaving his Clan leaders to rectify the situation as he fought for calm. It baffled him, enraged him, that when war was waged among men it was the women and children who suffered, hungered and endured pain and, often, humiliation tenfold that of their men. Proof of that resided here in his own dungeons, where he would have sworn it never would. And yet he had also seen courage that would have compared favorably to that of any warrior he had known.

As he exited the large dungeon cavern, he halted in surprise at the sight of the human who stood just outside the door, accompanied by two of his own soldiers.

"What do you do here?" Dearn asked him, weariness weighing on his body as he faced the quiet man.

King Derek Sutton had been raised by the Clans from his tenth birth year to his sixteenth. He was the product of an agreement between his father and Dearn's that was to have begun an alliance between the Clan and human forces. An alliance that promptly fell through after the boy's return to his own city and Dearn's father's refusal to send Dearn to the human king.

Sutton was tall for a human, well past six feet, with broad shoulders and a stocky, muscular body. His wheat-colored hair and gray eyes were a startling contrast to the darkly tanned skin of his face. He was big and proud, his shoulders thrown back, his eyes narrowed in contemplation as he regarded the man he still called friend despite their fathers' disagreements.

"And it's nice to see you as well, my friend." Sutton grinned slightly. "Perhaps I could have a bit of your time and a sip of your wine, and we will talk of the reason for my visit."

Dearn would have preferred a bath, a hot meal and a long nap, but he nodded abruptly before moving past his old friend and leading the way back to what had become a meeting room.

"I wondered if it was by your order that the women and children were placed in the dungeons," Sutton remarked as Dearn handed him a glass of wine minutes later. "I was checking on this myself when I heard you speaking to them."

His tone was questioning, though it carried an edge of anger that the captives had been there to begin with.

"My people are angry and frightened, Derek." Dearn shrugged as he took his seat and leaned back in it wearily. "Much is happening, too quickly."

Derek nodded slowly, taking one of the seats before the desk as Dearn continued, still confused as to why he would be there.

"And what has brought you here? Travel within the mountains has become hazardous, indeed. How did you make it past the Vulture troops lying in wait?"

"I came in regards to a letter I received from a friend of my father's, King Alfred. He accuses you of killing his daughter, Dearn."

"Have you ever seen the Princess Allora, Derek?" Dearn asked him, frowning.

"Several times. A frail, timid child who seemed always in pain."

Dearn grunted.

"She was in pain because the monster had her wings bound to the point that she now carries naught but winglets upon her back," he growled, ignoring Derek's shocked exclamation. "I returned from Cayam with the princess this dawn. She had been imprisoned within a tower room, held as payment to the Vulture leader for aiding Alfred in this insane war he has begun against the Clans. She lives, Derek, but by the gods, I don't know how."

Dearn gulped the wine in the goblet, waiting for the soft heat as it hit his belly and moved through his body. Gods, he was tired.

"So, the rumors were true." Derek shook his head. "This is what I needed to know. I would like to see her before I leave, then I will return to Bracken and lead my forces here. We will join you in battle, Dearn."

Dearn looked up, surprised by this announcement. He had not expected that the soldiers of the large northern city of Bracken would even consider such a maneuver.

"We are friends, Dearn. And more than that, we are allies," Derek reminded him, reading his shocked look. "I will give you what aid you need, just as you have done for me."

Dearn sighed wearily. Years before, a distant cousin had threatened to wreak havoc with Derek's rule by leading a large band of rebels against Bracken. Dearn had come to his aid without being asked, flying his warriors about the town and joining in battle with Derek to drive the cousin and his forces from the city. Bracken had never been attacked again.

"I want no more innocent deaths in this, Derek." He shook his head as he leaned forward. "Our forces are strong enough and large enough to win the war. I only seek to minimize the losses in whatever manner I can."

Quickly, he outlined the situation and the plans he was making. He didn't want a long, bloody battle where allies were forced to shed blood. Clan forces alone could conquer those coming for the Fortress, if he timed it right and weakened King Alfred properly.

"A complicated plan." Sutton nodded. "And one worthy of you, as well. But should you change your mind, you have only to send for us. I have three thousand men who will come to the aid of the Clans, should you need it."

"And I thank you for that, my friend. But there is one favor I would ask. When you reply to King Alfred's request, do not deny him outright. Allow him to believe you are thinking on this matter. Perhaps that will buy us some time. Something I am greatly in need of right now."

"This I can do easily enough," Derek agreed, extending his hand as they rose to their feet. "'Til we meet again, my friend. And, please, you can fly the distance much easier than I can ride it. Visit Bracken sometime—you would enjoy it, I think."

"Soon. I promise." Dearn shook his hand, then Derek saluted him casually before walking from the room. He was thankful, as he had not been before, that his father had begun the alliance with the humans in Bracken so many years before. It meant having a friend and ally now where could have been an enemy instead.

* * * * *

Hours later, the human women and children were safely asleep in beds rather than on a stone floor. The Clans had been informed of the decision, and despite the leaders' fears they were satisfied with Dearn's decision. Soon, Dearn promised himself, he would sleep as well. The afternoon was now well under way, and still he had found no time to rest. He would not be able to delay the matter much longer. The brief naps he had allowed himself over the past days were doing little to restore his strength.

"So, what do we do now?" Brendar poured a healthy measure of wine and swallowed it in one gulp. "We have nothing to use against the king or Canton. Do we rely on luck?"

"You rely on using your brains."

The princess's human maid, Mary, walked slowly into the room, nervously smoothing down the front of her dress. Five men turned to look at the distinguished old woman.

"I thought that was what we were doing," Havar murmured as he surveyed her. Dearn would have been amused by his advisor's interest if he had had the time.

"You are running yourselves around in circles." She poured a small glass of the wine, and as she sipped her eyebrows lifted in approval of the potency and taste.

"Very good wine, Your Highness," she complimented Dearn.

"Thank you, my lady." His tone bordered on sarcasm, but it was late and she had yet to state her purpose for being here. "How may we help you tonight?"

"You have already helped me by saving my princess," she told him softly. "It is I who come to help you. I know the single weakness General Canton possesses, which will aid you in dealing with him."

Once again silence reigned. Dearn glanced at the other men and saw reflections of the same surprise he was feeling.

As she let them come to terms with her announcement, she emptied her cup.

"And that weakness is?" Dearn leaned forward to fill her cup as she reached for the decanter.

"The Princess Allora," she informed him as he refilled her glass. "Canton goes to war because he believes the Clans murdered his beloved. He will turn his men back should he learn that she lives and Alfred's words are lies."

"There is no rumor of this," Brendar objected as the words sank in. "Were this true, then the people of Cayam would have known about it."

Mary shook her head.

"They would not speak of it if those involved told no one," she pointed out. "King Alfred ruled over Allora with an iron fist. She has rarely gone against his edicts. And Canton said nothing for fear of King Alfred's refusing his suit when Allora came of age to marry. The only problem was, when she came of age he believed she was dead."

"So the human general has a weakness after all." Dearn refilled his own cup this time, staring up at the woman as he did so. "Please, sit down." He gestured to Havar to bring a chair.

"I will aid you, Sire, in any way I can," she stated as she sat and sipped her wine. "Whatever information I can give you, I will gladly do so. My princess would have died had you not taken her from that prison. He tortured her for no reason other than the wings upon her back."

"For this, he will pay as well," Creidon spoke up. "I am her uncle by marriage, madam, my wife the sister to Demetria. I know well the pain the family went through at her disappearance all those years ago."

"It is nothing compared to the pain Demetria went through." Mary shook her head at her own memories. "She tried many times to escape but was foiled at every turn. Finally,

Alfred aided her in her quest and pushed her from the tower window. He made her death appear an accident."

"Why did she not use her wings?" Havar asked her, frowning.

Mary swallowed, turning her face away from them as she fought to control her emotions.

"King Alfred had her wings cut as far as the surgeons dared to remove them. What was left was bound, as Allora's have always been bound."

Horror and disbelief crushed Dearn's heart as his own wings shuddered. The barbarian had dared to cut her wings from her body? The pain would have been agonizing, the bleeding profuse enough that it could have caused death by itself. How could he have done such a thing?

"There were few who knew who she was, or from where she came." Mary took a longer sip of her wine now, and Dearn knew her memories of her queen's pain must be horrendous. "The few times Demetria tried to get a message to her people she was betrayed. She finally gave up. When Allora was born without wings, she assumed the child would be safe. But when the Princess turned three, the wings began to appear."

The story Mary related of the king's fury and the instant attempts at surgery to remove the wings had Dearn clenching his fists, his body tight with his rage. To treat a child so cruelly, to force it to endure such pain, was monstrous.

"Allora will know no more pain." Creidon moved forward as he spoke, refilling his own wine to numb the gut-burning fury raging through them all.

"This information is best kept within these chambers, Sire." Damar sat slumped in his chair, his wings shuddering from his emotion. "Should my mother know her sister and her niece suffered so, it may kill her. Especially coming so soon after Mera's death."

"I agree with you, Damar." Dearn sighed. "This information shall stay within this chamber and go no further.

But I am certain Mary has other information we can use against the king and his cohorts." He looked now to the maid with a raised brow.

"I know many things, Sire," she whispered with a tremulous smile. "And I will tell you all."

And she did. For long hours notes were taken, names were listed, and Dearn began to get a clearer picture of the rise of the Elitists and the insanity of the human king.

Canton was Alfred's weakness, not the princess. But the princess was Canton's weakness, and Dearn would use it. He would show the general his beloved, and the lies the king had perpetrated. He would have his victory, and he prayed to the gods it would not come with the blood of innocent men on his hands.

As soon as he slept then plans would be made, and Dearn swore that the end of this war would see the destruction of both the Vultures and the Elitists they aided.

Chapter Nineteen

A breeze blew through the small crack of the window in Allora's room. It wafted over her skin, and its haunting whisper through the canyon eased a part of her soul. Nothing could completely ease her fears, though. She lay in the dark, huddled in the huge bed beneath the thick quilts, motionless as she fought the betraying tears that fell from her eyes.

Tears had never helped the pain before, and she knew they would not help her now. Yet neither could she stem the betraying proof of the soul-deep emptiness she felt inside.

Mary had disappeared early that morning, leaving Allora alone in the cool silence of the room to face the curiosity of those who brought her food and clothing. Just hours before the one called Tamora had helped her into bed, urging her to sleep after the long hours she had spent pacing her room. Allora feared she would never sleep again, knowing the deceptions, the savage hatred and evil her father had practiced against her. How did one sleep with the pain and indignation of a lifetime rising like a black plague inside her soul?

She should be flying, relieving her pain by soaring on the wind as she laughed and reveled in freedom. Instead, she was lying abed, feeling the cool wind from the mountain pass and hating the need to feel it caress wings fully grown.

What were these people, these Winged Clans, she wondered, that just the knowledge she should have wings on her back would turn their ire away from her? Was she not still King Alfred's daughter? Why had their hatred been deflected?

She remembered the woman from the courtyard, the one who claimed to be her aunt Saran, who had come here to watch with tears wetting her cheeks as Allora was shown to the bathing room. In a small rock pool of heated water servants had lathered and rinsed her. Her hair was washed, her body dusted with a lightly scented powder after she was dried.

She dressed in a long, warm gown made to accommodate wings that still fit comfortably despite her deformed winglets. She wished she could cover them as she always had before. Nothing had ever felt so alien as having the air on them.

"Princess, why do you weep?" Tamora whispered.

In the dim light of dawn, she rose from the cot set up across the room and came to the bed. Her wings were taller than her body, arching above her head by several inches, and the long bottom feathers only just swept the ground at her feet.

They were slender columns of strength, a kind of cloak of pride and dignity. Allora wanted to rage aloud at the hopelessness she felt whenever she looked at them.

"I am fine," she whispered. She wanted no pity; she only wanted peace.

Tamora sat beside her, considering her with kind violet eyes.

"I have a sister," Tamora said. "She is much younger than I am and lives with my family in the Clan stronghold. She says I am easy to talk to, if you would like to talk."

Allora shook her head. What could she say that would make sense? She turned her head, avoiding the gentle offer of sympathy.

"My brother broke a wing once. When he was very young. He cried loudly for days and nights, nearly driving us all mad. Finally, in desperation, Father took him out, holding him while he flew about the mountains. This seemed to ease my brother, but he told me later that it only made him sadder because he could not fly himself. But he cried no more, because on that flight our father told him that, even were he to never fly again, he would still be a warrior and a man one day. The loss of his wings would not take that from him."

"I have never flown. I have not your brother's problem." Allora grimaced, wishing the other woman would just leave her in peace.

"You are nearly a replica of your cousin Mera." Tamora's voice was now laden with pain. "Even your voice sounds similar. I wish you could have known her."

Silence extended through the room then. Allora could only regret all she had lost, but she had done that for many years. Finally, when she said nothing, Tamora gave a small sigh.

"Mera was Saran's daughter. The wife to Dearn's dearest friend and cousin. Their family was one of the first that Dearn found murdered. To find you now eases some of Saran's loss."

"I am not Mera. I cannot fill that place in her life." Allora swallowed tightly, wishing with all her might that she could fill a place in someone's life.

"This is not what Saran would want. But it would ease her, as well as you, if you allowed her to comfort you. There is nothing as peaceful or as soothing as being held within the comfort of a loved one's wings. Would you let me call her to you? She is sleeping in the next room."

Tamora tempted her with a promise of the kind of comfort Allora had always dreamed of. She could not say "no," yet neither could she say "yes." Fear held her in its grip as surely as her father had once done in his. These people had shown her nothing but kindness, acceptance so far, but she had never known either from anyone but Mary. The vast unknown, the sympathy and tenderness being extended terrified her. She didn't know how to allow others to care for her, and was terrified of rejection that might come later. Often, the cruelest blow her father had dealt her was delivered after his gentlest moments with her. She had learned to stay withdrawn from such overtures. She could not reach out, knew nothing but how to draw away.

Tamora seemed to understand. She went to the door and spoke to the guard. Long minutes later—surely, Allora thought, it wasn't the hours it felt as though it was—Saran appeared, and when Allora saw her, the tears fell faster. She had but one portrait of her mother and, dear Ashrad, but Saran looked just like her. It was the first thing Allora had noticed about her aunt.

Tamora left them as Saran replaced her on the bed. A whimper broke the silence, and Allora was surprised to realize it had come from her. Saran took a deep breath, and she felt as though the other woman was as frightened in some ways as she was.

"You are not much younger than my Mera." A soft hand touched Allora's hair. "She would often cry silently, just as you do now, because she knew her tears would cause me to move the sky and the stars to ease her pain."

Allora swallowed tightly.

"Tears solve nothing." She tried and failed to stem the liquid rolling down her cheeks. "Why do I cry? Why do I ache so, when I know this?"

"My precious, precious child." Saran's voice sounded strangled as she touched Allora's cheek. "You ache for all you have lost. And this is a part of nature. But look now at all you have found. Come, let me hold you and share your tears. Come, child." She held her arms out, the soft white of her wings seeming to unfold like a beacon of comfort.

Allora didn't know when she moved, but she was in the woman's arms, her tears soaking the gown beneath her cheek as the warmth of the wings wrapped around her. Her tears were no longer silent—great sobs tore her chest, as though the soft haven around her released some demon of agony that refused to stay mute any longer.

"I want to fly." The cry was ripped from her, her body heaving with the misery, the loss that only now she understood. "Gods save me, Momma. I want to fly."

* * * * *

Saran bent her head against that of the child sobbing so desperately at her breast and wept with her. She rocked her as the soft inner down of her wings, her mother's feathers, enfolded the heartbroken girl.

Momma, Allora had cried. *Gods save me, Momma.*

Saran could hear her own child's voice, the voice of her sweet Mera calling to her, and she clutched Allora closer, rocking her, sharing her sorrow.

As they cried, Saran realized they were no longer alone, but she knew they would not be. The sobbing would have brought the other women of her Clan—the aunts, the cousins, the women who recognized a child's cry of pain and to whom it mattered not whose child it was.

Saran's mother in turn wrapped them both with her wings, and Saran felt her tears against her cheek. Soft croons and velvet whispers echoed around them, and one of the women began to sing a lullaby.

"You are no longer alone, child," Saran murmured as Allora's sobs waned. "And the monsters may have destroyed your wings, but they can never destroy your spirit. I swear this to you, each day a warrior of your Clan shall take you to the wind and, Allora, you shall fly."

Saran prayed the words would give comfort, and she sensed perhaps it did, for slowly the weeping ended and the girl rested weakly within her arms. The lullabies, the soft, relaxing mothers' croons drifted through the room, and soon Allora began to slip into sleep.

"Momma?" Her voice was drowsy, hesitant beneath the enfolding wings and still laden with tears.

"Yes, my sweet?" Saran had to fight the agony that lost, nearly hopeless voice gave her.

"Don't leave me alone again, Momma." The whisper was on the edge of sleep.

"Never again, my sweet," Saran swore. "You shall never be alone again." There was a pause, then Saran whispered tearfully, "A child of my body taken, a child of my heart returned. The gods, indeed, know mercy."

Allora didn't answer. Saran knew by the soft droop of the slight body, the last hiccupping sobs that healing sleep had finally claimed her.

And the women still crooned. They stroked the child's back through Saran's wings, they comforted Saran and they held a vigil of love over a child that was no longer a child, yet still needed the healing touch of a mother's hands and a family's heart. This, they all knew, she would never lack again.

Chapter Twenty

ஐ

The next morning, Allora stood in shock, the comfort of the night before erased as she listened to Dearn's plan and his request.

"All you have to do is give us a message that Canton will be certain it came from you," he told her. "That will ensure his willingness to be flown here and see for himself that you are, indeed, alive."

Allora took a deep breath, fighting the instinctive need to scream out her protest. If they did this, they would show him the wings on her back and reveal a secret that could turn him from her forever. Canton would know the shame of her past and he would see the deformity of her body—all she had hoped to hide from him.

And Mary. Allora had trusted her maid; she had never imagined she would go to Dearn with this. Surely, there was some other way to halt the war.

"Allora, Canton can stop the war, this you well know." The betrayer spoke up. "He will come here if he knows you await him."

"There must be another way," Allora argued, ignoring the look of shock Dearn and Mary shared. "There must be some way to end this without bringing Canton here."

Silence descended, and she watched shock become frustration.

"Allora, there is no other way," Dearn insisted. "To turn the army away from us we must discredit your father and show his insanity for what it is. To do that, Canton will have to know the truth. It is he the men follow, not your father."

"But why must you bring him to me?" Allora cried out. "I will send a message, and you can just tell him I am alive and what my father is doing. There is no reason to bring him here. Take one of the women who were with me last night to him — they will tell him I live."

Astonishment filled Dearn's expression, and Allora knew he would not heed her. He and Mary were determined Canton would see her and know her for what she was.

Allora sensed her aunt near, felt the soft stroke of a wing tip as it touched her arm in comfort. How strange these people were, always touching, stroking, comforting. But there was no comfort for the pain they wanted to bring her.

"Allora, Canton loves you," Mary whispered as she came to her, one hand falling gently on her shoulder. "He will accept nothing but seeing you himself. You know this, so why do you fight us on it? Do you want the deaths of your people, both human and Clan, on your conscience?"

Allora stubbornly stared at her feet. Mary was right — Canton would accept no one's word in this matter. He would insist on seeing her.

"Daughter, what is it that you fear?" Saran whispered.

Allora turned to face this surrogate mother, this aunt whose bounty of love had healed a part of her wounded soul the night before.

"I would have spared him knowledge of my deformity," she explained as she clasped her hands tightly at her waist, fighting to gather the remnants of courage left after years of abuse. Moments later, she turned back to Dearn. "But you are right. He will accept nothing but the sight of me."

"Allora, those fragile wings will not cause one who cares for you any distaste," Saran assured her. "Canton's affection for you will not change. Even should it do so, you have a family now. We will do all we can to bring you happiness."

Allora shook her head, turning from them to stare past her balcony into the valley. The breeze fondled her hair, whispered in her ear and ruffled the feathers on her back. After the narrow prison of her tower, this place was heaven; yet now Dearn was asking her to risk a reminder of hell. Could she live if she saw the same disgust and fury on Canton's face as she had seen on her father's each time he saw her wings unbound?

"Once," she said finally, "Canton kissed me." She ignored Mary's surprised look. As far as the older woman knew, Allora and Canton had never had a moment alone. Alfred had always been careful to have them watched. "Tell him I would not be frightened the next time he should try to do so."

These words would bring Canton to her and, in the process, destroy her single dream of happiness. But, what choice did she have? Her father had to be stopped, and Dearn was right. The army didn't follow her father. They followed Canton, with his easy smile, his dark eyes and his quiet laughter. It was to him they looked for orders and from him they sought answers.

"Allora, you will see," Dearn promised, touching her shoulder gently. "This is the best thing. No one dies this way."

"I understand that." She raised her eyes to the blue sky, blinking back her tears, her regrets. "No one dies this way." Nothing was lost except the secret dream held deep within her heart that Canton would never know her shame.

Chapter Twenty-One

ॐ

"Inept fools. The gods give them the strength to fight, and how do they repay the gift? By allowing the most evil of all the demons to escape." King Alfred shook with rage as he sat on his makeshift throne and stared down at the Vulture who had just wrecked his tent. "What sort of warriors did you bring to me? Why did you not heed Cinder's commands and bring to me only your best, only those strong enough to fight for his vengeance?"

"Stop your prattle, old man." Edgar's chest heaved with his harsh breathing.

No control, just like the other demons, the king thought. *This one, too, is inferior.*

"You allowed her to escape!" He pounded his fist on the padded armrest of his chair. "It was your task to keep her imprisoned. It had fallen to you to punish her for her sins, and you allowed her to escape."

Alfred wondered why he had expected the Vulture demon to succeed. Why had he been so foolish as to allow the guards Edgar had chosen total control over keeping her imprisoned? He had known better, had been warned, and he had not heeded the warnings. It was his sin and yet, too, was it theirs. Even more was it their failure, for allowing such evil to escape into the world.

"I am tested in many ways for my faith," he moaned in prayer. "This is just one of those tests. My god will give me control. My prayers will be answered in my quest for patience."

"Your nattering is becoming more deranged each day." Edgar paced the tent, throwing his hands up as his wings appeared to vibrate in rage with each step. "This is no test from your god, you fool. This is a war, and if you don't get your head out of your ass we're going to lose it."

Disrespectful, lacking in any godly qualities, the demon raged and paced like a caged animal. How Alfred wished he could cage him. And he would, as soon as he completed the mission Cinder had revealed to him the black demons would accomplish. Then, they would all be caged, and they would all die.

He clenched his fists, fighting not to jump from his chair and bury his sword in the beast's heart now. Patience. He must have patience, or all would be lost.

"You have no vision of Cinder's will, Edgar," he growled as he stood. "You have no belief in his plans or how he will smite our enemies. We will be victorious."

They would be victorious, he reassured himself. Hadn't Cinder sent the handmaiden to him with the message of the conception of his son and the destiny in store for them both? Alfred would be a great king, and he would clear the world of the winged beasts so his son could rule and his people could cover the land. His son had been born healthy, as Cinder had sworn. Of course, Alfred had been unable to allow the mother to live. He wanted no feminine force turning his son from him, cursing him as Demetria had cursed his daughter.

"The escape of the harlot and her maid will not matter. It is too late for her to save her soul. Born of a demon, unrepentant of her sins, which manifest themselves in the vilest of deformities. She will pay, just as the other demons shall pay. They will pay with their lives."

Edgar stopped pacing and faced Alfred. His face was flushed, and his eyes seemed to bulge in his fury. He kicked the chair lying beside him.

"You and your mad ramblings are slowly making me as insane as you are. Will you please tell me how we are to get Allora back? You promised her to me. She is mine." He thumped his chest to emphasize his ownership.

"Poor besotted, lustful fool." Alfred shook his head as he resumed his seat, leaning back to watch the Vulture clench his teeth. "Ashrad allowed the demons to take her, tempting Cinder as he always has. You are Cinder's sword as well as I. Would you taint your soul with one so evil? Would you taint your mission with lust for one in whom Ashrad finds favor? She is our enemy. Find a woman who will sanctify you in Cinder's glory."

"She is mine!" Edgar's voice was louder, more furious. "I care not for your gods nor your mad ramblings. I want Allora; you promised her to me."

"She is gone. There is naught we can do about that. We must now strengthen ourselves against the damage she could cause. It is a test, Edgar. You shall have her back when the time is right." Yes, Alfred decided, Cinder was merely testing them and their resolve to do what must be done.

The Winged Clans had gained no victory, he assured himself. They were only following the destiny Cinder had written for them. She would be their downfall, just as she had nearly been his.

Her evil would be destroyed, the Winged Clans would be destroyed and Cinder would rise from the prison of the Seven Hells and be free. It was written that only when Cinder's followers had wiped Brydon clean of those with wings could he ever be released from the punishment Ashrad had given him.

Alfred wanted to close his eyes and drift back into the visions Cinder brought him of his life after this war. The peace he would bring to Brydon, the streets he could pave with the gold his men had found in the mountains, the diamonds and precious jewels his mining experts assured him were plentiful.

The Clans were sitting on the gods' own treasure, and Cinder had told Alfred it would be his if he could just rid the land of their presence.

"And how are we supposed to pass this test?" Edgar sneered at him, and Alfred reminded himself once again that it was too soon to kill the demon upstart.

"By careful planning, of course." He shrugged. "We must find a way to counter any move they make to reveal Allora to the people. If it comes to it, Edgar, she must die to keep Canton from ever seeing her again."

"It would be easier to just kill Canton," Edgar snarled, resuming his pacing.

Alfred watched him kick at the pieces of wood and glass that had once been furniture and dishes. The man had no control of his temper. *Control is virtue*, Alfred silently recited, hands clutching the padded armrests of his chair. Displays of temper were for fools and demons, not the swords of Cinder.

"We cannot kill Canton. He leads the soldiers; they will fight for no one else. He must live at least until the end of the war." After that, Alfred didn't care what happened to the man. The spirits of lust had infected Canton the moment he saw Allora. There had been no hope for him after that.

"Then what do you think we should do, old man?" The perpetual sneer Edgar wore became broader.

"If she is seen, then she must be killed. The Clans will fly her out to the soldiers as they near the pass into the Fortress. You will have men watching for her, and you will have her killed."

"Killed?" Edgar burst out. "You would have her killed after promising her to me?"

Dear Cinder, you test my faith to its limits with this demon you have sent me.

"She will do you no good if she turns the soldiers back, you fool. Might I remind you that you have only three hundred men? The Clans are three thousand strong. Because you neglected to make quick work during the nightly killings."

Edgar's lip curled. A child on the verge of a sulk.

How am I ever to win this war with warriors such as this fighting the battles, dear Cinder?

"We thought to have more time," Edgar mumbled.

"You knew the date of the yearly celebration as well as I did." Alfred shrugged, while inside he cursed the ignorance of demons. "You knew they would be missed. You also knew the moment their bodies were found all Clans would be called to the Fortress. You knew all this, yet still you tarried to play games with the women."

Lust and lies and ignorance abound in the hearts of demons. I am being tested; I am being punished for lying with the demon Demetria and allowing her demon child to live. I shall persevere. Alfred closed his eyes, breathing deeply as he sought the vision of his god once again.

"Wake up, you old fool." Edgar threw a table leg, kicked an unbroken bowl and shattered it. "What about the women and children they took, the families of your captains? Your men will not fight if their families are used as a shield."

"My men will fight if their families are killed as they watch." Alfred opened his eyes, staring at a point above Edgar's head as he saw the vision. "They will fight to their deaths, if need be."

"And how do you intend to pull this off?" Edgar was shaking his head when Alfred looked at him.

"That is your area. Cinder has shown me the way, but you must do a little work yourself, Edgar." Alfred smiled at the demon. Yes, Cinder would see that it all worked out in his favor. Had he not killed the lustful demon Demetria as he had been told to do? Had he not kept the demon child from tempting men with her lustful ways? Cinder would make him victorious against all odds.

* * * * *

Edgar narrowed his eyes. Alfred sat, relaxed now in the huge chair. His face had a childlike expression, as though he had discovered some new and unimagined wonder. He could only shake his head again at the man's crazed expression.

"My god has shown me the way, Edgar."

A chill chased down his spine as Alfred looked at him. In the depths of those faded blue eyes a flame seemed to smolder.

"And what has your god shown you, Alfred?" he raged. "Has he shown you a way into that damned Fortress other than the pass you showed us? Has he shown you yet how to take back Allora without killing her first?"

"You dare to continue to mock me?" Alfred frowned. "Cinder will smite you, Edgar. He will take you from this world and send you to the depths of the Seven Hells."

"He'll have to catch me first," Edgar sneered, knowing the words were guaranteed to incite the old fool.

Alfred's face mottled then flushed a bright red while the skin around his mouth paled.

"You dare to say such things!" His voice thundered through the tent as he rose from his chair, the black-and-blue velvet robes he habitually wore billowing around his wide body. "You dare to mock Cinder, when it was by his hand you were brought here to do his work? You dare to mock all he has promised you, should you defeat the demons and take the mountains in his name?"

"I dare to mock you, you crazy old fool, for you have none of your god but much of insanity, I believe," Edgar raged back, sickened by the petty excuse Alfred used for killing the Clans. "You are not fighting for your god," he went on. "You are not even fighting for the gold and veins of precious gems. You are fighting out of some crazed desire for revenge against the queen you killed and the child she left you."

"You will stop this!" Alfred screamed. "Cinder will strike you dead for this blasphemy against him."

"My blasphemy?" Edgar laughed now, amused to see Alfred's eyes widening in amazed horror at the disrespect. "What of your blasphemy, old man? You use your god to explain your killing of innocents, and your lustful thoughts toward your own child. Do you think I haven't seen that crazy light in your eyes each time you speak of her? You want her dead because of your own weakness and perversion."

Alfred gasped for breath, paling, flushing, fury tightening each muscle in his body. Edgar wanted to laugh at the spectacle he presented. The king was insane, and that insanity served Edgar to a point, but now he needed the man either dead or clearheaded, whichever the old fool could manage in the next several days.

"I am Cinder's sword." Tears leaked from the old man's eyes, making Edgar want to kill him then and there. "He shall grant me grace, he shall grant me patience when dealing with the demonic specters set before my path."

"Would you stop praying and preaching to me?" Edgar threw up his hands as he screamed back at the old man. "You stupid, insane old fool. Your idiocy will be the defeat of us, not the Clans."

"Cinder will strike you dead for your blasphemy against his sword. I am the sword of Cinder, brought here to wipe this world of the demons that would destroy it. I am the sword, and he will smite you for your disrespect of me."

Edgar shook his head and gave up. He turned and left the tent, followed by the mad preaching of the king and threats that his god would kill him. His fury erupted again. How was he supposed to contain this insanity and reclaim the woman promised to him?

He tore into a troop of human soldiers and left them lying, then ripped at the tent they had been heading for. Imbeciles. Stupid. The humans would pay for this setback with their lives one day, he swore. And that mad King Alfred would be the first. He would bury his sword in the old man's gut and watch him slowly bleed to death. He would pay, as would the Clans, for stealing the woman he had claimed for himself.

* * * * *

Matte watched the violent eruption of temper as Edgar stomped to his tent and entered it with a vicious swipe of the heavy fabric covering the opening. She narrowed her eyes, surveying the camp, studying those interested in the display and wondering how much they knew.

It was incredibly difficult to learn what was going on within the human tents. She knew General Canton and his lieutenant, Jacquard, were very interested in whatever Alfred and Edgar seemed at odds about now. Of course, were they a bit more obliging in sharing information, Matte could have told them what they needed to know.

She leaned against the rough wooden post that held her tent upright and stared across the clearing at Canton and Jacquard as they struck the same pose across from her. Their eyes met. Matte arched her brow slowly, a grin edging her lips as Canton frowned darkly then said something to his lieutenant. Oh, they really didn't like her.

Matte's Bastard Breed warriors were the only units with women warriors. She had over two dozen of them within her camp, and they were as tough and as well-trained as any of the men. They wouldn't have been there if they weren't.

But Matte knew the prejudice the humans felt toward them. Women weren't supposed to fight; they were supposed to be at home baking bread and weeping for the men who had marched into battle.

Who wept for Canton? Matte wondered. Had the rumors been true about him and the princess? Had there been an affection there that had driven the general into this senseless war for his king?

Personally, Matte believed the rumors were true. The general had the look of a man tormented with loss, a man fighting equal parts fury and conscience. She wondered if he was aware to what lengths Alfred had gone to start this war. The lives that had been needlessly, cruelly taken away.

"You going to go see if you can settle Edgar down?" Stovar moved behind her, his voice soft and low as he, too, scanned the clearing. "One of the guards at the king's tent sent word that Allora was taken last evening. He'll kill for this."

Matte took a deep bracing breath before she spoke.

"Send out a warning to our units to be prepared. I want them to stay out of his way, especially the women. Then, see if you can get word to the general to warn him as well. There's nothing I can do to ease Edgar's temper. He wants the girl, and I won't offer to take him to her."

"You won't have to. He'll order you to go in after her," Stovar warned.

"He might, but the time of our defection is drawing near. It won't be difficult to hold him off until we're gone. When he released my warriors, he signed his own death warrant." Matte pitched her voice so she had no chance of being overheard by anyone.

"King Alfred has ordered messengers sent to King Godfred in the Western Province," he informed her. "The messenger from King Sutton arrived last evening. It asked that King Alfred give him a while to think on the matter before he committed himself."

"Who is the messenger sent to Godfred?" Matte tensed. They couldn't take the chance that more soldiers would join these. The risks were too high.

"One of our own," he informed her. "He knows what to do."

Matte nodded. Her units were all well aware of her plans and the approaching betrayal of the Vultures. They had agreed far in advance what would regain them their homeland.

216

"Get ready, then. Edgar will be searching for the human women soon. I want them out of the way until he calms down. All we can do, other than that, is wait and see what happens."

Across the way, Jacquard left the general's tent and went to check on the human soldiers who had been unlucky enough to get in Edgar's way.

The humans are up to something, she thought. She wasn't certain what, and no rumors had yet to reach her, but she knew they were. Canton was too quiet—and much too unconcerned about his king's obvious insanity.

Canton was a bright man, and she couldn't see such intelligence blindly following the insane rhetoric of Cinder's followers. Yet he did nothing to deflect the king's mad ramblings and nothing to learn the basis of these odd meetings between his king and Edgar.

Oh, yes, he was up to something, she thought, watching as Jacquard slipped silently behind the group of soldiers then disappeared into the edge of the forest. She just had to figure out what.

Chapter Twenty-Two

ஓ

Meeting in the light of day was a dangerous thing, Matte thought as she hid within the shadows of the deserted aerie. Night was far better, with the shadows to shelter you and the three moons' glow barely enough to see your way. Then you had a measure of secrecy, slight though it was.

She had been surprised when the human boy approached her outside camp that morning.

"King Dearn would meet with you at half-day. In the aerie across from where first he saw you," the boy had whispered as he passed.

At first, disgruntled, foiled in her attempt to follow Lieutenant Jacquard, she had wanted to snap at the child to tell the winged king the pleasure to be found in the Seven Hells and how to get there. The knowledge that there was no way to learn why Jacquard had slipped from the camp so silently grated on her.

Then a thrill of pleasure had shot through her at the thought of seeing Dearn, this time in full light and knowing he would be coming to her as a friend and not a foe. She felt a nervous anticipation of the meeting after that. She had been so eager to rush to the aerie she had nearly forgotten the sword that was second nature to her.

She had remembered it, though, and much to Stovar's amusement had required several precious seconds when her hands fumbled with the buckle.

Now here she was, wondering where the hell he was. She was irritated with herself for that flash of excitement. Like a fledgling with her first crush, she thought in disgust, and for a mated man, no less — and a king, to boot.

Should Edgar suspect what she was doing, all she and the Bastard Breeds had dreamed of would be snatched from them. She would have to be certain to let this arrogant man understand the risks she was taking for him.

She sighted a troop of Clan warriors splitting up and flying over the area. At least they were taking precautions this time. She had done so herself before entering the aerie.

Minutes later, King Dearn soared through the valley, then circled back and headed for the aerie. Damn fine form, she thought as he moved gracefully along the thermal currents.

When he landed on the ledge, his wings folding gracefully along his back, she cursed her heart as its beat increased. *Not the man for you, Matte-girl,* she thought. *May as well forget the pumping blood because it's all for naught.*

"You made it." Dearn's teeth flashed white and clean in the dim interior. "I was afraid you wouldn't be able to."

"So was I." She crossed her arms over her breasts as she leaned against the cool stone of the wall. "Do you know the risk you took in sending that message to me? Are you trying to get me killed?"

He frowned at the irritation in her voice.

"I'm trying to save your pretty feathers," he snapped. "But to do so, I may need your help from time to time."

Her pretty feathers? It was all Matte could do to keep from preening at his words. Definitely, she was worse than a damned foolish fledgling with her first crush. This man was trouble.

"So, what kind of help do you need?"

* * * * *

Dearn tilted his head, his nostrils flaring as an intriguing scent filled them. It had to be coming from the woman in front of him.

"What?" Her baffled frown confused him, almost as much as the scent did. "I bathed before coming to you."

"What is that scent?" He moved closer, sniffing the air around her like a beast searching for prey.

"Scent?" Matte lifted her arm, her nose wrinkling. "Damned humans," she muttered in disgust. "Some silly female thing they use to cover their stink. I was in a hurry this morning and must not have realized the water girl put it in my bath."

"It's nice." He grinned at her. "It reminds me of the air after a storm. Invigorating."

"How is your mate doing?"

Dearn sighed, moving back from her, though the smile still tilted his lips ever so slightly.

"Tamora is not my mate, Matte," he told her softly, though he went no further in his explanation. "I have not mated yet. But as for your question, she is healing fine."

* * * * *

Not mated? Matte fought the surge of excitement she felt.

"Why did you ask for a meet?"

"Are you mated, Matte?" His question threw her off.

"Mated?" She frowned as she shook her head. "No, I have no need for a mate."

Now it was his turn to frown, and Matte noticed again how long and thick his lashes were and how his eyes glittered golden-brown beneath them.

"All women have a need for a mate, just as all men do." He stroked his fingers softly down her arm. "Perhaps you have a lover?"

Matte fought to still her wildly beating heart.

"I have no lover, either." She shrugged, feeling her feathers trembling behind her as she ached to touch Dearn's skin with feather tips even more sensitive than fingers and shivered at the thought.

Her eyes met his, and she knew he had seen the shudder and likely knew the cause for it. Within a second one of his wings unfurled, and a tip stroked her arm. She wanted to whimper at the sensual stroke.

"I wondered if your skin was as soft as I remembered it being," he whispered as he drew closer, staring down at her with eyes heavy-lidded, nearly drowsy in appearance. "And I see I was wrong. Your skin is much softer than I recalled."

Matte swallowed at the dark, husky sound of his voice. It sent heat racing through her body. A heat unlike any she had ever known before.

"Dearn." She gasped out his name as she moved away from that touch that so weakened her. Gods help her, but she could not handle this right now.

"Matte." He whispered her name. "Face me, at least, so I will know this thing I feel is not one-sided. I would know you feel it as well."

His voice was at the same time chiding, hopeful and firm. Matte turned back to him slowly, fighting for breath, fighting to find a semblance of control in the face of the emotions surging through her.

"You may touch me as well," he suggested in the same husky whisper.

"You are the King of the Clans." Matte shook her head. There was no future for a bastard such as she and a man who shared his blood with centuries of leaders.

"I am a man, Matte." His lips curled slightly in a smile that tempted her to caress them, just once, with her own.

"Touch me now as I touched you. At least allow me the same pleasure I gave you."

She stared up at him, seeing the dark need in his eyes, the desire to sense the same pleasure he had given her. She had never known such a need in a man, had never heard of one desiring such a touch.

Hesitantly, watching his face for the slightest sign of distaste, Matte allowed her left wing to partially unfurl and curve around her body. She drew the tip of the soft inner feathers along the bulging muscles of his bare arm.

Her breath caught as his face flushed and his eyes brightened as though with fever through his lowered lashes. The look was one of such intense pleasure, such need, that it was all she could do to keep from pleading with him to take her, to touch her as he had never touched another living woman.

"Matte." His whispered sigh of her name hung between them, as deep and arousing as a caress. "Feel what you do to me, Matte."

As his hands drew her closer, his wings enfolded her. The pleasuring touch of the softer feathers higher within his inner wing caused her to moan, a low, deep sound she had never heard from her own throat.

"No!" Matte jerked back, ignoring the surprise in his face, separating their wings and nearly ripping her heart out as she did so.

"I did not come here to be a king's plaything. I am a warrior. Would you treat one of your warriors in such a manner?" It mattered not to her that all his warriors were men.

"I must admit," he said, his voice strained, "I would not do such a thing to one of my warriors. But in my own defense, Matte, not a single one of my warriors is as lovely as are you."

They were merely pretty words, Matte assured herself, fighting to ignore the thread of heat and desire in his voice. They were merely words whispered by a man as well versed in the sensual as he was in tactical warfare. She had heard rumors.

"I assumed you had a reason to meet with me." Matte could not allow herself to be swayed by pretty words. "If there was none other than your need to play, then I will return to my camp. Otherwise, tell me why you had me risk my life to come to you."

Anger was building inside her now. Anger and hurt. He was a king, and he thought, as did all men in positions of power, that he could play where he pleased. He would learn that she was not a new toy he could amuse himself with.

"Very well." Dearn surveyed her intently, his gaze beckoning. "As for the meeting, I need your help in contacting the human general, Canton. I need to get him alone and possibly fly him to the Fortress. We have a plan, Matte, and it just might work."

He was once again the warrior. Matte saw him tamp down his desire and watched cool precision enter his expression as he brought his mind back to the business at hand. His passion, his desire, were forgotten. It pricked her female pride, but this she could understand better than she could understand any passion he had for her.

Besides, she had anticipated this. She knew the rumors of Canton and Allora's fondness for each other and had counted on their being true. Canton fought for love and vengeance, not because he believed in the war.

So she listened to the plan, inserting her own ideas as he outlined it until they finally reached a workable solution. If they could pull it off, then the war would soon end. If they didn't, they all could die in a battle so fierce that Brydon's rivers might well flow with the blood of both Winged Clans and humans before it was over.

An hour later, Dearn and his men flew from the valley and headed back to the Fortress. Within minutes, Matte's captain landed on the ledge and faced her with a question in his eyes.

Stovar had been more than nervous about this meeting, considering Edgar's sudden suspicion of everyone leaving camp. Thankfully, their excuse had been a valid one, as the sightings of Clan warriors had become more frequent.

Matte quickly outlined the plan to him and received a nod of approval at her agreement to help. Then he, too, began to sniff the air around her.

"Matte, are you wearing some scent?" He grinned at her teasingly. "I did not notice this before."

Matte felt her face flushing.

"Damn human women," she muttered. "I must have missed it in the bath this morning."

Stovar frowned. "It smells different, not like the human scents I have smelled before."

"Did you know he was unmated?" She was abruptly embarrassed as she realized the scent reminded her of Dearn.

"Of course, I did." He shrugged. "I happened to overhear it outside the human village we were watching last week. The woman was his lover, but not his mate. King Dearn has not yet found his mate."

"Why did you not tell me this?" she demanded, her arms across her chest as her eyes narrowed on him.

"I didn't know you would care, Matte." Stovar regained his grin, and Matte knew she had just revealed the interest she would have preferred to keep hidden. An interest she had never had in another man. Seven Hells, she thought, she didn't need personal desires interfering now.

"Go to Seven Hells, Stovar," she snapped, launching from the ledge and motioning her men behind her.

I should not care, she thought, feeling a prick of hurt at the thought. Bastard Breeds were not fit for the likes of King Dearn and she knew it, especially a Bastard Breed with Vulture blood.

Matte forced personal thoughts out of her mind and concentrated instead on how she was going to get the general away from camp and alone long enough to get Dearn's message to him. She had an idea. It would mean using one of Canton's own spies and was a bit of risk for her, but the end result would hopefully be worth it.

Chapter Twenty-Three

ɛᴏ

The camp was quiet. Canton stood at his tent entrance and watched the campfires burn as his men settled slowly around them to sleep. There were none of the winged bastards camped alongside these soldiers who would be dying in the battle to come.

The Vultures had flown out hours before, after snagging several of the camp women, to settle wherever they stayed at night. He had been unable to learn their location. Just as he had been unable to gather the evidence he needed that this war was being fomented by the Elitists and their winged beasts of prey. Those women would not return, just as the others had never returned. Sometimes the bodies were found, sometimes they weren't, but it was a certainty that if they were taken from camp they would not survive to the coming dawn.

Alfred had become infected by the Elitists' rhetoric years earlier, even before his marriage to Queen Demetria. That didn't explain Allora's death, though, nor did it explain why Alfred had sent for that bastard Edgar. There were too many questions, too much that his spies were unable to learn. Canton had tried to find a way to draw one of the Vulture or Bastard Breed warriors into his service but without success. Until he did, there was no chance of finding the answers he needed. And he didn't trust his king, or his king's explanation of Allora's death.

He was aware that a message of some sort had been delivered to King Alfred at first light. Edgar had nearly torn the camp apart in his rage after Alfred summoned him. The screams of the woman he had taken to his tent had continued well into the afternoon. The Vultures were hard on their

226

women, and from the looks of that one when she crawled away she would be good for no man for a very long time to come.

Canton had ordered a week before that all the women return to Cayam. Surprisingly—or perhaps it wasn't—Alfred had countermanded that order and sent for even more of them.

He did not want to be a part of the wholesale slaughter of the Winged Clans or responsible for the deaths of the soldiers who followed him. His army was outnumbered, even with the Vulture warriors who flew with them. The Winged Clans would decimate the soldiers who rode for their Fortress, and there would be no way to stop the bloodshed once it began.

Canton had tried every way he could think of to negotiate peace. He had even sent a messenger to the Fortress with a message for the king of the Winged Clans. They had found him days later on the trail, an arrow with the markings of the Eagle Clans in his heart.

There was nothing left for him to do. He could not betray his king without proof. He could not walk away from the battle and, possibly, the murderers of his beloved Allora.

How, then, should he proceed? He asked himself wearily. Surely, there was some way, some answer to end this madness.

"They're finally settling in for the night."

"'Bout time." Jacquard looked up from the maps and handwritten messages before him. "Have any of the informants shown up yet?"

"None." Canton frowned.

"Something's up." Jacquard shook his head as he lowered his voice to a whisper. "That Vulture that flew in at dawn was from the castle. I heard Edgar order him and another to stay and guard his 'treasure' as we were leaving."

"His treasure?" Canton swung his gaze to the other man. "What treasure?"

Jacquard shook his head once again, the dark strands of his long brown hair obscuring his face before he pushed it back.

"I have no idea, but thinking on it, we've had three spies die in the past year. Each one worked the west wing of the castle," he pointed out. "That makes me pretty suspicious, Canton."

"The Tower rooms," Canton murmured. "The Vultures sit atop the highest one each night. What treasure could they have there?"

Jacquard shrugged. "I've been pondering it ever since we left and can't come up with an answer."

He plowed his hands through his hair once again. Puzzles aggravated the man, and Canton knew he wouldn't rest until he found out what was going on. That was what made him such a good leader.

"Can't be gold," Jacquard continued. "Alfred keeps the gold locked in the stone room beneath the castle."

"Hard telling what those bastards consider a treasure." Canton poured two cups of comfrey tea from the metal pot sitting on top of the brazier in the middle of the tent.

"They're good for nothing." Jacquard accepted one.

"They're good for death." Canton reminded him. "I found several of the camp whores dead before we left the city. Alfred gave the Vultures leave to use them as they pleased."

Jacquard closed his eyes, breathing out deeply. Canton knew the senselessness of those deaths bothered the other man as much as it did him.

"There are reports several of the women of the city are missing. Women not known for whorishness, yet they disappear when before there were no such occurrences. I suspect the Vultures in that as well," Jacquard whispered. "Their games are such that the women would not have survived, especially those unfamiliar with the rougher passions of men."

"They are not men, they are monsters," Canton growled. "Brought here and condoned by our king. This I do not understand."

"King Alfred is crazy, Canton," Jacquard stated bluntly. "He's going to get us all killed with this fool war."

Canton could only shake his head. Surely, the man he had followed all his life knew the ramifications of what he was doing. He had thought, hoped and prayed that eventually Alfred would come to his senses and allow him to head a delegation to the Fortress, but so far he hadn't.

"Allora's death—"

"Affected him not at all," Jacquard finished for him. "He has used her death to give rein to his madness and to pull the rest of us into it. It's been coming since Queen Demetria died."

Canton sighed deeply. Jacquard was right; none had known Allora well enough to grieve for her save him. Only he had been allowed to get close to her, and only he had loved her. Alfred's paranoia after the queen's death had resulted in Allora's total withdrawal from society.

Yes, Alfred had grown worse after his daughter's death, but only in regards to his determination to destroy the Clans. There had been no signs of grief, no tears or any other sign of emotion when she died.

Canton's love for Allora was the only reason he had not objected when he learned of the Vultures' return and Alfred's plan to use them in the war.

"There's something else," Jacquard went on as he read more of the reports filtering in from spies sent out weeks before. "Did you know Alfred's personal guards, the Elitists and troops of Vultures have been murdering Clan members a family at a time? The reports on this are pretty gruesome, Canton. The Elitists and Edgar's guards began to campaign even before the Vultures arrived—and before Allora's death."

Canton accepted the handwritten page Jacquard held out to him.

"Gods!" he whispered hoarsely, raising his gaze to his lieutenant as shock speared through him. "When did this begin?"

"Months ago, near as I can date it. Alfred ordered this, knowing the consequences, Canton. I'm starting to think he wanted a war, not just to bring justice to those responsible for Allora's death."

Canton had believed Alfred when he swore that King Dearn refused to punish the Clan members involved in Allora's death. Now, he wondered. If the murders of Clan members had begun so long ago, then who knew the true reason why Allora had been killed?

He had read reports of murdered Clan members months before, but Alfred had sworn it wasn't true. *Lies*, Canton thought. He was catching Alfred in one lie after another.

The distinctive call of a woodchirp sounded quietly at the back of the tent. Canton and Jacquard moved as one, rushing for the tightly stretched fabric of the tent wall and raising the bottom of it enough for the young spy to roll inside.

"Damned Vultures," cursed the spy, a hearty youth named Sandor who worked as a castle page. "They're all over the damned forest. I 'bout never snuck through their patrols."

Canton motioned for Jacquard to check the area outside the tent for eavesdroppers. If there were that many Vultures still patrolling the woods, then there was the chance they had seen Sandor sneaking through and stationed someone to overhear the information Canton was receiving. *Hell of a way to run a war*, he thought in disgust.

"Have a seat, Sandor." He nodded to the small table and chairs. "I'll get you some comfrey."

Sandor was accepting the mug of heated brew Canton handed him when Jacquard slipped silently back into the tent.

"It's clear." He resumed his seat, waiting quietly until Canton sat as well. "The boy's right, though. Those Vultures are all over the forest. I thought they headed to wherever their nests are hours ago."

"I know why they're patrolling. They're searching," Sandor revealed in a low voice as he sipped gratefully at the energizing hot drink.

"Why?" Canton asked.

"There were visitors in the city after you marched out last evening," the boy explained. "Someone was taken from the West Tower room, and the wives and children of all the army captains were kidnapped as well."

"Alyssa and the girls?" Jacquard's strangled question burst out.

"I'm sorry, Lieutenant, but they were taken as well." Sandor shook his head. "King Dearn left a promise that they were safe for now, but he has them all. And that ain't everything," he continued. "Seems the Vultures attacked the Southern Valley the night before. The Clan troops saved the families there, but there's talk that the Vultures are now attacking any village, human and Clan alike."

"The Southerners would lie for the White Lance," Canton argued.

"I know Craete, the leader there." Sandor shook his head. "He wouldn't lie for anyone, General Canton. And he wouldn't send information unless he was certain. He says the Clans didn't start this, and that they had no part in the princess's death."

"Then who did?" Canton demanded.

"I don't know, sir, but I have a friend who saw the kidnapping from the castle. He says the women taken from the tower room looked an awful lot like Princess Allora and her maid, Mary."

Canton studied the spy closely, seeing only confusion and honesty in his eyes.

"Princess Allora is dead." Canton swallowed the cold, hard knot of suspicion forming in his throat. "We all saw her body. It had to be another."

"General, I know those who told me of this." Sandor again shook his head. "They would not lie, especially for the Winged Clans. But they swear it was Allora, and they swear it was none other than King Dearn who stole her."

It couldn't be. King Alfred would not betray him in such a way.

"Princess Allora is dead," Canton repeated. God's mercy, why was he being tempted in such a way? Had he not cradled her lifeless, torn body in his own arms? Had she not worn the gold bracelet he had given her on her seventeenth birthday?

"I only know what they're saying in Cayam, General." Sandor shrugged, watching him worriedly. "I came to you with it, just as I knew you would want me to. Regardless of who it was, they were being held in those tower rooms, I know that for a fact. I checked the area myself. The window was broke into the room, and there were several small feathers lying near the window. And all the clothes stored there were the princess's. I recognized some of the gowns. The doors were bolted from the outside, and the servants I talked to said only King Alfred or the Vultures were allowed near there. Whoever was there was pretty damned important, and someone King Alfred wanted hidden."

* * * * *

Outside the tent, Edgar raised his eyebrows in surprise as his gaze met Matte's. The general's spies had learned a lot in a damned short time. This wasn't good.

Alfred had warned Edgar that should Canton learn the truth their plans would be ruined. He knew the soldiers followed Canton, not him.

Not that Edgar blamed them. Alfred was a weak, spineless fool, and crazed in the bargain. He had always known Canton was their greatest risk. He had allowed the man to live only because of the authority he wielded over the human soldiers.

He would have to be watched. At the moment, it appeared he didn't believe the tale his spy carried about the princess, but the man was smart. He would put it all together quickly. When he did, he would have to die.

Edgar looked forward to being his executioner.

With a quick motion of his head he indicated to Matte they leave. He needed to decide what to do, and quickly. He couldn't take the chance Canton would decide to betray his king, and Alfred would never agree to the death of the general. For some reason, Canton was the one man the king seemed to have any fondness for.

* * * * *

Matte kept quiet as Edgar outlined his plans, but inside her guts were boiling with fury. Only luck could have made Edgar glance in the spy's direction as he slipped through the foliage earlier. They had already checked that area and found it empty. Now, she was going to have to move quickly if Dearn's plans were to work out.

Edgar intended the general's death and for it to appear that Clan warriors had killed him. If he succeeded there would be no halting the war until every human within the mountains had been killed. *Too many innocent lives,* she thought as her gaze met Stovar's.

"I want you to put a guard on Canton, Matte." Edgar continued to issue orders. "We'll take him out at dawn, day after tomorrow. It can be done then, for we will be camped closer to the Clans' positions. It will make it easier for our men to look like Clan warriors if the humans know we're close enough they would be able to sneak into the camps. I'll put the team together; you keep an eye on him until then, and make certain he doesn't head for the Fortress."

Matte nodded to Stovar, assigning him to watch over Canton. If they had to, they would get the man out themselves, but she preferred to let Dearn take care of this one. It would leave her men in place to fight later.

"I'll head out and see what I can learn in town, Edgar," she said as she grabbed a piece of bread and a slab of the meat left from dinner. "I should be back tomorrow afternoon. Maybe I'll know more then." And maybe she could get a message to Dearn to meet her. They would have to take Canton faster than originally planned.

"Good idea." Edgar nodded. "Report back to me when you return. And Matte..."

She paused.

"Kill the human responsible for that scent. It annoys me."

She nodded, her face flushing at the rebuke, and headed out of the cave Edgar had occupied at the base of the mountains.

Damned human women, she cursed silently. She had bathed twice in the stream outside camp and still that annoying scent persisted. To add to the problem, she was developing a rash as well, all along her arm. Not an itchy rash, but one highly sensitive. If she caught the foul creature who had slipped the poison into her water, she just might obey Edgar's orders for a change and kill them for sure.

Chapter Twenty-Four

හ

"You're making a mistake trusting them, Sire."

Brendar was the first to arrive within the large stone room Dearn had appointed for the assembly hall of his newly formed Council of Clans. Dearn turned to see the fierce scowl on his face, the light of anger in his eyes. What had happened to his general of late that all one saw was anger?

"And what mistake is that, Brendar? I thought you agreed with the idea of the Council of Clans." he said as he gazed around the room, checking that his instructions for outfitting it had been followed.

In the center of the room was a large rectangular table. Dearn's seat was at the head, and the eldest of the White Lance Spiritmen would take the seat opposite with his two advisors to the right and left. There were six other chairs along the sides for the twelve elders of the Clans, one of which would be Havar.

"The woman, Matte. You are making a mistake trusting her. What makes you believe that she has the honor of the Clans?"

"Logic," Dearn answered absently as he studied the shelves hewn into the stone walls. "That and careful investigation. I have not been sitting on my wings these past weeks, Brendar, have you not noticed? I know enough. Besides, it's not as though we have a choice at this point."

Well, they did, but it was an unacceptable choice to him.

"If she betrays us, we'll lose many of our best warriors, not to mention our king," Brendar argued. "You should either take a less dangerous role in this war or bow out entirely. Our people need you here anyway."

Dearn drew in a deep, steady breath. He was a warrior; he refused to sit on his throne and hope for the best while his men were out there fighting. He had thought Brendar not only knew this but also understood it.

"If she betrays us, then she loses forever the very thing she has come to this land to attain—a place for her people. I trust her because I know what she wants, and I know how she has dealt with her own men and the humans she has encountered. I don't believe she will betray us."

"She bargained with the Elitists and King Alfred to come here. She lied to them. What makes you think she does not lie to you?" Brendar persisted.

Dearn counseled himself to patience once again. It seemed his life revolved around fighting for patience to deal with men who had once been perfectly reasonable.

"She did what she had to, to get here." He felt as though he were repeating information to a child. "She has done what she could to lessen the number of deaths without endangering her own men. She is a commander, and she has led just as I would have myself in the same situation. I cannot overlook that, Brendar. Her people deserve the land in return for what they have already done for us, not to mention what she plans to do before the war's end."

"She is a Bastard Breed with Vulture blood. Their evil is a part of her."

Dearn began to heat with fury at Brendar's stubbornness.

"She also carries the blood of the Eagle Clans, just as Allora carries the White Lance as well as the blood of the humans. Clan blood always flows true, Brendar, it has been so since the beginning, and this you well know. I will hear no more of it."

Clan blood flowed true and with honor. The Clans had no explanation as to why, but it was well known that any who carried Clan blood had a measure of honor that would always ensure their word was true. Dearn trusted in that, and he would trust in Matte. He only wished his ancestor had thought of this centuries before.

"You are thinking with your passions, not your head, Sire," Brendar challenged. "You desire the woman, so you must believe in her."

"End of argument." Dearn glared at his general, hoping the look was dark enough to shut him up. He feared if Brendar did not stop the temper he was keeping under careful control could well erupt.

Brendar's lips thinned, and he could see the arguments rolling within the man's eyes.

"What in Seven Hells is your problem with this, Brendar?" he finally burst out in exasperation. "You have been either surly or angry for weeks now. What incites you so? And do not give me that featherbrained excuse of the dangers to my person or your distrust of Matte. Give me the truth, for a change."

Brendar ran his fingers though his hair in frustration.

"I worry, Dearn. There is much that could happen."

Dearn saw the lie in his eyes and in the guilty cast to his expression.

"Is this about Tamora, Brendar?" he asked.

"Tamora is being hurt," Brendar said, his teeth gritting until his jaw bunched with tension. "But it is not about Tamora."

"How is Tamora being hurt?" Dearn frowned. "Who would dare to hurt her?"

This was news to him, for he understood well the temperamental nature of the woman who had been his mistress. It would not be easy to hurt her because it was extremely hard to even find a way to best her with words. Dearn had often enjoyed the debates that raged between them, so he knew her feelings were not so tender as to be easily damaged. This left the matter of a physical hurt, and if that were so, then he would know now who was responsible and he would deal with it.

"You are." Brendar's words had Dearn staring at him in shock. "Your association with this Bastard Breed bitch will do nothing but—"

The accusation was cut off by the arrival of Dearn's dagger at his throat. Dearn didn't know who was more surprised, him by the offense he had taken at the insult to Matte or Brendar at the blade suddenly threatening his life.

"Speak of her again in such a way and I will challenge you for her honor, Brendar," Dearn threatened in a low snarl. "You would not insult one of the warriors under your command in such a way, and neither shall you insult her."

The blade lifted a fraction, enough for Brendar to nod very slowly, very shallowly. Dearn withdrew the dagger, watching his general intently, and replaced it at his waist.

"Look how you defend her, Dearn. She is more to you than just another warrior," Brendar accused him. "And look at Tamora, who sits here at this castle and awaits you each day, pacing the floor in fear for you. You are playing with her, and it is not fair."

Brendar's body trembled now with fury and the offense of having his king's dagger at his throat. Dearn could feel the slight tremor his equal rage caused in his own body. He fought to tamp it, and to once again find the patience he needed to deal with this subject.

"And it is not your business, as I have told you once already. Cease your demands where Tamora is concerned. When I find the chance, I will speak with her. Until then, either declare yourself to her or stay the hell out of my way," he ordered.

"Declare myself?" Brendar looked back at him in shock. "I would not declare myself to her. She is no woman of mine. I merely resent the insult to her."

Dearn smirked. He couldn't help it. Suddenly, Brendar's anger and his snide comments were making sense. He wanted Tamora himself. Dearn wondered why he hadn't seen it before.

"There is no insult to her." He shrugged, keeping his suspicions to himself. "Just as there will be none to Matte. When I have made my decision between the two, then will I state my intentions, and not until."

Brendar took a deep, controlling breath. "Made your decision between the two?" The words dragged from his tight jaw.

"Yes." Dearn nodded, fighting the grin he could feel at his lips. "When I decide which one shall share my bed. Or perhaps I will keep them both. My grandfather had four mistresses before he mated."

Brendar's fists clenched, and the struggle to keep his hands from Dearn's throat was clearly written on his face. Dearn ignored the threat, knowing it now for what it was. This jealousy of Brendar's he could understand, for he knew he would feel it himself if he had to deal with a competitor for Matte's affections.

Not that he wasn't certain he didn't have to, but he consoled himself that he had a better than average chance of winning, considering the effect his touch had on her.

"I would have thought better of you, Sire." Sarcasm lay thick and heavy in the warrior's voice.

Dearn shrugged.

"I am merely a man, and both are beautiful women. I would see which I like better before I choose, that is all," he repeated with feigned innocence. "Until I do so, leave me in peace. I have other matters to attend to besides my passions right now."

Brendar's wings vibrated furiously. The soft rustle seemed magnified in the dimensions of the cavern. No doubt, the warrior would have spoken again, but a loud knock sounded at the council chamber doors.

"Come in," Dearn called, though he did not take his eyes from his general.

"Sire, a message has come for you." One of the castle servants stood at the doorway. Dearn's eyes narrowed. He remembered the girl being the one who had brought his dinner, the same one who had caused such confusion in him. Her wings, though close enough in Eagle color to pass general detection, were not close enough to escape his notice now that he recognized the muted tones.

"Come in, Lenora, and close the door behind you." He observed the slight narrowing of the girl's eyes at his demanding tone. He'd wager she didn't take orders worth a damn under normal circumstances. What made her think she could serve others in his castle when taking such orders set her back up quicker than a poisonous mountain slither could strike?

She wore the loose white pants and tunic of a serving girl. He had seen her wearing the simple dresses the servants wore as well. He suspected they felt a shade different than did warrior's leathers on her body. A body he could easily tell was well-conditioned and used to more activity than trudging up and down castle stairs.

"What message has your commander sent me, Lenore?" he asked her.

"A meeting..." The girl's voice trailed off and her face paled alarmingly.

In disgust, Dearn reminded himself to talk to Matte about conditioned training against such reactions. When working as a spy, one must be better prepared for any eventuality.

Silence reigned now, and Dearn glanced at Brendar in time to see his eyes narrow as he recognized the unusual coloration of her wings, eyes and hair. Brendar would have grabbed her had Dearn not stopped him with an arm across his chest.

Likely it was a good thing he did, for he had seen the smooth tensing of muscle beneath the light clothing and suspected she would have beaten the general, more from surprise that a woman would fight him than from her excellent training.

"Did your commander order you to keep your identity hidden?" Dearn asked her.

Lenore swallowed, then straightened her shoulders and stood straight before him.

"My commander gave me no such orders, save those of serving here and watching out for your safety. I was not commanded either way about informing you who I was." Her voice was tight, self-disgust evident in her tone. Dearn would have expected no less from a warrior who had been caught so handily.

"You were told I have met with your commander already?" At her nod, he continued. "Why, then, did you not come to me?"

Lenora licked her lips then took a deep breath.

"I would have waited, by my own counsel, until the others of my Clan had openly joined you." She glanced at Brendar. "Many of your warriors doubt our honor, Sire. It would have jeopardized my own mission and interfered with help I could have provided at a later time if it were needed."

Dearn nodded shortly, understanding the woman's reasoning.

"You will continue as you are, but you will now report to me as well. Be careful of the few humans who still come and go within the Fortress. There are several we suspect as spies, and I would not have your commander endangered should they recognize you as one of her warriors."

Lenora smiled without amusement.

"There is little danger of that happening. Few humans understand the coloration of the wings, but I will do as you direct." She nodded.

"Very well. What is the message your commander sent?"

"Changes have occurred. She requests that you meet with her immediately within the same aerie to discuss this. Will that be possible?"

Changes occurring could mean nothing good, Dearn thought in alarm.

"I am heading out within the hour." He nodded abruptly then turned to Brendar. "Arrange for a troop to accompany me. We fly out as soon as they are ready."

"You are willing to trust one who has already betrayed you?" Brendar whispered the words, but the woman easily heard.

"I have betrayed no one, General Brendar," she informed him curtly.

"Neither were you honest," he accused her. "It amounts to the same thing."

"Does it now?" she asked him in a soft voice, tilting her head. "Does this then mean you meant your words last full moons when you swore devotion to me, should I share your aerie? If it does mean this, I shall, of course, reconsider my answer."

Dearn covered a grin as Brendar's mouth dropped open in shock.

"I was not myself. I had too much wine that night," he gritted out. "And I did not promise you devotion."

"Then you were dishonest?" She did not argue, but Dearn knew it was merely to save his general further embarrassment.

Brendar was silent as he attempted to stare the woman down, his expression coldly aloof.

"Point made, Lenora, and embarrassing the man who may lead you later is not a good idea," Dearn warned her as he turned to the general. "Go now, Brendar, arrange the troop so we may leave. I will be out as soon as I've changed."

Brendar nodded then left the room quickly. There was no longer time to argue, disagree or remember personal conflicts, and Dearn knew Brendar understood this as well.

"Lenora, is there someone you pass your messages to outside the Fortress?"

She nodded.

"Then go; tell Matte I will be there as soon as I can."

Lenore rushed quickly then from the castle and Dearn left behind her, jogging to his room. Something must have happened, something that affected the plans they had made days before. He changed into his warrior's leathers, strapped on his weapons and hurried to the courtyard and the troop already waiting for him. At his order they were in the air and flying fiercely for the aerie.

He worried over the reason for the meeting, but Dearn knew in his gut that his need to see Matte overrode every other concern. Soon, he would touch her again, hold her close and feel the pleasure of her body. Next time, he would not heed her objections so easily but would bestow upon those perfect lips the possessing kiss he had longed to give her since last he had touched her.

Dearn was well aware his priorities were in danger of being turned around where this woman was involved. He should be more concerned with the information than he was with seeing her. The warrior part of him was, but the part of him that was male, the part of him that burned for his woman, rejoiced simply in anticipation of the meeting to come.

Chapter Twenty-Five

ℜ

Dearn landed on the ledge of the aerie nearly an hour later, not certain what to expect. Some distant part of his warrior's pride was outraged that he should be so excited to see the woman. He should be aloof, distant, as he was in other matters of the heart.

The three moons shed gentle light into the aerie and softened Matte's stern features as she stepped from the shadows. Her body moved with a sensual grace that nearly took his breath and hardened every muscle in his body.

Her unique beauty was softer in this light, but the dark loneliness in her eyes seemed more defined. He wished he could wipe the loneliness from her, draw her into his arms and replace it instead with passion.

"We have a problem."

He liked the way she jumped straight to the point. In the back of his mind was the question whether or not she would be just as straightforward in bed.

"The spy made it to Canton with the information we planted," she continued, unaware of the direction of his thoughts. "But Edgar overheard the information being relayed."

Instantly, Dearn's ardor cooled, though only marginally.

"And Edgar's reaction was?" He fought the effect of her intriguing scent. This attraction was ill timed; he would do well to keep his mind on the battle ahead.

"He's going to kill Canton at dawn, day after next, using my men to take him and drop him from the sky so the humans will believe Clan warriors were responsible." Her tone was filled with disgust.

"Gods damn them," he cursed. Just as they had fooled the humans with Princess Allora's faked death, they thought to fool them once again with Canton's assassination.

"We'll have to move sooner than we planned," he decided. "First light. Can you get Canton to the stream beyond the camp limits? I can have my men waiting there, and we'll fly him to the Fortress."

The mists of the valleys would be thick then, making vision severely limited between the mountains. It would be the best time to take the human general.

"Edgar's men are patrolling the forest pretty heavily," she warned, frowning as she considered their options. "Perhaps your troops could position themselves farther along the river in the boulders at the base of the mountain. I can be certain the patrols there are otherwise occupied."

"You get him there and we will take him." Dearn nodded. "I'll have my men in place before dawn."

He estimated the time he would need to get the required troops together and place them. He should have hours to spare.

"Excellent." Matte took a deep breath. "I'll maneuver the patrols and, hopefully, you will get in and back out without being sighted."

Dearn nodded, noticing how nervous she appeared. Surely she was used to men appreciating her slender curves and the well-honed quality of her muscles.

"What are you looking at?" she finally snapped as his eyes strayed to her thighs.

"You." He grinned as her mouth fell open and her eyes widened.

"Me?" Incredulity filled her expression. "For what purpose would you look at me in such a way? It is my face you should be watching, not my thighs."

"Ahh, but you have such lovely thighs," he whispered. "They are quite distracting, Matte."

She blinked at him rather vaguely, processing his tone of voice and the way he looked at her. It was as though he could feel her mind working, trying to interpret this new development.

"I haven't time for this." She inhaled roughly, and Dearn noticed the slight trembling of her feathers in the dim wash of moonlight. She might not want to admit it, but her emotions were as attuned to him as his were to her. An excellent development, as far as he was concerned.

"Haven't the time for what, Matte?" He ran the backs of his fingers down her arm. Her skin was softer than any silk he had ever touched. Gods, how he longed to lie with her, to feel her body pressing against his own.

Matte jumped back, her breath expelling in a surprised gasp at his touch. Dearn frowned, wondering if he had somehow misread the interest he had seen in her eyes earlier. Then he hid a smile as he watched her flush a becoming shade of pink.

No, he thought, he had not misread the interest there. She wanted him, just as deeply, just as hotly, as he wanted her. She just wasn't as willing to admit it.

"I don't have time for a romp." Her voice was angry and filled with confusion. "I need to get back to camp and get this damn thing started. You should know better than this, King Dearn. Now is not the time for play."

He wondered if this woman had ever had time to play in her life. It was as though his soft teasing, his gentle laughter, confused her more than King Alfred's insanity did.

"Matte." He gripped her arm as she made to move past him, her body quivering with an excess of emotion. She turned her head to stare up at him angrily, and he lowered his until his lips were a breath from hers. He wanted to kiss her with a depth of need unlike any he had ever known before.

"When I decide to romp," he whispered, "I promise you I will choose a time and a place more appropriate. Until then, all I have on my mind is a taste."

His lips covered hers softly, an experiment, a testing of the flavor and texture of her skin. Instead, like a beggar confronting a banquet, he became a man possessed. The taste of her, the scent of her skin, the soft lips, hesitant, wary beneath his own, had hunger pulsing through his body.

Dearn's wings flared as his body began to harden in arousal, and before he actually meant to do it he had them wrapped snugly around her in the instinctive, primal position of the mating ritual as his lips slanted possessively over hers. His tongue pushed demandingly past the soft petals as he deepened the kiss, the taste, he was suddenly craving.

He heard the hitch of her voice. A whimper of surrender to the heat, then shyly, her tongue touched his, twining with it. Gods, she tasted so good. His hands clenched on her hips; his wings tightened around her, the sensitive, living feathers emerging, stroking over her, causing them both to moan into the kiss, to reach for more.

Dearn was unaware he had locked his wings around her. All he knew, all he could understand, was that he had to have her closer, he had to kiss her deeper, he had to bind her to him in a way that would forever brand her as his own.

His hands moved to her buttocks as he backed her slowly against the wall. He lifted her just slightly, holding her steady, bringing her closer until he could press the heat of his need close, firm, between the thighs of the woman who was burning him alive.

"Oh, gods!" Her strangled cry as his lips left hers to travel to her neck caused his shaft to clench in painful need. He thrust against her, holding her steady, feeling a flare of lust unlike anything he had ever known as she wrapped her legs around his thighs, her nails biting into his back as her arms went around his shoulders.

Her wings shuddered beneath his, the sensitive feathers ruffling, merging with his, sharing the delicately scented oils unique to each, merging into a scent that would mark her forever.

She accepted him. He groaned harshly in relief, feeling the inner feathers of his wings as they parted and slipped slowly past the outer feathers of his mate to the sensitive ones beneath. Dearn knew he was playing a dangerous game here. The mating rituals were old, and their instinctive processes impossible to deny after they reached a certain point. That point was quickly approaching as his blood began to boil in his veins and pool in his groin, hardening him to a point nearly agonizing in its pleasure.

"Again." Her cry drew a moan from him.

He stared into her dark, hungry eyes. His hand was beneath her breast now, and he could no longer resist loosening those laces. He felt her breath halt for a long second as he parted the material, his hand easing in to cover firm, hot skin. She cried out then, her head falling back as she arched to his touch.

He couldn't resist her taste any longer. His lips nibbled at hers, his tongue stroked in a slow demand that she eagerly accepted. Mating, their groans echoed through the aerie as they strained into the kiss.

Long moments later he tore his mouth from hers, staring down at her, fighting the pulsating demand of his body that he take her here, now. She stared up him, her eyes dark and glazed in the dim light of the moon, her body trembling against him as he caressed the peak of her breast, as his lips lingered a mere breath from hers.

Just one more, he screamed silently, closing the gap, his tongue plunging past them to mingle with hers as he pressed her tighter against the wall. He had to stop. He was at the limits of his control when her hot kisses slid down his throat, her teeth nipping his skin. She pulled at his vest as she fought to be closer. Gods, it was killing him, but now was not the time to complete the mating process.

The feathers of their wings were deeply entwined now. Matte's flared beneath his; the dazzling, haunting scent of passion enfolded them, drugging them with their mutual desire. They had to separate, but he anticipated the barren sense of loss that would result even before he did so.

She stared up at him, her eyes wide and dazed, her lips moist and kiss-swollen, her face flushed with passion. Confused pleasure filled her expression, her eyes dark with it but also with surprise at the depth of desire between them.

Slowly, excruciatingly, Dearn moved back from her, feeling the clasp of her knees loosen, her legs lower to take her own weight. Making certain she could stand on her own, he took his hand from her breast and withdrew his feathers until they disengaged from hers. She moaned with pleasure as the wings rasped against each other, and he closed his eyes in torment. The damage had been done; there was no backing out now. He might as well enjoy the touch while he could.

"A taste," he whispered, aware that he was still breathing harshly. "And your taste tempts me to continue, Matte."

"Dearn..." Her voice was breathless, and he became aware of the effect the small shudders in his wings had on the woman's sensitive skin as they completed their journey back to his own body.

Matte was right—they didn't have the time. And this new development was more than he wanted to handle at the moment himself.

"We have to talk about this, Matte," he told her softly, sighing inwardly at the conversations mounting up that would have to be dealt with. "Soon."

"Talk about what?"

She shivered as his wings made a final caress against her arms. Receptive, she understood the meaning of the clasp and the caress. Damn, he just didn't have the time he needed. She was his, and that knowledge lent an added worry to him as he accepted the fact that he would have to let her go for now.

"You know what." His voice was harsher than he intended. "You will be here tomorrow night, same time. I will deal with Canton then fly right here. We will discuss this then."

She shook her head sharply.

"Only if I can get away safely." She ran her fingers through her hair as she inhaled deeply. "I have to go now."

She didn't give him time to protest but flew from the ledge with a sharp signal to her men to follow.

Dearn took a deep breath, shook his head to clear it. The taste and scent of her still lingered on his skin, in his wings. He inhaled a deep breath, closing his eyes to savor it. Opening them long moments later he mentally berated himself for the momentary weakness, then left the aerie as well and headed back to the Fortress. There were plans to be made, and only a few hours left in which to make them.

He fought to get his desire under control, this new concern in perspective. The time would come soon to complete the mating. Then, he would show his new mate the pleasures he so longed to give her this night.

Chapter Twenty-Six

ఉౕ

It was barely dawn when General Canton made his way to the stream outside camp. He was tired, frustrated and not at all certain of the events that were progressing much too rapidly.

Alfred seemed to be slipping further every day into insanity. The previous evening Canton had tried to persuade him to delay the march into the Fortress until he could gain more information from his spies concerning the numbers they would be up against. The king became enraged, preaching from his makeshift throne of the gods' displeasure with Canton's continued questioning of his king's decisions, raging that the demon Clans must now pay for their betrayal of the gods and the people. He had finished by sneering with contempt at Canton and charging him with betraying the memory of the one they both loved, the Princess Allora.

It was enough to drive a sane man to desert, Canton thought, and he had to admit that was something he was giving careful thought to. He could not, in good conscience, continue to lead his men into a certain bloodbath. Besides, his heart was growing too heavy with his grief to continue seeking vengeance where he was no longer certain of guilt.

Allora's death was too much for him to bear. The past months had been agonizing as he sought a way to get through each day without her gentle presence. It had been hard enough before, with Alfred standing guard over each of their meetings. Now, denied even that small contact with her, he felt bereft.

When Alfred declared war against the Clans Canton hadn't been certain it was the wisest course of action, but he went along with it, hoping to find vengeance for Allora. He was even more uncertain now. The added complication of the Vultures was making his mind reel. Edgar was an arrogant, savage bastard whose sense of superiority never failed to set his teeth on edge. He cursed the day Alfred had brought the Vulture breeds from their exile, just as he cursed the Clan members responsible for Allora's death.

Bringing her killers to justice had been Canton's one thought, but now that he knew how King Alfred had been taking his own vengeance, he suddenly wasn't so certain they were doing what was right. Was it fair to punish a whole race for the actions of a few? Allora would have been horrified by this, and by his own part in it.

The reports of the kidnapping from the castle had only added to his turmoil. He remembered the body he held close in his arms, so broken, so torn that even her face was unrecognizable. But the clothing was; the bracelet was. Her long, white-blonde hair. Or had it been hers? He couldn't remember now, although he had thought that memory was forever entrenched in his mind. Had the woman he held been as tall as Allora? Had her skin been as soft? Why did it seem now that it was not?

If he were to believe it had all been a deception, then he would have to believe that his king, the man he followed all his life, had betrayed his own daughter. Lied to his people. Deceived—the reports sifting through from his spies now said little else. What would one more betrayal matter to such a man as King Alfred?

This was why he was nearly a mile from camp, following the written instructions he had found sticking out from beneath the tent wall earlier. Someone else evidently felt the same.

The danger of such a meeting passed fleetingly through his mind. The sun was barely up, and the mountain mists still lay heavily over the land. *A dangerous time to go seeking an anonymous informant,* he thought. Dangerous or not, he was there, his curiosity aroused by the reference to Allora.

As he neared the required location, Canton knelt by the stream, splashing his face with cold water then taking a long drink. When he raised his head, he jumped back, pulling his sword from its scabbard. It seemed his luck had run dry.

The King of the Clans, for Canton recognized him, did not appear at all anxious for battle. He stood across the stream with arms crossed over his broad chest, his golden wings folded placidly against his back while the mists rose around him as if they were in an otherworldly dream. He had heard enough stories of King Dearn's unusual coloring, and his quiet ways. How such a king could allow his people to begin a war as bloody as this one, Canton had no idea.

The wings rose from between his shoulders to the back of his head before arching gracefully over. They extended nearly to his feet in the shades of russet, brown and amber of the Eagle Clan. Other than the feathers, he looked as arrogant and strong as any other warrior Canton had ever seen. Perhaps even more so.

"Draw your sword, warrior," Canton challenged, his voice fierce.

The king remained silent for a long moment, unmoving, his amber eyes puzzled.

"When I was a fledgling warrior," he said at last, "my father began my training with a stern lecture on patience." A reminiscent smile crossed his face. "Each time I forgot my patience, my father would reinforce that lesson in sometimes painful, sometimes embarrassing ways to show me how I erred. I have come to realize, in these few brief weeks, that fathers of human warriors must not do this."

Canton shook his head, wondering what the man meant. Did he think patience would save him?

"We can debate training methods in the Seven Hells if you like," Canton sneered. "You'll not find me as easy to kill as Princess Allora was."

"Does love make all humans so gullible?" Dearn wondered, his expression becoming sober. "Did you see the body of your murdered princess, General Canton? Did you see her face, or anything other than the color of her hair and the fabric of her clothing?"

"There was nothing left to see, as you well know." Canton's voice was harsh with the fury that engulfed him. He stepped a pace closer to the stream, gauging its width and the best place to land, should he attempt to jump it.

"And if I were to tell you your princess lives?" the king asked him softly.

Canton stood still now, reminding himself that fury was weakening, logic and calm were required to defeat an enemy. Yet, such obvious baiting from the man standing before him was nearly more than he could stand.

"I would say you lie." His voice was low as he fought to ignore the raw, bleeding wound her death had left.

Dearn sighed and regarded him for long silent minutes.

"I tell you now, Canton, Princess Allora's death was a lie used to incite the people against us. If you wish to see her, then come with me. I will take you to her."

"Come with you?" Canton mocked, sneering his contempt to keep from pleading for assurances. "So you can drop me from the sky as you did Allora?"

The winged warrior shook his head as he smiled softly in sympathy.

"So she may assure you it wasn't you and your kiss which frightened her on a moonlit night. It was the passion you inspired, and the fear that you would learn her secrets."

Canton's arm weakened. His sword lowered and he could do nothing but stare across the stream in shock.

How well he remembered that night, the way Allora had torn from his arms and rushed back into the castle. It was the last time he had seen her, spoken to her. He had been haunted with that memory and the fear he believed he had caused her.

"How can she live?" he whispered in torment. "We would have seen her."

"Your mad king has kept her locked away within a tower that none can access except him," Dearn told him. "The few castle servants she managed to get messages to were found and killed before they could reach you. King Alfred has carefully kept her away from you, knowing that only your fury and your strength would give him a chance to defeat the Clans."

The messenger's words from the night before came back to him. The two women were said to bear a very close resemblance to Princess Allora and her maid, Mary. Canton had been unable to believe such a tale, but he could find no other explanation for the message brought to him now. At the time, he had dismissed it as a mistake. What he had just heard, though, now combined with it to increase his doubts.

Could it be true? he wondered. Could Allora truly be alive and awaiting him within the Fortress of the Clans? None other knew of the night he had revealed the truth of his passion against the softness of her lips. Otherwise, King Alfred would have surely confronted him over the indiscretion.

"She is well?" he asked, slowly sheathing his sword and watching the Clan king as hope spilled over in his heart.

"She is very well." Dearn nodded. "We have her at the Fortress now, awaiting your arrival. Will you disappoint her?"

"I have strived to do nothing but earn her approval for years." A thread of frustration ran through the words as he sighed deeply. "I will come to the Fortress."

Dearn shook his head. "There is no time for you to wait and come on your own, Canton. Edgar has ordered your death for dawn tomorrow. We must leave this valley and head for the Fortress, or we run the risk of being sighted. Your time here is over, until the Vultures are dead."

"Ordered my death? They would do no such thing without Alfred's consent," Canton scoffed.

"It will be made to appear that warriors of the Eagle Clan did the deed, just as they used the warriors of the Bastard Breed Clan to drop a girl already dead from the sky and convince you she was Allora. They will make you a martyr and ensure that the human soldiers will fight, regardless of the cost."

Canton knew Edgar had little regard for him and had expected the Vulture would try to kill him sooner or later. He had assumed he would wait until the battle was won, though, if it could have been won.

"So, I must be flown." Canton sighed heavily now, looking into the sky and gauging the distance he would fall should this king deceive him.

"You will be safe as a babe in his mother's arms." Humor was in the voice and the oddly-colored eyes of the man before him.

Canton shook his head, sighing again.

"I hope so, because I'd hate to be wrong about this. It looks like a hell of a drop, Your Highness."

Dearn's eyes widened.

"You knew? How?"

"Even this low in the valley we hear tales of King Dearn and his arrogance. Not to mention the odd gold color of his eyes." Canton was rather pleased he had surprised the man. He had a feeling under normal circumstances that would be hard to do.

"Rumors." Dearn shook his head. "I have a feeling that is the only grain of truth in all of them." He raised his hand and beckoned his men forward. "Now, brace yourself while two of my strongest collect you. I have a feeling you're heavier than one of them could manage alone."

Canton chuckled. He was as tall as the king and in superb fighting shape. Then, he was swiftly fastened into a padded leather body harness firmly attached to the middle of a sturdy pole. After the last strap was secured, they handed him the attached pole.

"Hold it over your head," Dearn told him.

When he did, two warriors hovering overhead swooped down and grasped each end, then lifted him into the air. He hung on, supporting some of his weight so he could breathe. *But what if,* he thought, *they grow tired and fall from the sky themselves?*

* * * * *

Dearn watched the warriors lift Canton into the air then, with a mighty push of his wings, began his own ascent. He was cautiously optimistic they would at least clear the valley floor before they were seen. He had men waiting past that point so that, should they be sighted, those carrying Canton could continue to the Fortress while the rest provided cover.

Within minutes they met up with the other twenty Clan warriors and were winging swiftly back into the mountains. However, they had no more than cleared the first mountain when they heard the excited call of a Vulture scout. Evidently, Matte hadn't been able to take them all out.

"Cover Canton's retreat," Dearn called out to Brendar as he aligned with the force that would halt the Vultures if they came within killing distance of the human general.

"Like Seven Hells, Sire." Brendar moved to his side. "You cover him. Get back from the fighting before you get yourself killed."

There were times, Dearn reflected, when being a king could be a drawback. Everyone kept trying to protect you even when you didn't need it.

"I order you to retreat, Brendar," he commanded.

"Your orders do not count when your life is in danger, Sire," Brendar retorted, checking once to be certain the Vultures were still far enough behind for safety. "Every man here will defend your life before that of the human. I would advise you to fly ahead before you cause his death."

Dearn glanced behind him; the Vultures were gaining on them swiftly. He motioned for the troops to fly harder—if they wouldn't let him fight then he would damned well see if they couldn't outrun their attackers first. If worse came to worst, he knew he could trust those who carried the general to continue on.

A flight on the edge of dawn through the dangerous cliffs and mountain passes was not advisable at the speed they were going. It was unknown territory for the Vultures, though, and Dearn hoped this lack of knowledge would slow them down enough to give his troops the edge for maintaining a safe distance.

Then again, maybe not enough of an edge, he thought as he looked behind him to discover he could now see the bloodthirsty expressions of the Vultures following them.

"They're gaining. Brace and fight!" he called out to the warriors carrying the general. "Get him to the Fortress. We'll cover your retreat."

The two men began to fly harder, balancing the human between them as they fought for wing space and speed on the air currents flowing through the passes.

"Okay, Brendar, we fight together," Dearn said as they drew their swords and circled to face the approaching enemy.

Chapter Twenty-Seven

ɞ

"No!" The harsh exclamation was rife with fear as Matte watched the Vulture troops launch into the sky. She had been too late, too slow in weeding out the scouts within the forest, and now Dearn and his men were in danger.

There had been only one sentry left. Only one of the Cinder-damned whoresons, and he had spotted the Clan troop and called the alarm before she could get to him. *Gods take him,* she cursed.

Body braced, she started to spread her wings to fly in aid but was caught securely from behind before she could. Twisting, turning, she fought the hard hands holding her down, determined to kill the man daring enough to keep her from battle.

"No, Matte!" Stovar's voice halted her frantic struggles as he kept her grounded. "You fly up there to help them, and Edgar will have the rest of our Clan killed before they know what's happened."

He was right. By the gods, he was right, but she had to do something. She couldn't stand idle while they killed Dearn.

Matte fought for breath, for sanity. She had to think of something, and quickly. Dearn was outmanned, his troop handicapped by the need to get Canton to the Fortress. He would sacrifice himself before he allowed those warriors carrying the human general to be harmed.

"Get ready. Give me ten minutes to set the signal, and if it looks like they're losing then we'll switch sides now. But don't fly into that mess alone." Stovar shook her as he spoke, his hazel eyes intent, commanding. She stared up at him, fear for Dearn filling her heart. "Do you hear me, Matte?"

She was losing control. She felt it, and she knew Stovar saw it as well. By the gods, what was wrong with her?

"I understand. Go," she ordered, taking a deep breath to calm herself. "Have the men ready to fly if they see us heading into the fight. Tell them to stay low—I don't want it known they were not fighting during this."

That would cause as much damage as being seen fighting for the enemy. Edgar would have the warriors killed without question—and her, as well. He would not tolerate even a whiff of disloyalty within his camp.

Matte watched anxiously as the Vultures grew closer to Dearn and the remaining eighteen members of the Clan troop. Eighteen against almost three dozen, and there would be many more if this battle wasn't over quickly. It wouldn't take long for another sentry or another warrior to see or hear the battle and head for the camp to alert the rest of Edgar's men.

Turning, she looked around frantically until she finally caught sight of two of her men watching from the trees farther away. With a quick, silent signal she sent them on a stealth course that would parallel the team flying the human to the Fortress.

She turned back to check the distance between the Vulture and Clan Troops. *Gods, too close*, she thought. They would never make it. They would have to turn and fight, and she knew every Vulture in Edgar's troop would target Dearn.

"I can't just stand here and do nothing," Matte whispered long minutes later as Stovar moved into the tree beside her. Her hands itched to release the bolt in her crossbow. She was a good shot; she could hit one of the attackers easily from the right location.

The Clan Troop had turned to fight, to protect the team moving steadily toward the Fortress with Canton. Among them was Dearn. Foolishness, Matte raged. The king should never, ever be in the front lines. It was not how battles were fought.

He was as inconsiderate as Thorne, her brother. Always rushing in where he was not supposed to be and making the lives of his commanders and captains a Seven Hells' experience. She would have to be certain to berate him over this when next she saw him. If she ever saw him alive again, that was.

"Patience, Matte. Remember what your mother taught you. Those Clan warriors are better trained and fiercer than Edgar's men. They may not need our help," Stovar reminded her

Matte heard him, but the fear pumping through her body demanded that she act, and that she act now. The Vulture warriors were close, and they were larger than Dearn's men, their fighting skills better honed by their battles with the scourge of that other continent.

"They are outnumbered." Her fingers clenched around the sturdy limb beside her. "The Vultures are bigger —"

"Means nothing," he assured her. "The Clans are ready for them. Give them a chance before we give ourselves away. It's better to surprise Edgar with our defection during the final battle than to play our hand now."

Once again, he was right. But, damn, doing nothing was killing her.

Look at him, Matte thought as she watched Dearn extend his wings, his big body braced for battle. His golden hair was haloed in the rays of the sun, and she could see the fierce, intent scowl on his face as he called out orders to his warriors. He was magnificent. His grace and bearing were a sight to behold...

She cursed. The Vultures would see this as well and head straight for him. What a coup the death of the Clans' king would be.

As she stood, her mind reeling, she heard Stovar sniffing behind her.

"Stop that." She turned on him furiously. "If you like the damned scent so well, go visit the human who makes it."

A brief, mocking smile crossed his lips.

"No human makes that scent, Matte," he muttered.

"Of course, they do," she scoffed, checking the area as a plan began to form in her mind. "Come on."

She jumped down, staying close beneath the sheltering branches of the trees as she flew for the top of the mountain directly beneath the fighting. She had an idea, and if done properly, and with a bit of luck, it just might work in Dearn's favor.

"Where in Seven Hells are you going?"

Arriving at the place she had sighted, Matte flew to one of the large trees growing there. Beneath the thick branches she landed and looked up at where the fighting had begun. Just as she had feared, the better part of the warriors were fighting to get to Dearn.

"Give me room," she ordered Stovar as she jerked the crossbow from her back and reloaded it, elbowing him to the side as he crowded against her.

"What are you doing?" He moved back, watching the sky anxiously. "Dammit, Matte, you'll get us all killed with this obsession you have for Dearn."

Matte knew they were too close to the fighting, and that the chances of being sighted were stronger here, but she couldn't hazard Dearn's life. Besides, if this worked, there would be no Vulture warriors of that troop left to carry tales to Edgar.

"I'm only evening the odds," she said as she took careful aim and pulled the small trigger. "Stop whining and help me out here, would you?"

Less than a second later the bolt found its mark in the wing of the Vulture moving stealthily up behind Dearn. With a vicious cry he began falling, unable to right himself or break the momentum he gathered as he plummeted to the ground. Matte smiled grimly as she reloaded and shot another of the deadly missiles toward the swarm of black wings. She dove back under the sheltering leaves. She couldn't take too many chances — if the Vultures were able to locate the source of the arrows there would be no hiding their identities.

"Insanity," she heard Stovar mutter as he checked the trees around them, knowing they would soon have to find new shelter.

"I'm keeping them away from Dearn." She turned on him, her heart beating in fear. "He's our ticket, Stovar. He has to live."

"I think he's a hell of a lot more than that, but we'll wait and see," he retorted, loading his own crossbow and aiming it carefully.

* * * * *

Dearn heard the Vulture's cry behind him. With a short, quick thrust he sent his sword into the wing of the one he was fighting then pulled free and turned to face the enemy behind.

There was no enemy behind.

From the corner of his eye he glimpsed two of them plunging into the canyon below but had little time to reflect on that mystery before he was faced with yet another sword.

With their longer arms and longer, heavier blades, fighting the Vultures in mid-air was not an easy task. The Clans' one advantage was their ability to outmaneuver the larger winged warriors. They were better equipped to attack from the side or below rather than face-to-face.

These were tactics Clan warriors were taught as fledglings. When faced with a larger opponent, you never fought in air face-to-face. You learned to countermove and weave among wings and swords as you cut a path through them.

It did not make for a quick battle, though, and Dearn was seriously worried that if they tarried too long the whole Vulture force would be on them. Luckily, it seemed there was a bit of help coming from below, which explained the Vultures falling to the floor of the canyon moments before. Well-placed crossbow bolts slammed into the largest of the attackers' wings. There was no aid that could have been more appreciated.

Matte. Dearn grinned at this insight. He could feel her down there; those were her bolts picking the enemy off one by one. His mate was more than a careful warrior; she could apparently also be a crafty one. He felt his heart swell with pride. She would bring a new strength and pride to his people when she was finally crowned his queen.

Dearn forced those thoughts behind him as another Vulture flew at him. With a grin he leveled his sword, calculated the line of flight of the dull black wings and made his own move. His blade sank into an unprotected side with a smooth, graceful motion. He heard the agonized cry then felt the drag as the Vulture's weight pulled him free and he spiraled to the ground.

Finally, the few Vulture warriors left were in retreat, and Dearn motioned for his own men to beat a speedy path to the Fortress and safety. Before he went, he sent a final salute to the trees, aware Matte would see it and know he meant to keep their rendezvous that night.

* * * * *

"Come on," Matte ordered Stovar briskly as she dropped from the tree and headed back to the stream where Canton had been taken.

"Why are we back here?" he demanded as he landed beside her, just inside the tree line. "What are you up to, Matte?"

"Hit me." She turned toward him, lifting her face.

"Hit you?" He gawked at her in confusion. "Why would I hit you?"

"Because it was my job to guard Canton," she whispered desperately. "You have to hit me hard enough to knock me out, Stovar, and just sit here with me until we're found. Then claim you had been searching for me. Come on, now, hurry."

"Matte," he protested, "this isn't a good idea."

"Do it now, or we'll die for nothing." She threw her crossbow to the ground, staring him down in determination. "You have no choice, Stovar."

Strangely enough, it wasn't reluctance Matte saw flare in her cousin's eyes but something closely resembling fear.

"Matte, you want to get me killed?" He grabbed her by the arm.

"You're not making any sense," she told him, checking the clearing quickly. "Do it before it's too late — this will be the first place Edgar checks. Now, hur —"

Without warning the blow came. As the blinding pain shattered through her head, she could have sworn she heard Stovar praying to Aleda, the goddess of mercy, that Dearn wouldn't kill him.

* * * * *

Stovar stared down at his unconscious cousin with a resignation he knew he would eventually regret. He was aware Matte had no idea the king of the Winged Clans had mated with her. Seven Hells, she had never seen such a mating before, had never heard of such a thing.

But Stovar had, and he knew his feathers were in some deep trouble when Dearn saw that bruise on her face. The king had told him just the night before as he started to leave the aerie after Matte that her protection was in his hands.

"Let no harm come to my mate, warrior." There had been cold steel in that voice and in the hand that gripped his arm as Dearn stared at him. "I will hold you responsible."

"She's the commander, not me," Stovar had attempted to argue, knowing well that there was none who could protect Matte unless she wanted to be protected. Which she would not.

He knew well Matte's stubbornness and determination. Seven Hells, even Thorne, King of the Bastard Breeds, had not attempted to place her safety in any hands other than her own. It was the height of foolishness to think it could be done.

"You are her captain, and the one who fights by her side," Dearn had snarled. "Let one bruise mar her delicate skin, and your hide will suffer for her."

Her delicate skin. Stovar rolled his eyes at the thought of that one. There wasn't a delicate spot on Matte's body, and this he well knew. He had trained with her, fought with her and fought beside her. Matte was the toughest woman he knew.

But Dearn was the most savage warrior Stovar had ever come across, other than Thorne. He groaned softly as he sat down on the ground beside Matte's fallen form.

The bruise was bad enough, but it was made worse by the fact he had inflicted it. He kind of liked his hide exactly where it was; he wasn't looking forward to having Dearn tear it from his body strip by strip.

Minutes later Stovar rose as Edgar and his men came rushing into the clearing. Hailing them in desperation, he knelt by Matte's unconscious body as though he had been trying to awaken her.

"What happened to her?" Edgar stared down at her curiously.

"I just found her." Stovar shook his head, hoping his air of confusion was convincing. "She was supposed to be guarding Canton. I got worried when they never returned to camp."

"Damn. Someone managed to get the best of the little bitch." Edgar laughed as he crouched on his haunches to stare into her bruised, unconscious face. "Didn't think I would live to see the day."

"We need to find Canton. That human will pay for this." Stovar prayed Edgar was buying his act.

"Wasn't the human." Edgar sighed and he shook his head, his eyes flaring angrily. "Seems the Clans were a step ahead of us this time. They must have snatched him. I just lost two troops in an air battle against them."

"How many of Matte's men were lost?" Stovar allowed his forehead to crease in a frown. "Damn, Matte will skin those bastards alive."

"Thankfully, none of them." Edgar rose to his feet without taking his eyes off her. "Matte had them gathering information and preparing for the march on the Fortress tomorrow. Damn glad they weren't there. We'll need you Bastards during the final battle."

Stovar lowered his head, fighting to hold back both his triumph and his hatred of Edgar.

"We lost some good warriors, though." Edgar grimaced when Stovar looked back up. "They had a man in the forest with arrows. Damn good shot, too, from what I saw. Right in the wing muscle, every time. Hell of a shot."

"Did you find the man in the forest?" Stovar came to his feet as though preparing to head to interrogation.

"Sorry, Stovar, he got away. No one was there when my men arrived." Edgar shook his head and looked down at Matte once again, his eyes narrowing. "Still can't believe they got her. I guess there's a first time for everything." His tone indicated a suspicion otherwise.

Stovar had the uneasy feeling that things were about to get a lot tighter within the Vulture Clans. Edgar's interest, as well as his suspicions, were aroused. It wouldn't be much longer before he decided it was time to take action.

"Bring her to the camp, Stovar." Edgar sighed roughly. "When she awakens we'll find out what happened. Then we'll march on the Fortress and show King Dearn who can best who in a fight."

As far as Stovar was concerned, Dearn had already proven that one, but he kept his own counsel, lifted Matte into his arms and headed back to camp. She would awaken soon, and when she did she would be raring to head back to that cursed aerie and her mate's arms.

Stovar would have chuckled at that one if he had been alone. He couldn't wait until Matte learned she had mated Dearn. Her fury would be a sight to behold, and then the king would see the handful he had chosen to mate with.

Matte was no man's plaything. She would rip into the king with the force of a mountain storm and bite into his hide harder than a streak of devil lightning. Seven Hells, it would be worth his own flayed skin to see that show. At least, he thought it would be, because he was fairly certain his skin would be flayed when Dearn finally got around to him.

Chapter Twenty-Eight

ဆ

The Clan Troop landed in the courtyard, shaking dirt and sweat from exhausted bodies and wings. More than one of them sighed loudly as his feet touched the ground.

Canton, having freed himself from the harness, was not the least bit ashamed to admit he would insist on walking off the damned mountains and into the valleys when it came time to leave. Flying was for the Clans of winged warriors, not for humans.

"Come with me." Dearn's voice was weary and terse as he motioned for Canton to follow. "Allora should be awaiting you."

Allora. The thought of seeing her sent the blood thundering through his body. He would not let her get away from him this time, he swore to himself. He would be certain to protect her better in the future.

As he entered the vast Great Hall, he saw little to generate happiness there. Tables had been set up to hold the bodies of the families still being discovered in the more remote aeries. The remains of women and children, as well as those of seasoned warriors, were being prepared for the ceremonial fires by the weeping women of their Clans.

"Your King Alfred's work." Dearn paused as he pointed to the nearest, a family of three. Father, mother and a teenaged daughter were laid out, their bodies pale and cold. "They were caught in the forest and dumped in the valley leading into the Fortress. The young girl on the end?" He pointed to her slowly. "She was only sixteen. She was raped before she was killed, as was her mother. They rape our women, then slice into their skin just enough so they slowly bleed to death, too weakened to fight or to even crawl to help."

Canton thought of the horrific tales he'd heard of the degradations performed on the whores in Cayam. That a young, innocent woman should be forced into such a nightmare sickened him to his soul.

"I was unaware of this, Your Highness." Tears clotted Canton's throat as he saw the severity of the carnage.

"That is the only reason you still live, Canton." The bitterness in Dearn's voice was a clear reflection of the pain he felt for his people. "We have endured a nightmare these past weeks. I warn you now — Alfred will die by our hands, whether you wish this or not. There is nothing or no one who will be able to prevent his death."

Canton could only shake his head. Alfred had lost all reason when he put his plans into effect, and he had lost all loyalty Canton had for him with the deception of Allora's death and the proof of the atrocities being inflicted on the Clans. Perhaps he could have continued to believe in his king were it not for the madness he had begun seeing himself, the women Alfred willingly allowed Edgar to abuse and murder.

"His plans for Allora were the same," Dearn told him as they moved on to the stairs that led to the upper part of the castle. "He had her in that tower room waiting until the Vultures succeeded in their war, then he was to gift their leader with her."

Canton halted in mid-step, staring at the king in shock. *Give Allora to that demon Edgar?*

"No..." He shook his head slowly, unwilling to accept that Allora had lived with the nightmare of that threat. "He wouldn't have done such a thing to her."

"You may ask her yourself." Dearn shrugged. "She heard the plans and knew the future facing her if her father succeeded. Come, she awaits you. But be careful, Canton. Her mind is fragile at this moment—it would be easy to damage her."

Canton felt fear burst through him.

"Has she been...? Was she...?" He couldn't complete the questions, so fierce was his fear that she had been harmed in ways she might not recover from.

"She has not been raped. But Allora has a secret, Canton, one she fears you cannot accept. Tread carefully, or you may lose her to her own insecurities as surely as you would have lost her to Alfred."

Dearn stopped in front of a huge door constructed, it appeared, of a single slab of wood. Such huge trees, Canton knew, grew only within the forests that the Clans ruled. He opened it then stood back so Canton could enter alone. Canton stepped inside with caution, distantly aware of the door closing behind him. His entire being was concentrated on the silent, sad woman who stood facing him from across the room.

How beautiful she is, he thought, held in silent wonder as he gazed rapturously on her small, heart-shaped face. The deep, dark pools of blue that were her eyes stared back at him, silent misery welling in their depths and threatening to spill along her alabaster cheeks. The long silken strands of her pale hair had been pulled back from her face and braided into a thick magnificent rope that fell over her shoulder and nearly to her waist.

She was beauty. She was his heart, standing there so silent, her small hands clasped tightly, her body so tense he feared she was stone rather than the warm, gentle woman he had known before.

"Allora." He whispered her name huskily, wanting only to hear his name upon her lips.

For two years he had courted her, fighting the obstacles her father put in their path, fighting his own dark demons that he, with his rough soldier's hands and common blood, could never hope to touch one so perfect, so pure.

Allora didn't speak. A tear passed slowly down her cheek as a whimper escaped her lips, and she turned her back on him. A back bared by the clothing worn by the Clan women, a back with the small, disfigured forms of two tiny wings. Those small, twisted shapes seemed to shudder, the white feathers ruffling as though caught in a breeze.

And then Canton understood. He remembered the bulky cloaks she always wore, how she was always certain to never allow him to see her back. He had assumed a deformity of birth; never had he imagined she was descended from the graceful, mystical, white-winged Clan of the White Lance.

Crossing to stand behind her, he reached out, his fingers just brushing the soft perfection of the little feathers. The wings shuddered once more, and he heard her muted sob.

"My dearest, dearest Allora," he whispered, bending his head to place a whisper-soft kiss atop the wing closest to him. "Why, my love, did you think you must hide such beauty from me?"

Allora turned so quickly he knew his expression of reverence had been caught. So, he did not attempt to wipe it away or to change it. He allowed her to see the naked, fearful devotion he had always had for her.

Confusion filled her eyes.

"You do not find it distasteful?" She frowned. "It is not a deformity in your eyes?"

Canton heard the naked fear in her voice, the husky terrors of a woman made to feel less than perfect.

"Your father did that to you?" he asked her. "Was it he who made you bind such perfection, to hide your heritage?"

Slowly, she nodded.

"And our Queen Demetria? Did he do this to her as well?" He remembered the often-frail, pain-ridden Queen, who had been said to prefer seclusion rather than the company of her people.

"He had the wings cut from her body, but they never healed properly. She bled...often." Allora's whisper was choked by tears.

"And you thought this would change my devotion to you, Allora?" Canton felt his heart tighten with anger, that she should so doubt him. "Did I seem so shallow to you, my lady, that I could not recognize beauty when I saw it?"

"No, Canton, never." Allora shook her head fiercely. "But Father has always told me it was a deformity, that you would be disgusted —"

"And you believed his lies over the many times I swore my devotion to you?" He shook his head as he cupped her face in his hands, his eyes staring intently into hers. "Who would you believe now, my princess? That monster or the man who stands here begging for your heart? The man who has always begged for your love?"

Like sunlight, her smile began to bloom. The dark misery in her eyes lightened to joy, and when she reached up to cover his hand with hers, Canton felt peace unlike any he had ever known suffuse his body.

"I have always loved you." She smiled tremulously. "I tried so many times to tell you. So many ways, Canton. There is no need to beg for my love, for always has it been yours."

With thumbs made rough by his profession, Canton softly smoothed away the tears and felt the silken perfection of her face. His head lowered, his lips touching hers.

"You will be my wife," he told her. He would not ask her, for he could not accept a denial.

"I will, when you ask me properly." Allora smiled up at him, aware of his warrior's pride and his own insecurities. Still, she showed surprise when he went slowly to one knee, one of her smaller hands cupped between his.

"My lady, grant me the honor of your heart. The joy of your love," he whispered. "I beg of you, grant me your life in marriage."

Outside Allora's room, the guards who stood by her door exchanged satisfied glances at the sound of laughter. The entire Fortress knew that peace likely rode on Canton's acceptance of his princess and her heritage. By the sounds of bliss from within the room, he had accepted more than just that heritage.

Chapter Twenty-Nine

ဢ

Dearn was exhausted. He breathed a sigh of relief when he finally reached his chambers and saw the door to his bath open, wisps of steam issuing from it.

There was tender mercy in the world after all, he thought as he anticipated the relaxing feel of the hot water over his tired muscles. Never in his life could he remember a time when he had been so weary, so battle-worn.

His leathers were stained with blood, his body aching with weariness. He could sink into the warmth and pray that Aleda would ease the ache in both his body and his heart.

He had delayed coming to his rooms so he could inform the newly formed Council and the Clan leaders of the battle and the aid Matte and her people had given them. He cautioned them to silence, for fear the human spies within the Fortress would hear of it before Matte's forces could join his own.

Then, one of the guards at Allora's doors had met him on the stairs with a message from Canton. The princess had accepted his proposal of marriage. Canton could now govern, holding the throne in stewardship for Alfred's son, should they be able to find him. He couldn't actually claim the throne—the child would inherit the moment Alfred died. Until he reached his majority, Canton would be his regent.

This habit of passing the throne from father to son confused Dearn. What if the son was not strong enough, or not qualified to lead? What, then, happened to those who followed him?

The Clans had eliminated this. The throne could pass down from father to son, but the son must prove his leadership abilities above those of all the other warriors who would vie for that seat of power. And there were often many.

Strength was not all a warrior needed. Logic, patience, and the ability to plan and to guide the troops were also requirements. The Clans were thus made stronger by the man who sat at their head.

But Dearn was content with the measure he had taken of Canton. He was a true warrior and a good man. For a while, at least, the humans would have the rule of someone who deserved this seat of power.

Relief filled him as he headed for the bathing chamber. The huge tub, hewn from stone and connected with a series of pipes running from the hot springs within the mountains, would be full and awaiting him.

He stripped, closing his eyes in relief when he felt the cool breeze against his naked skin. The leather was perfect protection during battle, but the sweat and dust after the excitement faded gave it an uncomfortable damp feel.

From the open balcony doors Dearn could smell the hint of rain moving in, and it reminded him of Matte and the scent she carried. It also reminded him of the aerie; his shaft hardened uncomfortably at the memory.

Gods, the feel of her, the pleasure of their wings mingling, melding, creating oneness. It was unlike any pleasure he had ever known in his life. And that scent, the scent of rain and heat, and the unbearable excitement of his senses.

He realized suddenly that he had noticed a similar scent about Tamora before she was attacked, and again before he left to fetch Canton. The scent had grown increasingly bothersome when Tamora got too close to him. It wasn't an offensive odor, but it had produced an unpleasant sensation whenever she touched him or reminded him of their prior relationship.

Dearn understood the significance of the scent on Matte's body. It was his scent. It was the result of an ancient mating ritual, one nearly forgotten within the Clans in recent generations as they took up the practice of mating ceremonies instead of waiting for the instinctual process. He must have placed it on her that night in the forest when his wing tip unconsciously caressed her bare arm. That was the first step in the ritual, and the moment when her spirit had accepted him as her mate. Within hours her body would have developed the mating scent. A scent that all other Clans would recognize for what it was.

All Clans with the exception of the Vultures. Vultures did not mate with their women. *Gods, what would happen to Matte if the Vulture leader realized? If he somehow learned of the significance of that scent?* Fear burned through his veins for her. He would not be able to tolerate this situation much longer. Matte would have to abandon her plans and come to the Fortress immediately.

The day in the aerie when his wings enfolded her, he had known the moment he felt his soft inner feathers caressing her flesh and her reaction to it what it meant. She had accepted him as her mate, and now her body carried a scent unique to the two of them, not unlike the smell of the mountains after a storm.

Tamora carried a darker odor, that of a midnight flight, one he suspected belonged to Brendar.

Dearn sighed. He wondered if Tamora was aware she had mated with Brendar. It was obvious the general knew, for he had been furious with Dearn for many weeks now.

So, why had they not asked for the mating ceremony? Tamora acted as though nothing had changed, that her affair with him continued.

Shaking his head in confusion he walked wearily into the bathing room.

Tamora awaited him in the steaming water, her long auburn hair bound attractively atop her head, damp curls escaping to curl about her shoulders. She watched him with apprehension. The confidence that had always been a part of her seemed to be missing. The room held the faint fragrance of the midnight scent.

Her heightened emotions, her fears, would cause the scent to deepen. It would never become overpowering. The mating scent was always elusive—there, then gone, then once again present—warning Dearn that he was treading on claimed territory.

Amusement lanced through him for an instant as he wondered how Brendar would view a scene such as this. He knew he would kill the man who dared to see Matte in such a way. He reached for one of the towels in the stone shelf beside the tub and wrapped it around his waist.

Tamora frowned. "Aren't you going to bathe?"

Dearn took another towel and held it out to her.

"We have to talk," he told her, wondering if he should call Brendar or just take care of this himself. He didn't want to cause undue strife with the mating couple, and he knew Tamora's behavior was out of character. She had a great sense of honor and would never deliberately betray her chosen mate.

"Dearn?" Her face revealed her confusion.

"Cover yourself, Tamora, and I will meet you in the bedroom."

He turned and walked to the balcony doors to wait. He wondered tiredly how he was supposed to handle this, as weary as he was.

"Dearn?" She stood behind him, and he turned slowly to face her.

The towel wrapped about her body, but the amount of skin showing was indecent in the context of the situation. Once again he shook his head, fighting off his own morbid amusement and wondering how Brendar would feel.

He didn't have long to wait to find out. As he opened his mouth to speak, the huge oak door thundered against the wall, an enraged Brendar standing within the frame.

"Do come in, and close the door behind you."

Dearn crossed his arms over his chest and fought against ordering them both to their rooms until they could talk reasonably. The door thundered closed, making him wince. He was thankful it was made of the heavier oldtree wood and not prone to splitting.

"I will not have this, Dearn," Brendar roared as he advanced into the room, his fists clenched in fury. "You surely know by now we have mated?"

Dearn started to speak.

"Who is mated?" Tamora beat him to it, rounding on Brendar in surprise.

Dearn felt no small amount of confusion at the anger in her voice. How could the woman not know she had mated with the general?

"You and I have mated, woman," Brendar snarled into her face. "How dare you stand here dressed like that? How dare you deny me and come running to Dearn instead?"

"Mated with you?" Tamora yelled in disbelief, her face suffusing with color. "Why would I mate with you, of all people?"

Dearn watched Brendar's face flush with anger, his hazel-and-violet eyes glittering with the emotion her statement sent surging through his body. Violence would erupt in a matter of seconds. Their emotions were out of hand, and he did not want to be witness to the culmination when they finally collided.

"Enough." He raised his voice as Brendar moved toward Tamora. "We will discuss this reasonably, or it won't be discussed at all." Then to Brendar, "Did you take the time to inform her what you had done when it happened, or did you just expect her to know?"

Abruptly, he asked this same question of himself. *Gods, surely Matte understood…?*

"She carries my scent, she should know she has mated with me," Brendar stated roughly, staring at Tamora in torment.

Dearn looked at Tamora and watched her face drain of color. Shock and comprehension filled her, and he saw the moment she must have remembered the mating of the wings — or perhaps even more, for her entire upper body seemed to flush a rich, bright red.

"No," she whispered. "I would not…"

Amused pity welled in Dearn. Poor Tamora, to realize how she had longed for Brendar then denied the yearning because of loyalty to him. To have her body, her heart, take the decision from her mind must be a confusing, frightening realization.

"You carry his scent, which means you accepted the mating, Tam. If you didn't want it, then you would not carry his scent, no matter the number of times his wings wrapped around you."

Tamora shook her head, shooting Brendar a look filled with anger.

"I was distraught. I didn't know what I was doing."

Dearn smiled and would have spoken had Brendar not erupted in male fury once again.

"Listen to her deny me," he raged as he ran his hands through his reddish-brown hair. "She has denied me since the day she accepted the mating. What woman does not know what is meant by the melding of wings?" He turned to her, his expression thunderous. "Did you think the melding of wings merely a game, you foolish woman?"

Dearn watched Tamora's face. Watched the pride flare in her eyes at the insult, then watched as confusion replaced it. *Poor Tam,* he thought. She had no idea what she accepted when she allowed the mating.

"Tamora, go dress," Dearn ordered her. "Then I want you to leave this room and go with your mate. How the two of you handle this is not for me to decide. But it is for me to decide that the mating ceremony will take place when this war is finished. Brendar will be fighting again, Tamora. Think carefully before you deny him and send him into battle with such internal chaos."

Once again Tamora's face paled, but she did as he ordered, aware there was no longer any choice but to face the truth. Dearn hoped his own mate was as willing to accept her fate.

"You knew I mated with her..." Brendar charged, turning on him.

Dearn shook his head in denial. "I did not know until this day, Brendar. Not until I mated myself did I recognize the signs."

Brendar's eyes widened in astonishment, and Dearn could not blame him, for he realized it rather astonished him as well.

"You mated? With who? And when?" the general demanded in confusion, for it was well known all the Clans had expected him to mate with Tamora.

Dearn sighed deeply, closing his eyes as he finally admitted the truth aloud. "I have mated with the female commander of the Bastard Breeds. A woman warrior, Brendar, can you believe it?"

"You mated with her?" Incredulity lined Brendar's face as he shook his head. Then gradually, awareness dawned, and he remembered the dagger his king had held to his throat. "I take it, then, you have made your decision."

Censure was rife in the tone. Dearn laughed aloud at the sarcasm in his general's voice.

"I had made my decision long before, my friend. I was just unaware that you, too, had made such a decision, and I was merely guiding you into admitting to it."

"You were merely playing your usual games, Sire," Brendar snarled. "This time, it was less than amusing."

"But well worth the time given to it." Dearn sighed as he sat back down, arranging the towel to properly cover his body. "But now I find myself in much the same position you are."

Brendar looked at him questioningly. "Your mate teases you with another man as well?" His anger was still holding strong and steady.

"Your mate hasn't teased you, Brendar." Dearn breathed out roughly. "Much as my Matte, I fear, Tamora was unaware of the instinctual mating rituals or their process. We have lost much of our heritage over the years in becoming so civilized. Our mates are women, Brendar—strong, courageous and independent women. They will not accept easily that their bodies and their hearts are stronger than their will. I have a feeling we both have a fight ahead of us, and I'm not talking about this Seven Hells' war with the humans, either."

Understanding finally lit Brendar's face. He would have spoke, but Tamora chose that moment to return from the bathing room.

"You truly did not know we had mated?" Brendar asked her, still filled with anger but more willing now to hear his mate's explanation.

"I still say such has not happened, Brendar." Her head lifted arrogantly, her violet eyes sparkling.

"Then you have not deliberately denied me?" A small smile etched his lips.

Tamora frowned, and Dearn fought to hide his grin at her display of temper.

"I have fully meant to deny you. But perhaps..." She glanced at Dearn. "Perhaps my heart has accepted you. We shall see."

"Well, see somewhere else. I need some rest," Dearn mumbled through a yawn. "Go, get out of here so I can bathe and sleep. And for the sake of the gods, have someone send me something to eat. I'm famished."

He didn't wait to see if his orders were obeyed. He dragged his body from the chair and trudged mindlessly to the bathing room and the water that Tamora had hopefully left within the tub.

Chapter Thirty

ℬ

When Matte awoke in her tent, there was no feeling of disorientation, no questions or hesitation. Within that first second she knew what she had done and feared she had made a vital mistake when she saw Edgar sitting beside her cot and Stovar standing close by.

"Did you get the Seven Hells thornhogs who hit me?" She looked at Stovar, praying to Aleda that Edgar had not learned of their betrayal.

"'Thornhogs' is a hell of an insult coming from you, Matte." Edgar laughed at her. "Be damned if you don't reek nearly as bad, though."

Matte sniffed the air but could detect no unusual scent. She would have challenged Edgar had she not caught the warning light in Stovar's eyes. *What was this Cinder-cursed scent?*

"Yeah, well, you tangle hand-to-hand with one of the cursed knots of wood and see if you don't come out smelling the worst for it." She touched her face gingerly. Stovar had more power in his fists than she thought. Her head felt three times its size and throbbed worse than an infected wound.

"How long before you'll feel up to leading your men?" Edgar asked her, his gaze brooding as he considered her. "I want to begin the final march morning after next. We'll meet the Clans outside the forest edge, I would assume. Will you be ready?"

"I'll be ready." She would have nodded but knew the pain would vibrate through her head.

There was silence and Matte closed her eyes, hoping she appeared unconcerned with whatever suspicions Edgar had.

"They have Canton, now, Matte. We'll have trouble with the human soldiers if they see him with the other side. I need you waiting for that. I want that cursed human dead the moment he's sighted."

Matte reopened her eyes, glaring at Edgar with what she hoped was convincing fury.

"Then they managed to capture him after all. I was hoping they would merely kill him."

"No such luck." Edgar sat back in the wooden chair he had moved beside the cot. "They would have been out to capture him, not kill him. They have Allora, so they must know the human's affection for her. This will complicate things."

"Complications are what make the fights more amusing." Matte laughed softly, intentionally using a phrase he had uttered himself many times. "It will make the killing better."

Edgar laughed, too, a lighter sound than before, and Matte hoped it indicated his renewed faith in her. He was as suspicious as any Vulture ever made, but she had never betrayed him before, had always fought at his back despite his cruelty during her first battle. He seemed reassured she would do so now.

"We will attack the Fortress ahead of schedule then." He slapped his leg and rose. "Be ready for blood, Matte, for we will spill much of it."

"I will be more than ready, brother." Matte heard the hatred and passion in her voice as she thought of taking Edgar down, but she was confident he would interpret it as her anticipation of seeing the Clans' blood flow.

"Excellent. I shall leave you to rest then, and hopefully to wash off some of that stink. It's becoming quite unpleasant." He paused, his eyes narrowing. "I would hope you remember, Matte, the punishment for betraying me?"

Matte fought real rage now. Oh, yes, she remembered well his manner of punishment.

"Betrayal of what?" She frowned, pushing to her feet as though to confront him. "How dare you threaten me, Edgar? Have you forgotten who has watched your back since we landed in this cursed place?"

A small smile curved his cruel mouth as he tilted his head in acknowledgement.

"I just wanted to be certain, sister, that you remembered," he said softly.

He left her tent, waving for the warriors who had come with him to follow. Matte turned to Stovar, her head angled questioningly as he watched the Vultures leave. He put a finger to his lips, warning her of spies outside her tent.

"Have a bath drawn for me, Stovar." She sat back down on the bed gingerly, holding her head. "Then find Carin and tell her to bring her healer's poisons. I have an ache in my head that will bring me low do you not."

She wanted to discuss Edgar and the suspicion she'd read clearly in his eyes but knew well that now was not the time.

"You should rest, Matte. The blow you took was a hard one. I think perhaps the thornhog who hit you thought your head was harder than it actually is."

Matte heard amusement in his voice, but she saw worry in his eyes. She shook her head just slightly, assuring him she was fine.

"It was a puny blow." She smiled back. "They merely had luck on their side. A bath and Carin's potion, and I'll be fine. I want to get a troop out in a few hours and see if I can't find one or two Clan warriors to vent my wrath on."

"You should rest." Stovar gave her a fierce glare at this idea. Too soon, too dangerous — she knew his thoughts, but she had to assure herself that Dearn was well and that Canton had reached the Fortress.

"I am fine, Stovar. Do as I ask." She made her voice brisk, commanding, as the spy would expect. "I want blood for this day. And blood is exactly what I intend to have."

Stovar's lips thinned, his handsome face set in lines of anger as he stared at his cousin. He walked to the tent entrance and called one of Matte's warriors over. With quick instructions, he sent that man for Carin and others to draw the water for Matte's bath.

"Tell Carin to fetch me when she is finished, and we'll discuss this raid you seem intent on. But I still think you should rest."

He started to leave, but Matte stopped him with a silent gesture.

"Send a message to Dearn to meet with me. Four hours," she mouthed to him.

Stovar shook his head violently.

"Do it!" It was a silent order now, her face setting in lines of determination. "Do it now!"

Stovar clenched his teeth in a silent snarl. He stared at her for long moments then, with an abrupt shrug of his shoulders, nodded tightly.

Matte waved him away. She wasn't going to argue, her head was throbbing too fiercely. Perhaps it wasn't as hard as it used to be, she thought as she probed the area with her fingers, flinching at the contact. She'd be damned if she didn't feel as though she had been run over by a wagon and the harebeasts that pulled it.

Lowering her head into her hands, she took a deep breath, fighting the nausea rising in her stomach. For a blow, it had been a harsh one, but she knew her cousin had meant her no harm. Seven Hells, she had taken harder, so why did she ache so much worse this time?

She dropped her hands from her face and stared at her feet. Edgar had hit her harder during that first battle on her sixteenth birthday. He had not knocked her senseless, though. She had been awake and aware through every moment of the rape and had sworn vengeance that day, and again later in the night when she lay staked to the cold ground, knowing that soon the Bats would fly and they would find her laid out for a meal, a ready feast for their cannibalistic tastes and their fierce lusts.

It was only by the grace of the gods that Thorne had come looking for her. He had untied her, his dark face hard and cold as he covered her with his shirt and held her while she cried. She had been unable to fly, so he strapped her to his own body and flew her home, leaving her to the care of her mother and sisters while he sought out Edgar and his men. The rape of a Bastard Breed woman might be no longer a crime, but it still had not gone unavenged. Thorne had punished him and the warriors involved.

Even so, Matte had sworn the day would come when she would repay Edgar herself. That day had come.

* * * * *

Late that evening, hours before Dearn was due to meet with her, one of Matte's men was spotted within Fortress territory. Dearn dressed and flew with only two guards for the aerie.

He ignored the flash of excitement he felt at the thought of seeing her once again. He was worried, though. She had sent for him rather than meeting him as they had arranged. That could only mean Edgar had somehow changed his plans and would be moving more quickly.

As he sat within the depths of the aerie and awaited her, he wondered once again how well she was going to accept the revelation that they were mated. He had no doubt she was unaware of it. She displayed the same confusion at her response to him that he was certain Tamora had with Brendar.

He didn't have long to wait. The gentle breeze of her descent drifted through the cave as she landed on the ledge. Her feet barely touched stone before she was running to him, and Dearn opened his arms to embrace his mate.

"Thank the gods you're all right," she murmured.

His wings enfolded her, and this time, he felt only peace when the inner feathers of his wings caressed her skin. He cupped her head in his hands, tipped it back, and his lips took hers in a kiss of thankfulness. Never had he been happier to see another alive and well. The danger she faced would worry him into an early grave.

As he raised his head, Dearn frowned. Her face appeared shadowed, but the moons' glow should have cast the shadow on the other side. He smoothed his thumb over the area, and outrage roared in him as she flinched.

"Who dared to strike you?" The words felt as though they were being ripped from his throat.

A tight fist of rage clenched around his chest, his stomach, that anyone would dare to touch her.

"Oh, it's nothing." She smiled up at him. "Stovar had to knock me out—"

"He will die tonight!" He saw her incredulity, but the fury riding him would not allow him to hear the rest of her words. "Tell me now where the bastard waits."

"At her back, where he has always been."

Dearn pushed Matte away, his wings flaring to protect her as he turned and unsheathed his sword in a single movement. He faced the Bastard Breed warrior with cold steel and the flames of vengeance burning him.

Stovar didn't back down, nor did he draw his sword. He faced Dearn from the shadows, standing tall just inside the aerie.

"What in the Seven Hells is wrong with you?" Matte came from behind his wings with a fierce glare. Then she turned on the intruder. "And why are you here, Stovar? Why did you follow me?"

"Better me than Edgar or one of his warriors." Stovar shook his head at the sight of them. "You're taking too many chances, Matte. Besides, it's better to meet the man intent on killing me than to look over my shoulder always expecting him."

"Have you gone insane? Why would Dearn want to kill you?" Matte questioned, irritated by the hostile looks passing between the two men. Something was going on here they weren't telling her about. "Does war make all men lose total control of their senses?"

"We can't blame this on the war, cousin," Stovar informed her before returning his attention to Dearn. "It was necessary to save her life. Edgar was already suspicious of her because of the scent. He would have killed her had he not thought a Clan warrior knocked her out to get to Canton."

"So you hit her in the face?" Dearn growled. "There were any number of ways you could have achieved your purpose. There was no need to hurt her so severely."

"It was quickest. Edgar was upon us." Stovar observed the tension in Dearn's body lessening a fraction.

"What scent?" Matte broke in, anger vibrating in her voice. "You two are making as much sense as Edgar and Alfred."

Dearn sighed. He should have known. After Tamora, he did know—he just didn't want to admit it could happen to him as well. And he doubted Matte would be very eager to accept a mating at the moment, considering she likely knew nothing about it.

"Your mating scent, Matte." Stovar, on the other hand, clearly had no qualms about hitting her with it. "The two of you are mated."

Dearn cast the warrior a dark, quelling look. He would have preferred to tell her himself. The points the other man was storing up were not exactly on the positive side.

"You are as insane as Alfred." Matte laughed, but the sound was strained. "I haven't mated with anyone."

"The scent you can't wash off? The rash on your arms?" Stovar pointed out. "You are mated, Matte, and sooner or later Edgar will remember the signs as well. It's not uncommon for it to happen among the Bastard Breeds."

Dearn met her accusing gaze with a confidence he didn't feel. Who knew how this determined woman would accept such a revelation?

"You mated with me and did not inform me?" she demanded in a soft voice that nearly made him wince. There was an edge to it that did not bode well for him.

"To be honest, Matte, until earlier this day it did not occur to me that you were unaware of the ritual." He kept his own voice soft and showed none of his internal turmoil.

"I do not have to accept it." She shook her head. "Now is not the time for this, and I don't have the time to deal with it."

"It's too late to worry, in either case," he informed her. "It has happened and must be dealt with. My only concern now is Edgar, and how much he is aware of."

"Little at this point," Stovar informed him. "But he's suspicious, so it won't be much longer."

"He begins his march toward the pass morning after next." Dearn could tell Matte hoped to put the subject of the mating behind them. "At the speed he and Alfred intend to push the men, they will be at the pass before dusk tomorrow."

"And we will deal with them," Dearn told her as he watched her closely. "What are the plans you have made for your people?"

"When the battle begins, we will fight alongside the Clans."

"No," he commanded. "You will have your Clans defect tonight." Then, when she would have argued, "You cannot push this, Matte. Bring your people together tonight and fly for the Fortress. I will have my troops waiting to escort you."

"It won't work that way." Matte turned on him fiercely. "We don't know all Edgar's plans yet."

"His plans do not matter at this point." Dearn heard the edge of anger invading his voice. "If Edgar has noticed the scent on you, then he will remember what it means eventually. You are endangering yourself and your Clan."

"You endangered them." Matte's finger came dangerously close to his nose as she pointed it at him. "This is all your fault."

Dearn's eyes widened. The woman was inflamed, her cheeks flushed, her feathers trembling with emotion. The emotion was not all anger, though. Her scent became a shade stronger, enveloping him with sweetened tendrils of equal parts desire and tenderness. He would have smiled were he not so taken aback by her fury.

"Might I remind you, it would have never happened did you not want it." He was amazed at his control. "It is not as though it were possible to force it on you."

"That's exactly what you did," she charged. "You of all people should know better."

Dearn stepped back as that finger jabbed into his chest. Never had he been so berated by a woman, and in front of another warrior, no less. How did one control such a being as this? In his experience there was only one way. He wrapped her within his wings, his lips covering hers, the inner feathers of his wings caressing her skin, calming her, preparing her for him.

Chapter Thirty-One

∞

The Fortress courtyard was filled with Clansmen, warriors milling around, captains shouting orders, preparations being made for the coming battle.

Pure Clan colors mixed with the diluted, muted shades of a race long vilified for what was no fault of their own, except that they were the living evidence that the honor of the Clans had been shattered by deception and violence. The Bastard Breeds mingled with the Clans, some uncertain, some still filled with the heady excitement of finally coming home, and all with eyes glazed with the wonder of the Fortress.

The courtyard appeared to be a mass of confusion, but despite the shuffling, hurried bodies, Dearn could see the order that existed within the chaos. The cream-colored wings of a Bastard Breed captain stood side by side with the pure, brilliant blue-black of a Raven leader and the rich russet of the wings of an Eagle captain as they discussed yet another battle strategy.

There had been no true battles in centuries, only what were little more than skirmishes with human thieves intent on raiding the Clans' dallion stone or gold and silver mines. The Clans were ready to fight, though. Dearn could feel it in the air around him. They were prepared—strong and determined to exact vengeance for the deaths of their people in a way no human could ever understand.

Most of the Clan warriors were older than their Bastard Breed counterparts, but still none had ever been to battle until this war. Many within the troops had never taken a life. They had trained for it—a Clan Warrior's life was spent in training to some degree or another. However, Dearn knew from experience that no amount of training could prepare them for inflicting death.

The humans were riding quickly for the sheltered pass that led into the Fortress, and Dearn was determined to get there before they reached it. The last scouts had just returned with the news that Alfred's army was now nearly through the forests that separated the mountain ranges. It was only a matter of hours before they reached the pass that led directly to the Fortress.

"Matte, is your Clan ready?"

Dearn turned to his mate, feeling pride well inside him. He already knew her Clan stood ready, and she fearlessly before them. Her warrior's leathers lovingly clung to each curve of her body, emphasizing full breasts and slender thighs. He hid his wince as he noticed his warriors looking at her with male appreciation. He didn't care much for their glances, but he knew he could expect little else. His Matte was a beauty, and she was his. He knew he need not fear that any of those who admired the gentle curves would attempt to touch what was his. They had all noticed the scent that marked her, the proof of their mating that had intensified after the night she had just spent in his arms.

That night of pleasure had come with a price, though. He ignored the snickers of Clan members as they glanced at the bruise that covered one eye and the better part of his cheek. Stovar, Dearn was certain, had spread the information that Matte had left that particular souvenir in repayment for the "handling" he had done of her in the aerie.

His Matte was a fierce one, but he contented himself with the fact that later he had silenced her most effectively and made her lose any desire to use her fists.

"We're ready." Matte, too, ignored the snickers. "They will head out in a few minutes to position themselves along the cliff walls. King Alfred's special guards have no families and will be likely to hide with their crossbows ready. They'll expect us to show up on time."

That had been the plan that would allow a handful of Vultures and a paltry army of under a thousand human soldiers to defeat the Clans. The humans had learned much from the Vultures in the art of deception and warfare.

Allowing Matte to return to the Vulture camp to finalize the plans with Edgar had required all the courage in Dearn's warrior heart. Even now, he broke into a sweat remembering the terror-filled hours as he awaited her return.

"The captains will defect, but many of the soldiers might still follow King Alfred's commands." Canton moved forward. "The wives and children were a good move, Dearn, but you'll still have a battle on your hands. They have been trained to use those crossbows effectively, and they will take out as many of your men as they can."

Canton was more than ready for the coming battle. Dearn could see the light of vengeance glowing in the other man's eyes. His fury over Alfred's cruelties to Allora had spread through his system faster than any poison. He wanted King Alfred dead and had no reservations over how that death occurred.

"How many do you expect to turn back after you're seen?" Dearn frowned as he considered this information. He was aware of it yet still had found no way to work around it.

"A hundred, perhaps a handful more." Canton shook his head. "My captains and those within my own detail are the only ones I really expect to turn back. The others will be too frightened of King Alfred's punishment not to fight. You'll have to capture him to stop them."

Dearn watched as Matte drew nearer, a frown marking her forehead.

"The humans owe more loyalty to you than that, Canton," she disagreed. "You lead those men, not Alfred. More will defect, I believe, than you think."

"But if I die and Alfred doesn't, their punishment will be severe." Canton shook his head. "We can't rely on that, Matte. It is better to be prepared for the worst."

"What about the women and children?" Matte turned to Dearn. "Surely, you aren't going to fly them out there into the middle of a battle."

Dearn shook his head. That had been the plan until he discussed it with Canton. The suspicion that it would turn back few of the soldiers had changed his mind. He could not in good conscience risk innocent lives in a plan that had such a low chance of success.

"We will take Canton and Allora only," Dearn told her, well aware of Canton's dissatisfaction with this plan. "We will send them with a special troop, responsible for their safety alone."

It was another point he and his mate disagreed on. Dearn had not made his final decision until they left their room to meet with their troops. That he had decided in ☐efenc of sending the princess out surprised her, he could tell.

"They will try to kill them first thing," she protested fiercely. "Protecting the princess will be no easy feat, Dearn."

"I'm aware of that, Matte." He looked down at the intense expression on her face. "We have no choice. The soldiers have to see both of them, and they have to be aware of Alfred's lies. This is the only way."

Matte took a deep breath as she nodded slowly. They had discussed it earlier, before dawn had made its appearance, and neither of them could come up with another solution.

"I have my own crossbow, Matte," Canton assured her. "I won't be ☐defenseless. I'll take care of Allora. And I carry a drawn plan of the maze of aeries within the mountain. We shall be fine."

The plan was to deposit Canton and Allora on a deserted aerie ledge within the first cliffs the humans would reach after exiting the forest. There, they would confront the soldiers.

When the battle began, Canton would take Allora into the maze of tunnels that ran through the cliff and hide there with her. Should the Vultures send anyone after them, the couple would thus have a damned good chance at survival. The tunnels, deserted aeries and long corridors would be impossible for one who was unfamiliar with them to search without a detailed map.

"Make sure of it," Matte grumbled. "I'd hate to have to see Dearn choose another leader for the humans when this is finished. As Allora's husband, you will have a much easier time of it."

The White Lance priests would officiate over the marriage after the battle had ended, but when Canton faced Alfred they would allow the king to believe this had already taken place.

Canton grinned, his smile full of pride and satisfaction. Allora's heritage and her wings had done nothing to cause the general's love for her to waver. That they would rule their people together when the battle was done was just an added benefit.

"Dearn, we have everything prepared." Brendar moved up to report. "We're leaving a minimal force here within the Fortress, mostly the youngest and oldest of our warriors. The rest of us are ready to fly. Princess Allora is on her way and ready to go."

Dearn turned and looked at the men, who were suddenly turned toward him awaiting his command. Varied Clan colors glittered beneath the rays of the new dawn; their faces were intent, and their gazes sober.

He took a deep breath as he extended his hand to his mate. Without hesitation her leather-gloved hand slipped into his, and she moved unresisting to his side as he drew her close. Together they faced both his people and hers, those former exiles who had dreamed of fighting side by side with their brothers in defense of the legendary Fortress of the Clans, the one place above all others that Ashrad had blessed.

"There have been a lot of changes." His voice rose through the courtyard. "We've lost many of our people, and seen death as we never thought we would. Now, the time has come to fight back."

A cheer went up among the men, rising in volume as they prepared to meet the enemy.

"We outnumber them," he announced as the din died down. "But that means nothing in this battle. There will be those in hiding, their arrows flying to pick us from the air. We'll also face larger warriors, warriors who relish the sight of blood. May Ashrad and his children be with us in our battle. Good luck to you all."

A second cheer resounded. A call to arms, a shout of dedication. More experienced warriors, maybe, but never more determined ones, Dearn thought.

As the cheers died down, Matte stepped forward and gave her men the signal to fly. Loaded with arrows, their crossbows and with a determined glint in their eyes, they stepped onto the wall and dropped smoothly into the air. Minutes later, Dearn watched as his men collected their bows and the small barrel-shaped quivers that strapped securely to their legs and made loading the crossbows so much easier.

Now it was he who stepped onto the wall with his personal troop of warriors and fell soundlessly into the valley.

Chapter Thirty-Two

ဆ

The sun was high when the human forces reached the edge of the forest. There, as though a line had been cut to dissect the cliffs from the trees, the woods ended and the mountains rose sharp and high. Alfred felt satisfaction pierce his chest. The soldiers behind him were quiet, praying, he knew, to the damned gods they yet worshipped. Soon, though, he swore to his own god, they would worship the one who was greater than all others. Soon, the shrines that graced the land would disappear and the altars that gave glory to Cinder would replace them. Soon, soon, it would all be as he envisioned it.

"Alfred."

The force stopped, as did he, in surprise as the insolent voice called from the cliffs above. It couldn't be, he thought in sudden fear. Surely, Cinder would have found a way to silence that voice forever.

"I do believe we've located your general and your lovely daughter," Edgar sneered from beside him.

Alfred fought for composure. They had known the Clan warriors would be here, but there had been no reports from the scouts that Canton and Allora would be here as well.

"Answer him," Edgar demanded. "Let's get this over with so we can get on with killing them."

Alfred glanced back nervously at the army now shifting behind him in wonder. They had been told Allora and the general were dead. Seeing them now sent a thread of dissent through the ranks. Had their king lied to them?

"Traitor!" Alfred shouted. "You have betrayed your king, Canton. I sentence you to death." He ignored Edgar's wince and disapproving look. Stupid Vulture. Didn't he know Cinder was watching over them?

"And you have betrayed your people, Alfred," Canton called back. "I claim the throne of Cayam in the name of its people, and by right of marriage to your daughter Allora, your firstborn heir and successor."

The men began to murmur amongst themselves. Like a slow-moving procession, the mutters of dissent grew as Allora stepped from behind Canton to face her people.

They stood upon a wide ledge high up on the cliff the forces must pass to begin the ascent into the mountains and the road that led to the Fortress. At sight of his daughter, moving with the grace and beauty of her mother, Alfred felt rage seethe in his belly—rage, and a need he could neither admit to nor assuage.

"Heathen! Fool!" Alfred screamed, causing his mount to become skittish beneath him and dance nervously against the reins. "I will not relinquish my throne to you nor to any other. I am King of Cayam, and you will bow before me."

He shook with his anger. Canton held in his arms the woman that had tormented Alfred's nights as none other ever had.

"You are a liar and the murderer of your wife," Canton accused him. "I stand here with the daughter you imprisoned and swore to kill. Your heir, Alfred, is now my wife. Soldiers, I order you to lay down your arms and to walk away from this battle. Your king is mad, and this war against innocents should stop now."

"And what of our families, Canton?" Alfred jerked as Jacquard, the most powerful of the captains, stepped forward. "Where are our wives and our children?"

The men behind Jacquard began to murmur their support of the question. They all worried and feared for those families.

Traitorous bastards, Alfred cursed. Didn't they know those sacrifices to Cinder would assure them of victory?

"They are safe in the Fortress of the Clans, Jacquard," Canton assured him. "You know me, and you know my word. No harm will come to your families regardless of your decision. But I tell you now to walk away or to join me in my fight against the demon of Brydon. Your king, Jacquard, and the plague he brought back to our land is that demon."

"No!" Alfred screamed, his voice hoarse with the ire running through him. "Demons, those with the wings who sit in their stone houses and plot the temptation of the gods-fearing. These are your demons, and I order you to kill them now. We are the swords of the god, and so shall we strike the demons from the air."

Alfred turned on the army, glaring them down in his fury. They would fight, he swore to himself, or he would kill them all with his own hands.

"Why have you lied to us, Sire?" A soldier's voice rose from within the crowd. "You said the princess was dead, and that Canton was murdered. Why have you lied?"

"Treasonous bastard." Alfred spat at the crowd. "Step forward so I may run you through with my blade."

None stepped forward, but he could tell by the angry dark looks that his men were not ready to back down.

"We are the swords of Cinder!" He raised his blade above his head as he faced them. "You will fight, and you will fight now. Begin by killing that treasonous Canton who stands before us, aligning himself with the demons we seek."

No one moved. Cinder was the most despised of the gods of Brydon, and there were few men alive who would fight beneath his sword. In his frenzy, Alfred had forgotten this.

"Give it up, Alfred." Edgar laughed behind him then spoke to the soldiers. "Go ahead and run. Your day is coming either way. When the Vultures win this battle, I will punish you for your defection. I will bleed you into troughs as I rape your wives and daughters and plant my seed strong within their bellies." He laughed once again at the horror reflected on their faces.

The cool confidence, the cruel gleam in his eye had many of the men stepping back. By the hundreds they slowly moved away, their crossbows raised and ready should they be attacked.

"General Canton, what are your orders, sir?"

Alfred felt his brain burn with the call Jacquard made to the general.

"Bastards." The word spat from his lips as the soldiers slowly backed into the forest.

"Fight, Jacquard," Canton called back. "Fight as though your lives depend on it. Because they do."

Edgar raised his arm, his signal to his forces hidden in the cliffs and the trees. From beneath the shelter of the leaves, human soldiers began to scatter, their war cries echoing around the cliffs. Then he took to the sky, aiming for where he had seen Allora and Canton. She was his, and he would have her while that damned human watched in agony.

* * * * *

"Let's go." Canton pushed Allora into the aerie, then through the back rooms where the tunnels led deeper into the mountain. He had seen the Vulture heading for the cliffs and knew Edgar would be there quickly. He had to get Allora to the caves.

He scanned the map he had fought to memorize before standing to face Alfred. The turns were clearly marked, the hidden rooms that would lead to but more rooms indicated with a bold slash.

"This way." They hurried into one of the tunnels, the torch in his hand barely lighting the thick darkness.

* * * * *

Edgar made it as far as the aerie ledge before the first arrow nicked his wing. Cursing, he turned, drew his crossbow and fired at the Clan warriors soaring into the valley.

Damn, there were more of them than he had expected, and they were hard to hit. It wasn't like targeting the broader, more cumbersome wings of a Vulture or the wide, tightly stretched wings of a Bat. These Clan warriors were able to weave in and out of the volley of arrows. Their wings lifted, twisted, and somehow they managed to evade harm.

He turned back and started into the aerie; the next arrow barely missed his head. *Son of a bitch.* Where the hell was the bastard shooting at him? Edgar ducked, and then was forced to fly from the ledge as another volley flew toward him.

Where the hell was Matte? Edgar looked around as he drew his sword and flew into the melee. She was supposed to cover his ass, and now she was nowhere to be found.

Chapter Thirty-Three

🔊

Dearn moved through the clashing warriors, his sword striking and blocking the heavyset Vulture warrior facing him. Fighting the bastard while blocking arrows from below was becoming increasingly difficult. Half his force was on the ground searching out and engaging the human soldiers still loyal to Alfred, while the other half was dodging the damned arrows in an effort to fight the Vultures trying to clear their way to the Fortress pass.

If even a small force made it through, the Clans were doomed. The women and children in the Fortress could easily be held hostage to make them surrender. There had been no other safe place for them, though. The Fortress was their last refuge.

Dearn blocked a swipe at his head as he shifted his wings and moved to the right to dodge the arrow flying toward him. Three had managed to lodge in the tight weave of feathers of one wing, but he had been lucky—none had pierced the muscles used in flying.

"You'll lose, you mangy Eagle." The Vulture in front of him laughed as, with his longer reach, he nearly pierced the tough leather covering Dearn's midsection.

"We'll see about that." Dearn's grin flashed as he saw his opening and swung full-force toward the Vulture's undefended side.

A scream of anger and pain followed the blow as the Vulture pitched sideways to keep the blade from sinking into the unprotected flesh. As he did so, Dearn turned, his arm bracing as he slashed the vulnerable wing muscle at the Vulture's back.

The blade hit its mark. Blood spewed from the lethal cut, the wing lost its ability to function and the Vulture plunged to the hard ground below them. He wouldn't survive, Dearn knew, so there was no need to follow him down and finish the job. He turned instead to the new attacker moving steadily toward him, fury twisting his face, his bloodied sword held above his head.

The blood of a Clan warrior stained the steel, Dearn knew. The sight of it sent his rage spiraling upward. Enough of his people had died; it was time to end it.

His war cry sounded as he met his foe. As blade slashed against blade, the hoarse cries of the victorious and the vanquished melded into one for him. From below, the arrows of both human and Bastard Breeds crowded through the sky. Vultures fell as Clan warriors wove and dodged.

Brendar was at his side, locked in hand-to-hand combat with a Vulture twice his size. As Dearn passed them, he ducked the blade coming toward him and swung his own at the wing muscle of the Vulture attacking his general. A second later he spun back and buried it in the belly of his own antagonist.

That accomplished, Dearn sped to the sharp slope of land where Matte had taken position earlier. There were three human soldiers rapidly closing in on her, having realized the arrows coming from her bow were taking out human and Vulture forces instead of Clan warriors.

"Get out of here. Human soldiers are moving this way. Get your forces farther up the point."

Matte nodded, sending out a shrieking whistle to signal her people to move farther up the mountain. It would be harder for the humans to attack them there. It would also be harder to avoid an accidental hit to the Clan warriors.

Dearn covered her. Strapped to his arm was a lightweight, though deadly, bow similar to the heavy crossbows. He fingered the launching mechanism for the lethal little arrows loaded into it as it lay along his palm, his sword held ready in the other hand.

He glanced up. The Bastard Breeds moved swiftly to obey Matte's signals, covering each other, fighting as extensions of the group instead of as individuals. It was a strategy he had not seen before and admitted would work well with his own warriors.

As Matte's forces cleared the area, Dearn lifted back into the air and once again joined the fight.

* * * * *

As Edgar avoided the sharp blade of a Clan warrior, he noted one had landed at Matte's position. Eyes widening, he watched as the warrior and Matte spoke, then Matte's forces began to move to higher ground.

Amazement shattered the calm he needed to fight, then fury flooded his system. Of course, he should have realized. In a blinding second of clarity he remembered the scent that had suddenly been ever-present on the whore. She had mated, damn her, and from the looks of it she had mated with none other than the thrice-cursed king of the Winged Clans.

Bitch! The word thundered through his brain as he understood the Bastard Breeds had betrayed him. When? Why? He kicked at the Clan warrior, catching him beneath the chin and sending him crashing into a wall of stone, then turned and headed for her. He would make her pay for this betrayal. The whore would pay with her life and the lives of those who followed her.

* * * * *

Satisfaction thundered through Dearn's blood as he realized the number of arrows was lessening, proof that the warriors on the ground were slowly taking the soldiers loyal to Alfred out of the fight. The Vultures still airborne were fewer as well. Soon, he prayed, the battle would be over.

He confronted another of the stinking enemy, but as he fought, he was careful to watch Matte's progress. Rage burned high in the cursed slithers now that they realized she had joined the Clan forces.

He sent another Vulture to the Seven Hells and in the next instant his heart nearly stopped.

Matte was once again covering the Clan warriors in the air, unaware of the shadow slipping through the brush and boulders around her. But Dearn saw him clearly, and the maniacal expression on the man's face as he raised his sword over his head and prepared for a killing blow.

"No!"

* * * * *

Matte's eyes narrowed as she sent another arrow into the wing muscle of an attacking Vulture. The battle was slowly winding down, the Vulture forces thinning out as the Clan warriors overwhelmed them. As she reloaded, a shadow and a sense of impending doom sent her leaping to the side an instant before a scream of fury accompanied the sword strike that sent sparks flying from the stone that had just been in contact with her breast.

"Whore!" Edgar spat as he came at her again, giving her no time to regain her footing or draw the sword at her side. His blade struck the ground, spattering clumps of dirt where her leg had been but a second before.

Without a breath's pause he raised the sword two-handed over his head again, aiming it like a giant dagger at her heart. Matte fought to find purchase on the loose soil as she scrambled away. Her wings flared in an effort to gain stability as she desperately evaded a blow that nearly took her legs off, then another that would have bisected her had it landed.

"I'll enjoy killing you, Matte," Edgar sneered as he slashed relentlessly. "I'll make you pay for betraying me. Then Thorne will pay when I leave him and his cursed brood there as food for the Bats."

Matte had expected him to do that no matter the betrayal she had dealt him. Thorne knew the Vultures would not be able to risk bringing the entire Bastard Breeds Clan across the seas, for they knew Thorne would eventually end up banding with the Clans and destroying the Vultures.

"As long as you die as well." She rolled to the side, feeling the whoosh of the steel as it glanced along the back of her feathers. Finally finding traction, she regained her feet and was able to yank her sword from its sheath in time to parry the next blow.

"I should have taken you when I had the chance, bitch," he snarled, his brown eyes glittering with hatred. "Now, I'm just going to have to wait until your body is dead and cold."

"That's the only way you'll ever have me again, you dirty slither," she hissed back, blocking his attack again. "Remember, Edgar? I warned you when you left me staked out for the Bats I would pay you back."

Fierce satisfaction brewed in Matte's gut as she detected an edge of fear in Edgar's expression.

"I should have sliced your heart out that night."

"That you should, brother," she sneered. "You should have never left me alive and given me the chance to repay you."

The memory of that rape, of being tied to stakes and left as a snack for the ravening creatures that ruled the night speared through Matte. The terror, the knowledge that there was no way to escape, surged through her as fresh as it was then, lending the strength of rage to her sword arm. She sliced, but the swipe against his hard leather vest was too light to cause much damage. Matte still took satisfaction from his yelp of outrage and the thin red streak that appeared on his skin.

Size and the rage that coursed through Edgar gave him the edge. With a merciless forward assault, he slammed his sword into hers, the force of the blow numbing her hand, and she dropped her blade. She tried to retreat, but suddenly the ground beneath her gave, sending her onto her back.

"Goodbye, Matte," Edgar sneered, saliva dripping from the corner of his mouth as he prepared to send his sword plunging into her body. She could never move fast enough to avoid the oncoming steel.

Then, suddenly, the threat was gone. With a cry of fury a body slammed into Edgar's, knocking him to the ground as a large fist slammed furiously into his shocked face.

Matte blinked. For a moment her heart stopped as she stared at Dearn, straddling the Vulture leader, the blood lust in his face transforming his features into those of a savage predator.

"No!" She jumped to her feet as Dearn prepared to plunge his dagger into Edgar's chest. She gripped his arm, her eyes catching his, and fear lanced through her at the wildness she saw glittering there.

"He is their leader. Let the Clans punish him, Dearn. It is their right." She refused to let go despite the force he applied to be free. "Let them have justice, Dearn. Let them heal."

For a moment, she feared he would ignore her plea.

"He would have killed you." His teeth were gritted, the words coming out in a savage snarl that sent ice through her veins. Dearn was not rational at that moment.

She touched his face, trembling from both weariness and the emotion surging through her.

"And you saved me," she whispered. "You promised the Clans they would have Edgar and Alfred for justice. The human captains have taken Alfred, and now you have taken Edgar. Take them back to the Fortress, Dearn. Let the Clans have their justice."

* * * * *

She was right. Dearn fought to release the blood-pounding rage rippling through his veins and muscles. Edgar had dared to lay hand on his mate. For that, he deserved to die by Dearn's hand. But, he had raped and murdered the wives and children of the Clans as well. Justice for the many outweighed his own personal need for vengeance.

Slowly, he released the dagger. With the leather ties he had placed on his thigh earlier, he quickly bound the Vulture leader and left him for collection.

It would take a while to gather the living Vultures and human soldiers who had fought against the Clans. It would take even longer to haul them up the mountain and into the Fortress. There, they would find their destiny in the valley below.

Dearn turned, jerking her into his embrace, his feathers flaring to enclose her as the memory of her brush with death once again washed over him. Gods help him, he could not survive if he lost her now.

The thought of that shot weakness to his legs, making them tremble as he held her close. Slowly, he sank to the ground, pulling his mate with him, unable to release her, unable to release the fear of losing her.

It was long moments later before his wings slowly retracted and Matte could lean back and stare into the hard face of her mate. She breathed a sigh of relief then rested against him tiredly. Only Clan warriors could be seen in the skies now, flying patrol while those on the ground collected the living. The day had been a long one, and the sun had barely reached its zenith.

But they had been victorious. Matte smiled, tilting her head to look at her mate, and she felt her blood heat with love for him. She had found more than she had ever dreamed when she stepped foot on Alfred's ship so many months ago. She had reclaimed the Bastard Breeds' home and found her mate in the man who would lead them all.

"We did it, Dearn." She breathed in deeply, her heart slowly easing from its thunderous pace as she let their triumph seep into her soul. "It's over."

"Was there any doubt we would?" he asked her, flashing a smile. His golden eyes glowed in the sunlight as the breeze blew gently through his silken dark-brown hair.

"No doubt," she laughed back, falling against him as he pulled her into his arms. "No doubt whatsoever."

She looked out over the mountain, watching as Canton and Allora made their way down from the aerie where they had been hiding. There was a new ruler for the humans and justice for the Clans. The war was over, but Matte knew her own life was now just beginning. The life she would share with her mate—Dearn, King of the Winged Clans.

Why an electronic book?

We live in the Information Age—an exciting time in the history of human civilization, in which technology rules supreme and continues to progress in leaps and bounds every minute of every day. For a multitude of reasons, more and more avid literary fans are opting to purchase e-books instead of paper books. The question from those not yet initiated into the world of electronic reading is simply: *Why?*

1. ***Price.*** An electronic title at Ellora's Cave Publishing and Cerridwen Press runs anywhere from 40% to 75% less than the cover price of the exact same title in paperback format. Why? Basic mathematics and cost. It is less expensive to publish an e-book (no paper and printing, no warehousing and shipping) than it is to publish a paperback, so the savings are passed along to the consumer.

2. ***Space.*** Running out of room in your house for your books? That is one worry you will never have with electronic books. For a low one-time cost, you can purchase a handheld device specifically designed for e-reading. Many e-readers have large, convenient screens for viewing. Better yet, hundreds of titles can be stored within your new library—on a single microchip. There are a variety of e-readers from different manufacturers. You can also read e-books on your PC or laptop computer. (Please note that

Ellora's Cave does not endorse any specific brands. You can check our websites at www.ellorascave.com or www.cerridwenpress.com for information we make available to new consumers.)

3. *Mobility.* Because your new e-library consists of only a microchip within a small, easily transportable e-reader, your entire cache of books can be taken with you wherever you go.

4. *Personal Viewing Preferences.* Are the words you are currently reading too small? Too large? Too… ANNOYING? Paperback books cannot be modified according to personal preferences, but e-books can.

5. *Instant Gratification.* Is it the middle of the night and all the bookstores near you are closed? Are you tired of waiting days, sometimes weeks, for bookstores to ship the novels you bought? Ellora's Cave Publishing sells instantaneous downloads twenty-four hours a day, seven days a week, every day of the year. Our webstore is never closed. Our e-book delivery system is 100% automated, meaning your order is filled as soon as you pay for it.

Those are a few of the top reasons why electronic books are replacing paperbacks for many avid readers.

As always, Ellora's Cave and Cerridwen Press welcome your questions and comments. We invite you to email us at Comments@ellorascave.com or write to us directly at Ellora's Cave Publishing Inc., 1056 Home Avenue, Akron, OH 44310-3502.

MAKE EACH DAY MORE *EXCITING* WITH OUR

ELLORA'S
CAVEMEN
CALENDAR

☥ WWW.ELLORASCAVE.COM ☥

Cerridwen Press

Monthly Newsletter

News
Author Appearances
Book Signings
New Releases
Contests
Author Profiles
Feature Articles

Available online at
www.CerridwenPress.com

CERRIDWEN PRESS

Cerridwen, the Celtic goddess of wisdom, was the muse who brought inspiration to storytellers and those in the creative arts.

Cerridwen Press encompasses the best and most innovative stories in all genres of today's fiction.

Visit our website and discover the newest titles by talented authors who still get inspired—much like the ancient storytellers did...

once upon a time.

www.cerridwenpress.com